THE MAPMAKER'S MONSTERS

VAMPANTHER ATTACK!

Rob Stevens is a captain with a major British airline and does much of his writing in hotel rooms around the world. He grew up in Bournemouth and graduated from Cambridge University with a degree in engineering before training to be a pilot. He lives on the Dorset coast with his wife and two young sons.

Also available:

THE MAPMAKER'S MONSTERS:
BEWARE THE BUFFALOGRE!

Shortlisted for the Waterstone's Book Prize

'A high energy fantasy of very strong order'
thebookbag.co.uk

'A rollicking page turner. 5 out of 5'
Amazon

'I have told all my friends about this book and I can't wait to read the next one'
Charlie, age 9

'Cool, clever and totally unputdownable!'
Amy, age 11

THE MAPMAKER'S MONSTERS

VAMPANTHER ATTACK!

Rob Stevens

Illustrated by Adam Stower

MACMILLAN CHILDREN'S BOOKS

First published 2009 by Macmillan Children's Books
a division of Macmillan Publishers Limited
20 New Wharf Road, London N1 9RR
Basingstoke and Oxford
Associated companies throughout the world
www.panmacmillan.com

ISBN 978-0-330-45672-2

3 5 7 9 8 6 4 2

A CIP catalogue record for this book is available from
the British Library.

Typeset by Nigel Hazle
Printed and bound in the UK by CPI Mackays, Chatham ME5 8TD

For my mother and father
for a lifetime of love

Prologue

Crouching low with his shoulder pressed against the cold stone wall, Marcello crept along the dimly lit corridor. All the while his gaze was fixed on the end of the passage where a towering, cloaked figure was guarding a heavy wooden door. Concealed by the shadows, Marcello edged to within arm's reach of the oblivious guard then lowered one knee to the floor and waited.

He was convinced that what he had been searching for resided in the chamber before him, and he wouldn't make his escape until he'd seen it for himself. For over an hour neither Marcello nor the guard moved a muscle. The only sound Marcello heard was the blood throbbing in his ears, until . . .

'Barbarus!'

The voice from the other side of the door surprised the guard, whose grunt masked Marcello's startled yelp.

'Yes, Master?'

'I should like to see you forthwith . . .'

The sentry hesitated, a frown of confusion puckering his pasty white brow.

'That means right now, you halfwit!'

'Well why didn't you say that?' mumbled the guard, rolling his crimson eyes. Raising his voice, he called, 'Yes, Master.'

The hinges screamed as the guard pushed open the solid door and entered the room, swinging it shut behind him. Seizing his opportunity Marcello darted forward and wedged the closing door ajar with his satchel. Pressing one eye to the narrow opening he held his breath and peered into the chamber.

A few flame torches hung from the walls, making the room barely any brighter than the corridor and casting flickering shadows on the high vaulted ceiling. In the centre of the room, on a high granite plinth, stood a stone tomb carved with strange writing. Near the far wall stood a high-backed chair.

Marcello watched with intrigue as the guard entered the deserted room.

'Good evening, my lord,' said the guard. 'Did you have a good day's sleep?'

Suddenly a figure sat upright in the open tomb and Marcello snapped a hand to his mouth to muffle his gasp.

'Yes, thank you. What time is it?'

'Nearly midnight.'

Like the guard, the figure in the stone coffin was draped in a black cloak, with a high collar that hid most of its face, which Marcello could see in profile. Barely protruding above the collar, the top of its head was covered in short black fur and adorned with two tufty black ears. A shiny black nose was just visible on the end of its black snout.

'I'm thirsty,' barked the beast. 'Get me a drink – and do make sure it's freshly squeezed.'

'Of course, my lord.'

'I'm sure I don't need to remind you what happened to the last guard who tried to get away with giving me an ageing pint from the cellar.' As it spoke the beast lifted a sword from inside the stone tomb and brandished it in two black paws to emphasize the threat. Even in the half-light provided by the torches Marcello could see that the sword's hilt was carved from a single incredible diamond.

This time he couldn't prevent the gasp escaping his lips.

Without waiting to see if he'd been heard he grabbed his satchel and sprinted back along the stone corridor towards the spiral staircase.

He burst out into the night, punching deep footprints into the fresh snow as he fled the castle. Certain he was being pursued he pelted around the edge of the frozen lake, only pausing to look back when he reached the opposite bank.

He saw no one.

'Calm down, Marcello,' he whispered to himself. 'It seems the coast is clear.'

He knelt down to catch his breath. Icy air stabbed his heaving lungs as he studied the castle gateway across the lake. Excitement and terror swirled through his blood as he contemplated what his discovery meant. Men had searched for the sword for many years but never found it – or at least never returned from their quest.

He took a quick swig from his soft leather water bottle, pushed a cork into its spout and slung its strap across his body. Then he pulled his map out of his satchel and unfolded it. Taking a pen from his bag he scribbled frantically on the chart.

'Damn this cold!' he cursed, but he knew it wasn't the frosty temperature making his hands tremble.

He folded the map and put it back in his bag then stood and began jogging towards the narrow slope leading up to the ridge. The swollen water bottle bounced rhythmically on his hip like a beating heart.

He had climbed the narrow slope on to the exposed ridge and was just starting to believe he would make it safely back to Lovdiv when he felt a sudden shiver of dread course through his body. As he spun round he knew immediately that all hope of escape was gone.

'Ciao, Signor Blanco.' Marcello managed a dry smile. 'Listen, I meant no harm. I was only visiting.'

Before Marcello even had a chance to react, the guard snatched his collar with both hands, lifting him clean off the floor.

'No one visits the castle,' he growled.

'Well, I can't say I'm surprised,' croaked Marcello, 'if this is the sort of welcome they can expect.'

'You must not leave.'

'I'd love to stay for dinner,' said Marcello with a quaver in his voice, 'but I have other plans. Maybe we should rearrange – for when hell is covered in ice?'

As the guard's grip tightened around Marcello's throat, thin blue veins riddled his waxy complexion.

'You know, they say you lot are all quite ugly,' Marcello croaked defiantly. 'But that's just not true. You're actually totally repulsive.'

'But the stories of our ruthless killings have not been exaggerated.'

'That's good to know! Anyway, what can I help you with?'

'My lord is thirsty.'

'Well, why didn't you say so?' gasped Marcello. 'Here, take my water bottle.'

'Very funny.' The sentry's blue-black lips spread into an evil grin.

Moments later, as Marcello felt the life begin to drain

from his body, he slipped his satchel from his shoulder and tossed it desperately into the air. The bag sailed silently over the jagged ridge and its strap flapped like a streamer as it plummeted silently out of sight. He kicked and punched with every ounce of strength he had but eventually his arms dropped to his sides, his legs hung limply and his heart beat no more.

Chapter 1

Hugo Bailey stood on the dockside watching another ship preparing to set sail. He was supposed to be selling souvenir maps that his uncle, Walter, had drawn but he had spent most of the day gazing out to sea.

'I bet that one's heading for India,' said Hugo wistfully to himself, a light breeze tugging at his unruly mop of blonde hair.

He imagined himself aboard the vessel as it skipped across the ocean, its full sails pushing it towards exotic lands. Noticing a sailor who was carrying a heavy-looking wooden chest towards the ship's gangplank, Hugo approached him.

'Excuse me, sir,' he said, tilting his freckled face up at the sailor and giving him a broad, gap-toothed smile. 'Are you heading for somewhere exciting like Africa or the Indies?'

The sailor stopped and turned to Hugo, his cheek squashed up against the side of the chest. 'Much more exciting than that,' he said, laughing.

Hugo's eager blue eyes widened.

'This here ship is going sailing in search of the ancient civilization known as . . . Grimsby.'

The sailor turned and staggered up the gangplank, chuckling to himself as he went. Hugo smiled and rolled his eyes.

A short distance away half a dozen grey-brown mice were gathered on the dockside amongst a cluster of wooden kegs. In their midst, a white mouse with a black stripe running from its nose to its tail was standing on its haunches.

Not only was he remarkable because of his distinctive colouring, he also had unusually large ears that were pink and bald. What made him stand out most of all, however, was that he was talking to the other mice.

'. . . then, without a thought for my personal safety, I scampered on to the buffalogre's head and let him have it right between the eyes.' He threw a couple of sharp punches by way of demonstration. 'Now this monster was at least ten feet tall – but it's true what they say, the bigger they are, the harder they fall.'

The white mouse scanned the faces of his audience. Twelve beady black eyes peered blankly at him.

'Maybe I didn't quite make myself clear. This monster was *huge*. An absolute beast.'

Six noses twitched curiously.

'I mean, the clue is in their name . . . buffal-*ogre*. With the emphasis being very much on ogre.'

Silence.

'So what I'm saying is that if I can defeat a ferocious buffalogre, there's no reason for any of you to be afraid of rats. Or even cats for that matter. Now, does anyone have any questions?

'Anyone. Anyone at all?

'Oh, I get it – you're the strong, silent types.'

One of the mice began scratching.

'OK, fellas. It's been a real pleasure chatting to you but I've got to dash. So remember, don't be afraid to stand up to moggies – deep down they're all pussycats really.'

He tucked back his ears and darted out on to the dockside.

A few yards from Hugo a woman screamed.

'Eeeaaaih! A rat!'

Hugo smiled to himself as he watched the ripple of heads bobbing as people yelped and leapt out of the rodent's path. The tiny animal scampered towards him, his claws making a ticking sound on the cobbles, then darted up his britches and dived into the pocket of his tunic.

A few people in the crowd glowered as Hugo turned and sidled away. When he was well away from the throng he lifted the flap on his tunic pocket. Two beady black eyes blinked up at him and a pinkish, whiskery nose twitched.

'Hello, Savage,' said Hugo, smiling warmly. 'I wish

you wouldn't make such a scene. Why can't you travel in the sewers like all the other rodents?'

'You know I'm nothing like the other rodents,' scoffed Savage. They had met about a year ago on a tiny, magical island in the middle of the ocean. He had been Hugo's permanent companion since and was his best friend in the whole world.

'I know, but it's like the parting of the Red Sea whenever you pass through a crowd.'

'Maybe Moses was a mouse,' said Savage.

'Don't you mean Mouses?' laughed Hugo, tickling his friend under his chin. 'So what have you been doing all day?'

'The usual,' said Savage. 'Hanging around with some of the field mice.'

'You haven't been stirring up a rebellion again, have you?'

'Doing my best.' Savage's eyes twinkled. 'Cats have had it too easy for too long. I don't see why they should get to do all the chasing – it's time for my coy cousins to take a stand. But try telling that to the mice in this town – I might as well be talking to myself.'

'Maybe they were just too in awe of you to respond,' suggested Hugo. 'Then again, it might have something to do with the fact that animals in this part of the world can't talk.'

It was late afternoon and market day was drawing

to a close. Market Square was deserted except for a last remaining stall selling fruit and vegetables and a couple of young boys playing. One was pretending to be clamped in the stocks while the other tried to pelt him with rotten fruit. Hugo stopped for a moment to watch their game.

'How many maps did you sell today?' said Savage, clambering up to Hugo's shoulder.

'What, altogether?' said Hugo.

'Yeah.'

'Including the ones I sold this morning?'

'Of course.'

'None.'

'None?'

Hugo shook his head sadly. 'I really wanted to do well today,' he said. 'I wanted to buy some food to take home and make Uncle Walter proud, but I ended up daydreaming all day about exploring.'

'Don't panic,' urged Savage. 'The day isn't over yet. I bet you can sell a map to the next person who comes into the square.'

'You really think so?'

'Absolutely.'

Hugo's back straightened. 'OK,' he said with a resolute nod. 'The very next person.'

CHapter 2

Savage's ears flared at the sound of horse's hoofs approaching.

'Get out of my way!' commanded a whiney voice. 'Very important nobleman coming through. Clear the way.'

Hugo recognized the upper-class accent before he saw the man on horseback. Then Rupert Lilywhite rode into the square wearing a wide-brimmed felt hat crowned with a huge pale blue feather. He had his nose in the air and an expression of utter disgust on his face. When his horse passed within ten yards of the boys playing, Rupert looked horrified. 'Coming through!' he shrieked. 'Keep away, KEEP AWAY!'

The boys stood still, wondering what all the fuss was about, as the strange nobleman rode nervously past, a comfortable distance from the stocks.

'He's afraid he's going to catch poverty,' laughed Hugo.

'If ever there was a man in need of a map, it's him,' said Savage. 'Why don't you go and say hello?'

'Do you think he'll remember me?'

'You spent the best part of a year sailing the

ocean on the same crew. Of course he'll remember you.'

Hugo began waving.

Bouncing up and down awkwardly in his saddle, Rupert Lilywhite remained oblivious to Hugo's gesticulations.

'He's not going to stop,' sighed Hugo.

'Oh I rather think he will,' said Savage.

The little mouse leaped from Hugo's coat and scampered across the cobbles. Stopping just a few yards in front of the horse, Savage sat up on his hind legs, fanned his ears out wide and started squeaking loudly. Or at least as loudly as a tiny mouse can squeak.

Whinnying wildly the startled horse reared up, clawing the air with its front feet. Then it began spinning round on the spot like a dog chasing its tail, bucking and rearing up alternately, its hoofs clattering on the stony ground. Rupert's response was instinctive and immediate. Demonstrating the full extent of his horsemanship, he wrapped both arms tightly around the horse's neck, closed his eyes and screamed for help.

Hugo rushed over and grabbed the horse's bridle. The mare reared a couple more times with decreasing vigour then settled down, neighing gently as Hugo patted its shoulder.

'Are you OK, sir?' he asked. As he spoke he felt Savage scurry up his tunic and perch on his shoulder.

'Yes, of course I'm OK,' snapped Rupert, sitting up and straightening his hat. 'Now get out of my way!'

'Don't you remember me, Admiral?'

Frowning, Rupert Lilywhite peered down at Hugo.

'Did I catch you stealing turnips from the market last week?' he asked.

'No, sir,' said Hugo. 'I sailed with you aboard *El Tonto Perdido*. I am the mapmaker's apprentice.'

'Ah yes,' said Rupert vaguely. 'Hector, isn't it?'

Hugo shook his head.

'I mean Henry. No? . . . Harry? Humphrey? Horrace?' With each name, Rupert's voice grew more and more shrill.

'Hugo, actually. Hugo Bailey.'

'That's right! Hugo,' said Rupert triumphantly. 'See? I never forget a name.'

'He's right,' Savage whispered into Hugo's ear. 'He never forgets any names – he just hasn't got a clue who they all belong to.'

Hugo disguised his giggle by pretending to cough. 'Are you planning any more expeditions, Admiral?' he asked.

Rupert stroked his thin moustache with one gloved knuckle and gave Hugo a smug grin. 'You know, Hubert,' he said, 'when you've been exploring as long as I have and achieved what I've achieved you'll find that your hunger for adventure has been quenched, your thirst for excitement satisfied.'

'But you've only been on one voyage,' said Hugo.

'I like to think of life as being like a bowl of fruit,' Rupert continued, ignoring Hugo's observation. 'There are so many flavours to try. You might feel like a pear one day, but the next you might feel like an apple.'

'If I was wearing that hat, I'd feel like a lemon,' whispered Savage.

'As you know, I don't like to show off but the truth is that I am by far the greatest living explorer in my whole family, out of my cousin and me. He's spent long enough living in my shadow, so I'm hanging up my explorer's . . . er . . . star-measuring thingamabob and letting him have a turn at the wheel.'

'Is he setting sail soon?' asked Hugo eagerly.

'Only across the Channel. Then he's heading east overland, hoping to reach China. He leaves tomorrow at the crack of midday, although why he has to set off so early is beyond me.' Rupert rolled his eyes. 'Anyway, I have to go. Father is throwing a banquet tonight to wish Sebastian luck on his travels and I simply mustn't miss the crab soup.'

Rupert tugged at his reins and his horse turned and trotted away.

'Excuse me, Admiral!' Hugo called after him. 'If

you're going to your father's mansion, you're heading the wrong way.'

Rupert pulled his horse up and looked around, studying the narrow lanes that radiated out of the square. 'Oh dear me,' he said. 'I seem to have completely lost my bearings. It must have happened when Bessie here was spooked. It really is so unlike me.'

'Perhaps you'd like to buy one of my Town Maps,' suggested Hugo, producing one with a flourish. 'They're only two groats each, and you'll be lost without it.'

CHapter 3

Hugo stood in front of the market stall, holding the two coins tightly in his hand. Savage clung to his shirtsleeve, his whiskers twitching as he sniffed the produce hungrily. The grocer, a large bald man with a big round belly and rolls of fat on the back of his neck, seemed oblivious to Hugo as he arranged the cabbages on his stall.

Finally he looked up. 'Right, who's next, please?' he said.

Hugo glanced around. He and the grocer were the only two people left in the square.

'Me, I think,' said Hugo. 'What can I get for two groats, please?'

'I know your game,' said the grocer, looking down at him suspiciously. 'You wait until my back is turned then you steal a handful of plums. Well, I ain't falling for it.'

'But . . . I'm not a thief,' said Hugo defiantly. 'I have two groats to spend at your stall.'

'Two groats?' laughed the grocer. 'That ain't exactly going to buy you a feast, is it? Let me see now.' He perused his fruit and vegetables, wiping his brow with a grubby handkerchief. It was a cool autumn evening but his head was gleaming with droplets of sweat, like a freshly rinsed watermelon. He picked up a plump, ripe cauliflower with lush green leaves and a crisp white heart.

'That looks delicious,' smiled Hugo, his eyes sparkling as he imagined the rich soup Uncle Walter would be able to cook up using the vegetable. 'I'll take it.'

'That'll be five groats then, please,' said the grocer with a mean smile.

'But I only have two.'

'Well, you can't afford this then, can you?' The fat man's belly shook as he chuckled to himself.

'I don't trust this guy,' Savage muttered. 'I think he's a couple of plums short of a crumble.'

After a moment's consideration the grocer composed himself and selected a pair of bruised, tired-looking apples. 'You can have these for two groats, and I'm doin' you a favour,' he said. 'Take it or leave it.'

Hugo hesitated for a moment. Realizing this was the best offer he was likely to get, and keen to take something home to his uncle, he reached forward to take the fruit.

'Not so fast!' exclaimed the grocer, pulling the apples away. 'I'm not falling for that either. You're not getting your grubby hands on my apples until you've coughed up. Otherwise how do I know you won't scarper without paying, you little toerag?'

Hugo sighed and handed over the money. The grocer dropped the coins into a leather pouch tied round his waist then put the apples back on his stall.

'Excuse me,' said Hugo sharply. 'Can I have my apples, please?'

'Apples?' repeated the grocer. 'What apples would they be?'

'The ones I just paid you for.'

'I don't recall you paying me anything,' said the grocer, rolling his eyes upwards as though trying hard to remember something.

'I told you he was a few tomatoes short of a salad,' whispered Savage.

'I just gave you two groats,' insisted Hugo.

The grocer bent down so that his face was inches from Hugo's. A gust of hot onion breath blew out of his mouth as he sniggered. 'You know that, and I know that,' he hissed, 'but it's my word against yours so who's going to believe a little runt like you?'

'I will!' boomed a deep voice to Hugo's right. There was a metallic chime and a curved silver blade appeared between Hugo's face and the grocer's, its point prodding at the fleshy bag under the fat man's left eye.

At that moment a gust of wind ruffled Hugo's curly blonde hair and he shivered. He turned to take a look at his saviour. The man had dark skin and emerald green eyes that twinkled with confidence. His black moustache curled up at the ends and his pointed beard was like a single brushstroke on his square chin. He was dressed all in black from his leather gloves to his leather boots, topped off by a black headdress that was wrapped around his head then flung loosely over one shoulder like a scarf. Seeing the fear in the grocer's eyes the stranger smiled broadly, showing off a row of dazzlingly white teeth.

'Whoa!' said Savage, watching eagerly from Hugo's shoulder. 'This guy is almost as good-looking as me.'

'Now, I suggest you give the boy his fruit or I will relieve you of an eyeball,' commanded the stranger, tracing his sword delicately around the stallholder's eye socket. His accent was like nothing Hugo had heard before, full of strange guttural emphasis.

'OK, OK,' stuttered the grocer. Keeping his eyes on the man he patted his produce blindly until he laid his hands on the two bruised apples. He picked them up and offered them to Hugo.

'Oh dear me no, this really won't do,' said the stranger. 'Two groats for those apples is daylight robbery. They're not even fit to be fed to pigs.'

'I can think of a certain flying pig who would devour them,' whispered Savage.

Hugo smiled at the thought of his old friend Pigasus whose favourite food was rotten peaches.

The stranger continued. 'I think the very least you can do is give this young boy some fresh apples – let's say half a dozen of them.'

He withdrew his sword a short distance while the grocer frantically piled six ripe green apples into Hugo's leather satchel. He looked at the stranger with wide eyes, hoping for approval.

'Let's throw in that nice crisp cauliflower as well, shall we?' suggested the stranger.

The grocer obliged eagerly.

'And how about a turnip . . . and a few handfuls of beans?'

Again the grocer complied.

'Now all you have to do is give the boy back the money you tried to steal and we'll call it quits.'

The grocer was about to protest but thought better of it when he felt the cold hard steel pressing into his flushed cheeks. He handed Hugo two groats, managing a sickly smile as he did so.

'Thank you very much, sir,' Hugo said to the stranger.

The stranger touched his forehead with two leather-clad fingers and nodded. 'At your service,' he said, raising one dark eyebrow in an expression that was both mysterious and quizzical. Without another word he turned sharply, his black robe billowing out behind him as he strode away.

Slowly Hugo shook his head and mumbled, 'Who on earth was *that*?'

Chapter 4

Hugo hefted his satchel on to the rough wooden table in his uncle's house in Peppercorn Lane and proudly displayed his wares.

'Goodness me!' exclaimed Uncle Walter with a chuckle. 'You must have sold plenty of maps today to afford such a feast.'

'Actually, I only sold one,' admitted Hugo sheepishly. 'Rupert Lilywhite bought it for two groats so he could find his way back home.'

'I'm glad to see his sense of direction is as keen as ever! It's people like Rupert Lilywhite who keep us mapmakers in business,' laughed Uncle Walter. 'Don't tell me you bought all this food for two groats though?'

'Of course not!' exclaimed Savage, leaping on to the table and sniffing the turnip. 'It didn't cost us anything.'

Walter fixed Hugo with a stern stare. 'I think you'd better explain yourselves,' he said.

Barely pausing for breath Hugo told his uncle about the mean grocer and the dark stranger who had leaped to their defence.

'What was his name?' asked Uncle Walter, intrigued by his nephew's story.

'He didn't say,' said Hugo. 'But when he left he saluted me like this –' he touched his forehead with two fingers to mimic the stranger's parting gesture – 'and he raised his eyebrow like this.' He raised one eyebrow at Uncle Walter.

'How very mysterious,' marvelled Uncle Walter. He tried to raise a quizzical eyebrow in return but both eyebrows climbed his forehead, expressing something more like surprise.

'That's not right!' laughed Hugo. 'Just arch one of them.'

'I'm trying!' smiled Walter. 'But I can't budge the left one without raising the right one at the same time. Oh, but wait – I can do it the other way round. Look!'

'You've got it!' cheered Hugo. 'That's how the stranger looked at me.'

'Is this right?' asked Savage, wearing an expression of total concentration and wiggling his big pink ears furiously.

Uncle Walter and Hugo exchanged puzzled looks.

'Perfect,' said Hugo.

Hugo pushed his bowl away and sat back, rubbing his full belly.

'That soup was delicious.'

'I can't take any credit,' said Uncle Walter, dabbing his thick white moustache with a cloth. 'It was one of your mother's recipes.'

Savage, who was perched on the rim of his own bowl, looked up from lapping at his broth. 'Your mother must have been a good cook,' he said, his nose drenched in soup.

Hugo glanced across at the iron pot suspended over the open fire and imagined his mother standing there. She would have been serving the soup with a long ladle, her wavy hair tucked away under a headscarf.

'Anyone would think you two hadn't eaten for a month,' she would laugh as she watched Hugo and his father devour their meal, wiping their bowls clean with hunks of homemade rye bread. 'It's like watching a couple of vultures at work!'

That vision was from another life – a time before his father had been lost at sea trying to earn enough money to pay their crooked landlord, and before his mother had been beaten by illness and worry. And yet the memory was so clear it was as if they were right there in the room. Hugo could smell the sawdust that always coated his father's clothes from head to toe; he could hear the soft warmth in his mother's voice. As he reminisced he clutched the wooden chess piece he wore round his neck on a string. His father had carved it for him just before leaving on the voyage from which he'd never returned.

'I don't suppose there's any more Stilton?' beseeched Savage, snapping him back into the present.

Walter placed a chunk of cheese in front of him. 'That's the last piece so don't eat it all at once.'

'You've really developed a taste for cheese, haven't you?' said Hugo with a smile. 'Just like an ordinary mouse.'

Savage looked up and nodded, his cheeks bulging as if they contained two whole hazelnuts. 'You're always telling me I should pretend to be *more like an ordinary mouse* when we're in public,' he said when he'd finally managed to swallow his mouthful. 'I'd stand out like a sore thumb if I didn't eat what the other mice eat.'

'But we're not in public now.'

'I'm simply trying to stay in character.'

'I see,' teased Hugo. 'How very noble.'

'One does what one has to,' sighed Savage, pushing the last of his Stilton into his already overloaded mouth.

Later, as Hugo and Walter played chess and Savage lazed in front of the fire, they were disturbed by a loud knock at the door. Hugo looked at Uncle Walter with a frown. 'Who could that be?' he asked.

'I've no idea,' replied Uncle Walter, arching his

right eyebrow to show off his newly discovered expression of intrigue. 'Who would call at such a late hour?'

Again there was a loud knock at the door.

'It's too late to be a social call,' said Uncle Walter, scratching his thick white moustache.

'Maybe the grocer wants his vegetables back,' suggested Hugo.

'Excuse me, folks,' said Savage, scampering on to the table and hopping impatiently from foot to foot. 'I don't wish to state the obvious but the solution to this perplexing mystery might become clearer if one of you opened the door.'

As Hugo headed across the room, Savage darted behind a pottery tankard. Hugo and Walter had decided he would be safer if he kept a low profile in England. A talking mouse would earn its owner a fortune in a circus sideshow and there was no telling what lengths some might go to in order to obtain such a valuable asset. To Hugo and Walter, Savage was much more important than a way of making money – he was one of the family.

Hugo turned the key in the lock and opened the heavy wooden door. The hinges creaked as the door swung inwards and a blast of icy cold air was sucked into the room, almost extinguishing the fire in the grate. Hugo peered into the darkness, shielding his eyes from the heavy raindrops that were peppering the cobblestones and plopping into the sewer.

The figure outside was wrapped in a long black robe billowing gently in the breeze.

'We meet again,' he said, touching his forehead with two fingers of his gloved hand.

'You're the man from the market square,' Hugo said, beaming.

The stranger bowed his head. 'At your service.'

'I didn't really thank you properly for helping me earlier.'

'Please think no more of it,' said the visitor. 'Somebody once stole something very precious from me so I will not abide thievery. Now, I apologize for the intrusion at this late hour but I am looking for the great mapmaker Walter Bailey.'

'He's my uncle,' said Hugo proudly. 'I'll just get him.'

As Hugo started to turn away he realized that Uncle Walter had already come to the door and was standing right behind him.

'Can I help you?'

'I very much hope so,' said the stranger. 'My name is Jadea Jafil. I come with news of your dear friend Marcello Giovanni.'

Jadea removed his cloak and unwrapped his headdress,

revealing long black hair pulled back into a tight ponytail. He strode into the room, slapped his gloves down on the table and crouched by the dwindling fire. Taking a poker he stoked the embers to life and held his palms up to their heat. Hugo watched the stranger in silent awe while Walter dished up some soup.

Jadea sat and drank in silence, finally setting his empty bowl on the table and fixing his intense gaze on Walter.

'I am indebted to you for your hospitality,' he said.

'Any friend of Marcello's is welcome at my table,' said Walter.

'Are you a mapmaker too, Mr Jafil?' asked Hugo.

Jadea smiled and shook his head. 'Not exactly,' he said. 'I suppose you could say that I am a hunter. My speciality is, shall we say, protection. Marcello and I travelled together on a number of occasions – across many deserts and over many mountain ranges. We ventured across Europe and much of Northern Africa together.'

'So it's your job to protect explorers from attack,' stated Walter. 'Were you present at Marcello's expedition to Scandinavia?'

Jadea's eyes narrowed and his jaw tightened, as if he was angered by the question, then he was calm.

'That was a dark night indeed,' he said flatly. 'I know what you must think of me, but please do not let my single failure eclipse a thousand victories.'

Now the fire was just an orange glow beneath flaky grey embers. An expectant silence fell over the room. Jadea and Walter eyed each other like two chess players trying to read their opponent's thoughts. Eventually Walter spoke.

'It is a pleasure to meet you, Jadea. Now – you said you had news of Marcello.'

Jadea confirmed this with a grim smile.

'I'm afraid so,' he said, looking deep into Walter's eyes. 'And I need your help. It is a matter of life and death.'

CHapter 5

Walter and Jadea held each other's gaze. Hugo's mouth fell open and he saw Savage squirm excitedly behind the tankard.

'Well, now you've got our attention you'd better tell us everything,' said Walter calmly.

Jadea stood and walked across to the fire, one hand cupped over the hilt of his sabre. The room fell silent. The raindrops drummed on the world outside.

'Marcello is missing,' whispered Jadea.

'Since when?' asked Walter urgently. 'What happened?'

'He was staying in Lovdiv – a tiny village in the northern foothills of the Transylvanian Alps, just outside the border of Demonica.'

'Yes, I know it,' said Walter. 'A little village clustered round an ancient Roman church – built in honour of Claudius the Ninth, I think.'

'You are correct. Ironically, the townsfolk used to believe the presence of the church would actually protect them from any murderous deeds.' Jadea grimaced. 'But I'm sure you know of the merciless violence wrought in that particular region by the one they call Lifereaper.'

Walter snorted inadvertently.

'You find my story amusing?'

'I'm sorry. I mean no disrespect,' said Walter, holding up both hands. 'But don't tell me you really believe in this Evil Lord who stalks mountainous regions preying on hapless travellers?'

'Have you heard of this Lifereaper, Uncle Walter?' demanded Hugo.

'Don't be alarmed, my boy.' Walter gave his nephew a reassuring smile. 'The existence of Lifereaper is no more than a fantastic myth.'

Jadea fixed Walter with a cold, hard stare, until the smile on Walter's lips began to wither. When eventually he spoke, Jadea's voice burbled like boiling water.

'Over recent decades hundreds of people have ventured into Demonica, never to be seen again.'

'Well, yes, the mountains within Demonica are notoriously treacherous,' Walter interjected.

Jadea continued relentlessly. 'Last year a large number of villagers disappeared from Lovdiv in one night alone. Their bodies have never been found but the beds where they were sleeping were stained with blood. Tell me, Walter, how would you explain these events?'

'I don't know about that, but the last I heard, Lifereaper was supposed to be living in the Pyrenees,' he reasoned. 'At least get your stories straight.'

Jadea nodded. 'There have been many rumours as to the precise location of this vicious lord's lair – the Pyrenees, the Himalayas, anywhere from Africa to Scandinavia. Wherever there is a spate of unexplained deaths, the idea that Lifereaper's residence is nearby soon follows.'

'What does this all have to do with my uncle's friend?' asked Hugo, shuddering.

'Marcello was in Lovdiv the night of that slaughter,' explained Jadea. 'As you know, Walter, he had spent many years searching for Lifereaper's castle.'

Walter nodded grimly. 'Since his family disappeared in the forest just to the south of Demonica his mind had been occupied by little else. Their bodies were never found so I supposed they had fallen victim to wild animals or become lost and perished in the snow. But Marcello was convinced that Lifereaper's hordes were to blame and he became obsessed with finding this imaginary castle.'

'He had become convinced the secret fortress was hidden somewhere in Demonica,' said Jadea. 'The last time I saw him his conviction had redoubled after meeting some phoney witch who claimed to have seen a vision of the castle in the kingdom. Out of sheer desperation it seems he decided to venture alone into the depths of Demonica and find Lifereaper. He hasn't been seen since – and for this you have my eternal sympathy.'

'There could be any number of explanations.' Walter's voice was full of bravado but his cheeks were pale and slack.

Hugo approached his uncle and placed a hand on his shoulder.

'I tried to warn him,' said Jadea. 'I told him he would be safer staying in Lovdiv but he was convinced that Lifereaper was going to wipe out the whole village.'

'You were in Lovdiv too?' questioned Walter.

Jadea nodded. 'When I heard of the slaughter, I went to help protect the village.'

'Why didn't you accompany Marcello into the mountains?' demanded Walter.

'Somebody had to stay to take care of the surviving villagers,' said Jadea defiantly.

'What happened to him?' whispered Hugo.

'At first it was thought Marcello might have fallen prey to the many crevasses and precipices of those mountains.' Jadea paused dramatically. 'But I now have reason to believe he was killed by one of Lifereaper's henchmen.'

'Oh please!' cried Walter. 'How can you possibly believe this nonsense?'

'Because I have evidence he found the Evil Lord's

castle,' Jadea retorted, his deep voice resounding around the small room.

'Evidence? What evidence, Mr Jafil?' inquired Walter. 'From what you've said Marcello has taken whatever he found, or didn't find, with him to the grave.'

'Not exactly,' said Jadea, arching one dark eyebrow. 'Some moons ago a small band of merchants was travelling along the riverbank, a few miles downstream from Lovdiv. It was early spring and the snow was beginning to thaw.

'One of them spotted something by the riverbank, crusted in ice. At first they thought it was the carcass of a small animal – a fox or a dog – but when they drew closer they realized it was a satchel. A leather satchel . . . Marcello's satchel.'

'Go on,' said Walter, resting his elbows on the table and leaning forward intently.

'The merchants salvaged the satchel and freed it from its icy tomb. Inside they found some fruit, almost perfectly preserved by the cold, some pieces of stale bread . . . and a map.'

Hugo caught his breath, his heart thumping.

'The map depicts a small section of mountains but what intrigued the traders even more was the coded message it bore. When they reached Lovdiv they found the village almost deserted but the priest, Father Romanov, remained. Curious about their discovery and eager to hear the priest's opinion, the merchants showed him Marcello's map.' Jadea sat back down at the table. His voice dropped to a husky whisper. 'He was just as baffled as the tradesmen by most of the code. But he understood two symbols immediately – a crisscrossed arch next to a black cat.'

'What does that mean?' asked Hugo.

'The arch depicts a portcullis,' said Walter. 'It's often used by mapmakers to denote a fort or a castle.'

'And what about the cat?'

'That is the symbol commonly used in those parts to denote Lifereaper himself,' said Jadea gravely.

'Well, Mr Jafil, you certainly spin a good yarn,' said Walter – then his smile disappeared. 'What comes next? Are we to learn that Marcello's map, the only piece of tangible evidence to support your claims, was taken by the traders when they left the village – never to be seen again?'

Jadea inhaled patiently and when he spoke his voice was slow and deliberate. 'You are right, Walter. Without the map I am no more than a madman spouting unbelievable fables. However, it just so happened that I visited Father Romanov soon after the traders had left his church. When I learned of Marcello's map I tracked them down. Naturally they were reluctant to part with their prize but let's just say I *persuaded* them to hand it over to me.'

Uncle Walter's voice was no more than a whisper. 'You have the map to Lifereaper's castle?'

Jadea nodded once.

Hugo realized he was holding his breath. 'How do you know it's the right castle?' he asked as he exhaled.

'Quite,' agreed Walter. 'Just because Marcello discovered what he thought was a secret castle doesn't mean the person living there is some ridiculous Evil Lord.'

'Let me tell you about this "ridiculous" Evil Lord!' snapped Jadea, his green eyes narrowing. 'Lifereaper is responsible for untold death and misery. Thanks to Marcello's courage I now have confirmation that he rules the small alpine territory of Demonica, spreading his evil within its borders and slaughtering anyone who dares to enter his kingdom. His evil minions terrorize victims far and wide, preying on the young and the defenceless, and have killed countless innocent men, women and children. Lifereaper himself executed my whole family some years ago. I was fortunate to escape his attack but my wife and child perished at his hands. Even my dog fell prey to his ferocious rage.'

'I'm so sorry about your family,' gasped Hugo.

Jadea smiled grimly. 'I appreciate your sympathy, Hugo,' he said. 'It's something that I have learned to live with. Their memory keeps me going from day to day. That and the thought that one day I will hunt him down like the dog that he is and make him beg for forgiveness.'

Hugo felt immense sympathy for Jadea's loss, but at the same time the anger in the stranger's voice sent a shiver through him.

'So you have actually come face to face with Lifereaper?' mumbled Walter, his eyes bulging. 'All this time I was sure he was no more than a fantastic legend. Is he as vicious as they say? What's he like?'

'Lifereaper is a beast.' Jadea smiled. 'But I am a hunter and Lifereaper is exactly the type of beast I specialize in.'

Hugo studied their mysterious guest with his dashing smile and his proud moustache and his strange curved sword. 'What sort of hunter *are* you?' he murmured.

Jadea laughed. 'It is better that I do not blacken your mind with the details of my godforsaken pastime.'

CHApter 6

'Oh come on, Jadea, don't be a spoilsport!' Overcome with curiosity, Savage had darted out from behind the tankard, the tips of his ears glowing bright pink. 'What sort of creatures do you hunt?'

Suddenly remembering that his ability to talk was something of a secret, Savage froze. His beady eyes looked sheepishly from Hugo to Walter and finally to Jadea. Jadea smiled.

'It's no good playing dumb now,' said Hugo, rolling his eyes. 'I think you've already let the cat out of the bag.'

'Or, indeed, let the talking mouse out into the open,' laughed Jadea.

'Jadea, this is Savage,' said Walter. 'He's a friend we met on our last voyage – to a magical little island in the middle of the Ocean Sea.'

'A talking mouse – how wonderful! The world is full of surprises, isn't it?' said Jadea. Then tickling Savage under his chin he purred, 'You're a handsome little fellow, aren't you? Cute enough to eat.'

'Yes, I suppose I am,' said Savage coyly, his ears

glowing even more brightly than before. 'Pleased to meet you, Jadea.'

'At your service.' Jadea grinned broadly. 'And to answer your question, allow me to say only this: the creatures I hunt are soulless and bloodthirsty and we would all be safer if they were eradicated from this earth.'

'But—'

'I think that's enough questions about Mr Jafil's profession for the time being, thank you very much,' said Walter sternly.

He stood and poured two cups of beer from a clay flagon. Handing one to Jadea he took a long drink and sat down. 'I am grateful to you for bringing me the news of Marcello,' he said, wiping frothy droplets from his moustache. 'But I still don't understand how you need my help.'

Jadea smiled. 'I intend to follow Marcello's map and kill Lifereaper,' he said simply, 'but I need an experienced navigator to guide me through those treacherous mountains. Besides, no one understands Marcello's mind like you do. As you know he used his own codes when he made his preliminary sketches. You are the only person who could make sense of them. I need you to decode the map and lead me to the Evil Lord's castle.'

'This all sounds intriguing,' said Walter. 'If

circumstances were different I would jump at the chance to head off to Romania and help you on your adventure, but I have Hugo to look after.'

Savage cleared his throat loudly.

'And Savage, of course,' said Walter. 'I have Hugo and Savage to look after.'

'At least sleep on it,' asked Jadea. 'I will leave Marcello's map for you to study. Come and see me at the Sailors' Inn tomorrow when you have made your decision.'

Jadea reached down and slid something out of the leg of his boot. It was a piece of parchment, folded into a small square, which he handed to Walter.

'Keep this bootleg copy until tomorrow,' said Jadea. 'The original is kept in a safe place known only to me. I hope you will change your mind about coming with me. There is still time to save Marcello but we must leave soon.'

'What?' said Hugo, propping up his head with the heel of his hand. 'I thought Marcello was already dead.'

'Things might not be quite that straightforward,' said Walter, running a hand through his wild silver hair. 'The last time I saw Marcello he told me about the existence of the mezzaghouls but once again, I dismissed his theories as pure fantasy.'

'What is a mezzaghoul?'

'My old friend believed that Lifereaper's victims – and those of his underlings – spend a year imprisoned in Lifereaper's castle as mezzaghouls,' explained Walter. 'During this period they appear to live normally but their souls remain in limbo, neither in their body nor consigned to oblivion. On the first anniversary of their death their soul finally dies, and Marcello explained that . . .' Uncle Walter stopped, as if he'd thought better of what he was about to say.

Hugo placed both palms on the table and leaned forward eagerly. 'That what?'

'That if Lifereaper should be executed then all existing mezzaghouls would be freed,' said Jadea. 'Their souls would return to their bodies, leaving them free to continue their normal lives without any memory of their awful experience.'

'Marcello dated his map the first day of February in the year fourteen hundred and ninety-five,' said Jadea.

'Mapmakers often date their charts when they are complete,' commented Walter. 'Marcello was certainly of that practice.'

'And the likelihood is that he disturbed Lifereaper's henchmen when he found the castle,' proffered Jadea. 'I doubt he lived long after completing his map.'

'Which means Marcello probably went missing eight months ago this very night,' whispered Walter.

'So we have only four months to rescue him!' gasped Hugo.

'That is not the only reason to act with haste,' said Jadea, standing to wind his headdress. 'It seems that the merchants who found Marcello's map were not as innocent as they appeared. I have reason to believe that before I reached them they had already made copies of the chart and sold them on the black market. I have since heard talk of a number of such maps exchanging hands in alleyways and taverns all over Europe.'

'Why would anyone *want* to go to that horrible castle?' asked Savage.

Jadea smiled. 'Lifereaper is said to possess a magnificent sword, its hilt carved from a single enormous diamond. There are plenty of bandits from here to Constantinople who would risk life and limb to get their hands on that weapon.'

'Would people really risk their lives just to steal a diamond?' asked Hugo.

'I'm afraid this is nothing new,' replied Uncle Walter. 'For centuries bounty hunters have been trying to lay their hands on this legendary Diamond Sword. I'd always dismissed their efforts as wild goose chases but perhaps I was wrong.'

'If it does exist, that sword would be really valuable on the black market,' remarked Savage, his eyes lighting up.

'Not just valuable,' corrected Jadea, flexing his fingers as he pulled on his leather gloves, 'it would be *invaluable*. Even split between four or five men, the proceeds from that diamond would be worth a handsome fortune.'

'So you think these bandits are already in the mountains searching for Lifereaper's castle?' asked Walter, opening the front door.

Jadea stepped into the night, his cloak billowing around him. 'They'd never find it without help,' he said, 'which is why I think they'll be coming for you.'

Walter laughed dismissively. 'How on earth would they know to come to me?'

Jadea fixed him with a stern stare. 'They will come looking here because Marcello addressed his map to you.'

Chapter 7

Hugo watched Uncle Walter on the other side of the table as he fingered the unopened map, considering the potential journey it could take them on.

Between them Savage sat up on his haunches, looking from one to the other.

'I don't know about you but I feel rather bewildered,' admitted Walter at last.

'You're not the only one,' said Savage. 'What's the difference between valuable and invaluable anyway?'

'Valuable means something is worth a lot of money,' explained Walter, 'but if something is *in*valuable then it's priceless.'

'Who is Marcello, Uncle Walter?' asked Hugo. 'I don't remember hearing you mention him before.'

'I haven't spoken of Marcello for a long time,' muttered Walter, 'but our friendship goes back many, many years – to a time when I was not much older than you, Hugo.'

'Were you fellow mapmakers?'

Walter chuckled quietly. 'I don't know if I'd say that . . . Perhaps *rival* mapmakers would be a better description, certainly at the beginning of our friendship at least. We met about thirty years ago when we were both hired by the King of Spain to establish a safe trade route through the Atlas Mountains. I think the King thought having two mapmakers to navigate the route would make life easier on the expedition but it had quite the opposite effect.

'Marcello and I couldn't have been less alike. He was artistic while I was scientific. I was trained to study the stars and measure progress with mathematical precision, whereas his approach to mapmaking was much looser – more intuitive. His answer to every problem was to march to the highest peak around to "get a feel for the terrain". While I obsessed over the tiny details he was concerned with what he called the character of the landscape.

'I thought he was cavalier and impetuous, he thought I was unadventurous and cautious, so we disagreed at almost every turn. And of course we were both as stubborn as mules. When he said east, I said west. If I said left, he'd invariably say right.'

'Sounds like chaos,' said Savage. 'I'm amazed you ever established a safe route.'

'We didn't!' Walter massaged his forehead with the palm of his hand. 'We got horribly lost. Luckily I'd made a map of our route so far which meant we could retrace our muddled steps back to our ship. I thought this was a great feather in my cap but Marcello refused to even acknowledge that I'd saved the day. According to him we could just as easily have headed for high ground and sensed our way home from there.'

'I can see why you didn't want to tell me about Marcello.' Hugo giggled. 'I mean, how embarrassing – the great mapmaker Walter Bailey, lost in Africa!'

'I was lucky to ever get any work again,' said Walter, blushing.

'You never worked with Marcello again?' asked Savage.

'Heavens, no! Although we did become friends on the way back to the ship. I suspect he secretly began to see the merit in taking careful measurements of your position while I learned to appreciate the beauty of the land I was recording. Marcello taught me that every country has its own unique personality that makes it special.' Walter pursed his lips. 'That's not to say that a flicker of competition didn't remain and we'd spend the long days testing each other with riddles and codes.'

Hugo smiled. 'And you stayed in touch after you returned home?'

'Marcello lived in Milan but any time he came to Plymouth he would write to me telling me of his visit,' explained Walter. He took a long drink from his tankard and continued. 'But Marcello being Marcello, he couldn't just write a straightforward message – he was forever testing me. He used all manner of codes and cryptic symbols to let me know when, and exactly where, he wanted to meet. It became quite a game between us and I would do the same if I was ever visiting Italy.'

'That sounds like fun,' said Hugo, beaming. 'Like a secret club.'

'Oh, we were like a couple of schoolboys,' laughed Walter. 'Marcello always annotated his coded invitations with a special symbol he'd designed to signify that we were perfect opposites. And whatever the venue of our rendezvous, he'd always wait for me at the highest point of the building – in memory of his tendency to head for high ground when he was lost. Once I remember deducing that he would be on a particular ship that was docked in Plymouth harbour. I arrived at the ship at the allotted time and headed straight for the aft deck.'

'The highest deck on the ship,' agreed Hugo, nodding.

Uncle Walter shook his head. 'Marcello was nowhere to be seen. For a full hour I searched that vessel before it dawned on me where he would be hiding. I climbed to the top of the rigging and found him sitting in the crow's nest with a flagon of ale and two tankards.'

Hugo grinned at the thought of his uncle as a young man, taking his friend's complicated treasure hunt so seriously.

'Did you always solve his clues?' asked Savage.

'Of course,' said Walter, his kind eyes shining for a moment. Then his moustache drooped. 'Unfortunately Marcello's family went missing about a year before you came to live with me, Hugo. He became convinced that Lifereaper's underlings were responsible and his desire to avenge their loss consumed his life. I assumed that the grief had driven him mad. For my part I was sceptical of the legend of Lifereaper and have remained determinedly cynical ever since – until tonight.

'Mr Jafil's visit and the existence of Marcello's map have made me reconsider. My old friend may have been fixated on tracking down the Evil Lord but he wouldn't have produced a map that might lure others into Demonica without good reason. I'm ashamed to confess that I lost patience with his obsession when it seems he may have been right all along.' Walter hung his head. 'Marcello was a dear, kind friend and I wish I'd supported him more when he needed me. It seems now it's too late.'

'But we still have four months before it's too late,' said Savage eagerly. 'Let's get down to Demonica and rescue Marcello. It sounds exciting to me.'

'I'm not sure "exciting" is quite the right word,' said Hugo.

'Which word would you choose?' asked Savage.

'How about *extremely perilous*?' said Walter sternly.

'To the point where, if we're not chopped into pieces by a band of violent mercenaries, eaten alive by bears or mauled by wolves, we would most certainly end up being slaughtered by Lifereaper himself who, if the stories *are* correct, is the most dangerous, evil character ever to have walked this earth.'

Savage blinked a couple of times and twitched his whiskers. 'Actually,' he muttered grumpily, '*extremely perilous* is two words.'

'What sort of character is Lifereaper anyway?' wondered Hugo. 'Is he a person or an animal . . . or a monster?'

Walter scratched his chin. 'The tales I have heard refer to a cruel and ruthless creature, but as to what kind of being he is . . . who knows?'

'It seems strange they would use a cat to symbolize him,' mused Savage. 'If they wanted to signify his power and potency surely they could have chosen a more appropriate animal, such as . . . oh, I don't know . . . a mouse? I mean, who could possibly be afraid of a cat?'

'I suppose we'll find out for ourselves,' said Hugo, 'when we solve Marcello's code and find Lifereaper's lair.'

'We?' repeated Uncle Walter. 'There's no "we" about it. If I decide to help Jadea then I'm going alone. It's too dangerous for you two.'

'So instead you're going to leave us here, all alone, at the mercy of a band of sword-hungry bandits who could come here looking for you any day?' said Hugo.

'Good point,' Savage chipped in. 'Bandits who would probably not believe us when we said you were overseas and who might resort to violent measures in order to ascertain your location.'

'I hate it when you two gang up on me,' blurted Uncle Walter, getting up and marching off towards his study.

'So what's it to be?' Hugo called after him.

'I haven't decided,' said Uncle Walter testily, slamming the study door shut behind him.

Hugo and Savage winced at the noise and looked at each other in mock astonishment.

'I reckon we should definitely think about packing,' said Hugo with a smirk.

Chapter 8

Inside the windowless study, Walter sat on a rickety stool, hunched over a solid oak desk. A lantern stood at one end of the table, throwing dim orange light and long shadows on to the rough walls. Jadea's copy of Marcello's map lay flat on the desktop, its surface divided into sixteen equal squares by the sharp creases of its folds.

His eyes narrowed as he studied the scrawled message in one corner of the map.

To Walter Bailey
Plymouth

'Why me, old friend?' he muttered. 'Can the legend of Lifereaper actually be true? All those years I doubted you! Did you really discover his secret castle amidst those frozen peaks? I truly thought you were losing your mind but I cannot ignore the evidence before me.'

In front of him lay a square of thick brown parchment of exactly the same dimensions as Marcello's map. With his nose so close he could smell the dried ink, Walter studied the lines Jadea had drawn and then reproduced them with well-honed precision.

As a mapmaker he knew better than anybody the value of having his own chart to navigate by and, no matter how things turned out, he didn't want to rely on anyone else for guidance.

In the silence of the night, every sound seemed to be amplified to deafening proportions. The nib of his quill scratched and squeaked as, slowly and steadily, it echoed the details of Jadea's duplicate. His breath rasped like a saw, filling the airless room with heat so that his creased brow was soon varnished with sweat. Even the crinkling of the thick parchment under his pen sounded like the crack of a bullwhip.

Satisfied with his work, he sat up straight, pushing his palms into the small of his back and rolling his shoulders.

He shook his head and massaged his chin as he considered Marcello's map – a sketch of a small segment of mountains accompanied by a scroll containing an incomprehensible string of letters and symbols.

He knew his friend had entered Demonica from Lovdiv but the evil kingdom spread across a wide swathe of the Alps. The castle's location was sure to remain a mystery unless he could solve the coded message his

friend had left him. Taking a fresh piece of parchment, he set about trying to do so.

'What were you trying to tell me, old friend?' he whispered. 'And which of our favourite codes have you employed?'

When Walter finally left the study two hours later he dropped his copy of Marcello's map, folded neatly into a small square, into a thick clay pot on a high shelf.

Chapter 9

Hugo woke early, his mind buzzing with the recollection of the previous night's visitor. He jumped up and ran out of his bedroom to find Uncle Walter pulling on his overcoat.

'You're leaving,' said Hugo. 'You're going to see Jadea.'

'Your powers of deduction are impressive,' said Uncle Walter, the wrinkles around his eyes deepening as he smiled.

But Hugo wasn't smiling. He felt like he'd swallowed a rock.

'What about me and Savage?' he asked, his breathing getting faster.

'What do you mean?'

'Were you just going to leave us here without saying anything? What if the bandits come here looking for you? What if something happens to you?' Hugo's tone progressed from disbelief to anger. 'What if I never see you again? Weren't you even going to say goodbye? How could you just abandon us?'

'I'm sorry. I was wrong,' said Walter, holding his hands up. 'Your powers of deduction are truly awful.'

Half asleep, Savage stuck his nose out from under the flap of Hugo's pocket and sniffed the air.

'How could you think I would leave without telling you?' said Uncle Walter.

'You said . . .'

'I said that I'm going to see Jadea.' Uncle Walter approached Hugo and placed a strong hand on his shoulder. 'I didn't say I was heading off to hunt down an Evil Lord with him. I'm simply going to return his copy of Marcello's map and tell him what I have gleaned from it.'

'Do you know what it means?' demanded Hugo.

Walter smiled and nodded. 'There are two coded sequences of letters which I have managed to decipher. It should be enough to set Jadea on the right track. Then the rest will be up to him.'

'So you're not going to Romania without me?'

'I'm not sure if I'm going at all. I desperately want to save Marcello but it's just too dangerous to take you there – and I'm not leaving you here either.'

'But we'd be safe with Jadea, wouldn't we?' said Hugo.

Walter's thick moustache twitched. 'I'm sure Jadea is a worthy adversary for anyone and he has surely proved to be an effective guardian to many travellers in the past. But he is not invincible.'

'What do you mean?'

'Marcello once told me of an expedition he made to Scandinavia. One evening, while the rest of the team were setting up camp, the expedition botanist – a Frenchman by the name of Guillaume – went into the forest to study some of the plant life. The expedition Protector went along too. It was an incredible night – the air was clean, the sky was a flawless inky blue and thick frost coated everything like diamond dust.' Uncle Walter shook his head ruefully.

'What happened?' asked Hugo.

Uncle Walter looked into Hugo's eyes. 'They were attacked in the forest.'

Hugo gasped and Savage pricked up his translucent pink ears.

'Guillaume died,' Walter sighed. 'The Protector must have fought valiantly against their attackers – when he emerged from the forest alone he was covered in blood.'

'The Protector was Jadea, wasn't it?' whispered Hugo. 'That's why you asked him about Scandinavia.'

Walter nodded. 'I'd never heard Jadea's name until last night but when he mentioned that he'd been across Europe with Marcello the sovereign dropped. It just proves that, while I'm sure he is a fine swordsman with the heart of a lion, he cannot be everywhere at once. He is only human.'

'Well,' said Savage, cockily leaning one elbow on

the edge of Hugo's pocket. 'I'm happy to say that being human is certainly not one of my limitations. If you're looking for someone to protect you, then maybe I'm just the chattermouse for the job.'

'Can I see the map?' asked Hugo.

Uncle Walter laughed and ruffled Hugo's curly blonde hair. 'I'll let you have a crack at it when I get back – I made a copy last night.'

'Why?'

'Just in case,' replied Walter, arching his right eyebrow mysteriously.

'And what if the bandits come looking for you?'

'Now that I've deciphered Marcello's code I'll know exactly where *not* to send them.' Walter winked at his nephew.

'About those bandits . . .' said Hugo tentatively. 'I've been thinking.'

'Oh dear, that's never a good sign!' Walter smiled.

'I was thinking that if they were to come here we could team up with them,' Hugo persisted. 'We could search for Lifereaper together – the bandits' ruthlessness might be an asset when we're battling, um, whatever we might meet in the Alps. When we found Lifereaper we'd kill him with his sword then give it to the bandits to sell on the black market.'

Walter's eyes crinkled. 'That's an excellent idea, Hugo. But Marcello used to say that if the Diamond Sword was ever used to kill Lifereaper it would disintegrate immediately, leaving no evidence that it ever existed.'

Walter turned to leave.

'Uncle Walter! Wait!'

Walter popped his head back round the door. 'I'm sorry, Hugo,' he said firmly. 'I know what an appetite for adventure you have and I am just as desperate as you to save Marcello. But, for the last time, we don't know Jadea Jafil and I'm not going to risk everyone's lives by heading into the mountains of Demonica with him to find a castle that no living man has ever seen. If you, young man, are about to try and persuade me to change my mind then I suggest that you save your breath.'

Hugo looked at his uncle with surprise for a moment then pointed at the floor. 'You dropped a glove.'

Walter's bushy white eyebrows shot up his forehead and a rosy hue bloomed in his cheeks. 'Ah, right – I see – I mean, thank you,' he blustered, picking up his brown leather glove and stuffing it into his coat pocket. 'These blessed gloves are always falling out of my overcoat – it's a wonder I haven't lost them by now. I'll certainly need them today – it's almost wintry outside. I've never known autumn to be so cold. It never used to be like this when I was your age.'

Still muttering about the weather, Walter closed the front door behind him.

Hugo looked down at Savage. 'Are you thinking what I'm thinking?' he asked, with a mischievous smile.

'That depends,' said Savage. 'Are you thinking about having some cheese for breakfast and then going out to chase some cats?'

'Funnily enough, I'm not.' Hugo laughed. 'I'm thinking that somewhere in this house is a copy of Marcello's map.'

He looked longingly at the study door.

'I think we ought to wait until Uncle Walter shows it to us,' suggested Savage, seeing the mischievous glee in Hugo's face. 'While he's out, why don't we go down to the docks and watch Lilywhite's cousin preparing for his voyage? It should be fun seeing him try to work out which end of his boat is the front. While we're there you can sell a few maps to make some money for breakfast and I can terrorize a few sewer rats.'

'The door's unlocked though,' said Hugo, 'which must mean that Uncle Walter wouldn't mind if we looked inside.'

'Or that he trusts us not to,' added Savage.

Hugo thought for a moment then sighed. 'Come on then,' he said, grabbing his overcoat. 'Let's go and scare some rodents!'

Chapter 10

Sebastian Tumbledown-Smythe strode purposefully across the deck of his modest ship *The Iron Fist*. Its flat hull sat low in the water and a plain white sail hung limply from its only mast.

Sebastian was tall and lean, with broad shoulders and sinewy, muscular arms. His knee-length tunic was cut from sombre grey wool and his black felt tricorne hat was unadorned by feathers or braid. His beady eyes darted around hyperactively beneath his low forehead and his square jaw was set in an expression of permanent menace.

As he patrolled his ship, Tumbledown-Smythe barked orders to his crew.

'Wilkins, lash that rigging before I lash my whip across your back!' he yelled, steam pumping from his nostrils like an angry bull. 'Jacobs, you 'orrible toerag, if you don't throw those sacks below decks forthwith I'll throw you overboard. Hawkins, are you going to run my coat of arms up the flagpole or shall I run my sword through your belly?'

The sailors leaped sharply into action at the sound of his voice – ropes were tightened, sacks were hauled below decks, and the flag was flown. It was a plain red rectangle bearing a simple white X from corner to corner.

Hugo watched the activity from the dockside with Savage perched on his shoulder.

'Who is that frightening man?' whispered Savage. 'And what has he done with Rupert's cousin?'

'I know what you mean,' agreed Hugo. 'It's hard to believe he's even from the same species as Rupert, never mind the same family. He's so forceful and, well . . . competent.'

'He's not just competent, he's *in*competent,' corrected Savage, nodding wisely.

Hugo chuckled. 'Come on, let's see if we can sell any maps today.'

Luckily a ship from France had just docked and two of its passengers bought one of Hugo's maps almost immediately. He spent the money on a loaf of rye bread and a slice of pickled beef from a stall in the market square, taking great care to hide his face from the fat grocer.

By the time Hugo got home his nose and fingertips were numb from the cold.

'We're home!' he called as he slammed the front door shut.

Silence.

He walked over to the table in the centre of the room and looked around.

'Uncle Walter?'

As he glanced down at the table, the unfinished chess game from the previous night caught his eye.

Hugo's chess matches with Uncle Walter often stretched over two or three days with countless breaks for their daily activities. During these intermissions the board was always treated as a no-go area. Neither player would so much as study the state of play, let alone touch one of his pieces, without the other being present. Until now.

One of the pieces had been moved since they'd stopped play.

What was even stranger was that Uncle Walter had made such a foolish move. He had placed his bishop right out in the open, where it could be taken by either Hugo's rook or his knight.

As he surveyed the board Hugo felt goosebumps pop up all over his arms and a shiver wriggled through his shoulders. He had a strange feeling that everything wasn't as it should be.

'Look at this,' he said, scooping Savage out of his pocket. 'Uncle Walter's been playing with the chessboard – on his own.'

'I never thought I'd see the day,' tutted Savage, perching on Hugo's knuckle to get a good view of the board game. 'And look! He must have been in such a hurry to leave the scene of the crime that he left his overcoat on the floor.'

'Hang on,' said Hugo, his heart hammering in his chest. 'Not only would Uncle Walter never ever leave his coat lying on the floor, he'd never go out on a day like today without it.'

'I know – it's freezing out there.'

'I think he's in trouble,' said Hugo shakily. 'I think he was forced to leave the house.'

'You mean . . . *kidnapped*?' said Savage. 'But by whom?'

Hugo and Savage looked at each other.

'The bandits!'

Chapter 11

'Come on,' urged Savage, leaping to the floor and scampering towards the door. 'Let's go after him. We'll teach those bandits not to meddle with us.'

He stood up on his back legs and clenched his front paws into little fists under his chin. 'If we can defeat a whole herd of buffalogres then I think we can take care of a handful of measly outlaws without even breaking into a sweat.' He unleashed a flurry of punches on an imaginary target.

'Oh, I don't doubt your fighting prowess,' said Hugo, smiling at his little friend, 'but we don't know where the bandits have taken Uncle Walter. We've been out for hours – they could be twenty miles away by now.'

'But we know they're heading for Romania,' Savage announced, spreading his arms with exasperation.

'You're right,' said Hugo. 'Let's go. We'll head for Romania and when we get there we'll just ask around a bit – see if anybody's seen a group of bandits and a hostage with messy white hair and a moustache.'

Savage nodded eagerly and turned towards the door, but he'd only taken a couple of steps before he stopped and turned back, fixing Hugo with a suspicious stare.

'You're teasing me, aren't you?' he said flatly.

'I'm sorry,' sighed Hugo. 'I just think we should spend a few minutes preparing for our journey.'

'You're right,' said Savage, fanning his ears out wide. 'Tell me the plan – I'm all ears.'

'I don't really have a plan, as such. Let me think . . .' Hugo paused for breath as the butterflies in his stomach began to feel like a flock of geese. 'We know Marcello's map starts in Lovdiv so that's probably where Uncle Walter will lead the bandits. If we haven't caught up with them by then, we'll have to follow them into Demonica. They'll be using Marcello's map, which we don't have . . . but we know someone who does!'

'What exactly are you saying?' asked Savage, frowning.

'Basically, I think now is definitely the time to pack.'

Hugo went to his bedroom and returned with his leather satchel before loading it with a compass, his battered leather notebook, some charcoal and a couple of blankets. Leaning against the wall in a corner was the sword given to him by Snowdon – prince of the remote island he had discovered on his first expedition. He grabbed the weapon and slid it into his belt, then he went to Uncle Walter's study and turned the door handle before pausing.

Savage clambered up Hugo's shirt and perched on

his shoulder. 'Don't feel guilty about going in,' he said reassuringly. 'I think Uncle Walter would forgive your intrusion given the severity of the situation.'

'I don't feel guilty,' said Hugo. 'The door's locked.'

He stalked across the room to the thick clay pot that sat on the high shelf. Standing on tiptoes he reached up and delved into the pot, just as he had secretly done on many occasions when Uncle Walter's study was still off limits. As Hugo felt around inside the pot, his fingers brushed against something that didn't feel like a key.

Intrigued and excited, he fished out the small square of parchment and unfolded it.

'This must be a copy of Marcello's map,' he whispered. 'It's got two codes just as Uncle Walter described.'

Savage scampered down to Hugo's wrist to have a closer look.

For a moment the two friends stared agape at the map and its strange coded message.

'What does it mean?' said Savage.

'We don't have time to work it out now.' Hugo folded the map up and slid it into his satchel. 'We have to get moving.'

Reaching into the clay pot again, he hooked out the key and unlocked the study.

'What do you need in here anyway?' asked Savage as they entered the tiny room.

'If we're going to navigate our way across a whole

continent we're going to need a chart to guide us,' replied Hugo, casting his eyes around.

He had been expecting to see the room ransacked, maps and charts strewn around in the aftermath of a frenzied search by the bandits. But the study was untouched. Uncle Walter's backstaff sat neatly on the top shelf as usual and the maps on the wall were arranged as they had always been.

As Hugo scanned the scores of charts he noticed

something that made him catch his breath. One of the scrolls on the shelf was jutting out about an inch further than the others.

He smiled triumphantly. 'Aha!' he said, withdrawing the scroll and brandishing it like a sword.

Spreading the map on the table, he studied its inky lines. He traced his finger along mountain ridges and through valleys, trying to picture the terrain they described. He imagined the clear mountain air in his nostrils and the squeak of fresh snow underfoot. Then to his surprise he saw that the region of Demonica was shaded with a criss-cross pattern.

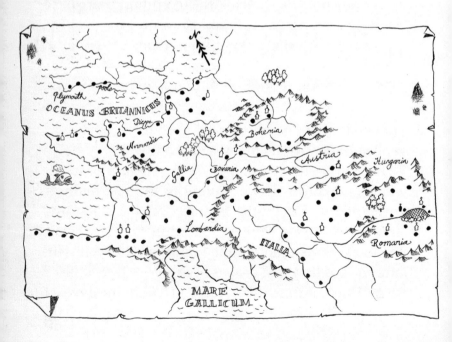

Its borders were marked clearly enough – a river to the north and a forest to the south, enclosing an elliptical region close to the Transylvanian Alps.

'Looks like Demonica is somewhat uncharted territory,' Savage observed.

'It's almost as if it's a no-go area,' said Hugo, feeling his pulse quicken. 'It's spooky to think there's this small but distinct kingdom in the mountains that no one has ever explored.'

'Or at least, never returned from exploring.'

Hugo began rolling the map up with short, sharp twists of his wrists.

'So how do we know which part of Demonica Marcello's map refers to?' asked Savage.

'That's easy,' said Hugo with a gappy smile. 'Or at least it will be once we've deciphered Marcello's riddle. And if we map Demonica ourselves as we go along, we'll know where his map fits in. Come on, we have to hurry.'

He grabbed the rolled-up map and the backstaff and strode purposefully into the living room.

'It's just occurred to me that Uncle Walter moved very little in the house, even though he must have been under pressure from the bandits,' observed Hugo, packing his leather satchel. 'Is it possible that he was trying to give us some sort of clues with the stuff he did move?'

'Leaving his coat on the floor certainly made us think he had gone out against his will,' recalled Savage, his nose twitching excitedly. 'Maybe he locked the study door to make you look in the pot for the key . . . so you'd discover the copy of Marcello's map.'

'It can't be a coincidence that the one map he'd disturbed in his study is the one that covers our route to Lovdiv,' added Hugo. 'But I don't understand why he moved the chess piece. Do you think that's a clue too?'

'Perhaps there's something we need to *check, mate*?' ventured Savage.

As Hugo pulled on his doublet, Savage hurdled the collar to avoid being engulfed by the garment.

'We don't have time to think about it now – we'll do it on the way.' said Hugo urgently. 'But first we have to collect someone else.'

Chapter 12

Hugo pelted along the cobbled alleyways, dodging and ducking through the crowds. Savage hung his head out of Hugo's pocket, ears pinned back in the slipstream, whooping with delight as he was bounced along and yelling things like, 'Go Hugo, go!' or 'Watch out for that horse!'

Hugo skidded to a halt outside the Sailors' Inn, immediately doubling over and resting his hands on his knees as his lungs convulsed. After a couple of deep breaths he stood up, still gasping, and entered the inn.

The guesthouse was a narrow building squeezed in the middle of a terrace constructed with a wooden frame filled in with wattle and daub. The innkeeper was a young wiry woman with lank hair under a grubby scarf. She wore a sludge-coloured dress with a woollen shawl wrapped around her bony shoulders. When she saw Hugo she stood up and gave him a wide, welcoming smile that showed off a row of rotting, festering teeth.

'Hello,' said Hugo, trying not to recoil visibly at the decaying contents of her mouth. 'I'm looking for a friend of mine and I was very much hoping you might be able to help me.' He was speaking ever so properly to endear himself to the lady.

'I ain't no missing persons whatchamacallit,' she replied, a look of bewilderment replacing her welcoming smile in an instant. 'Besides, I never heard of him.'

'But I haven't told you his name yet,' said Hugo.

'So you haven't – silly me!' she giggled. 'What's his name then?'

'Jadea. I do believe he's staying at your fine establishment.'

'Well, I definitely ain't heard of no Jadea and even if I had I couldn't tell you, I'm afraid,' said the woman, shrugging.

'Why not?'

'Some of my guests are very important and insist on total privacy,' she announced, folding her skinny arms proudly. 'When they stay at my guesthouse they can rely on my complete discretion, so they can. That's exactly what I told one of our guests this morning. I said to him, "You can rely on my complete discretion, Mr Jafil." That's what I said to him.'

Hugo felt Savage twitch with excitement in his pocket at the mention of Jadea's name, but he maintained a display of disinterest.

'And you are obviously a woman of your word,' observed Hugo. As he spoke he spotted a ledger sitting on the dusty countertop, with a quill nestling in the cleft of its open pages. 'I suppose the contents of your guest book are a closely guarded secret as well?'

'Of course. I am the only person what is privy to the details contained in there, therein,' she said, nodding at the book on the counter.

'Is that what you told Mr Jafil when he checked out today?'

'Oh, he ain't checked out. He's staying in room number . . . Hang on a minute!' Her eyes widened as realization dawned across her face. 'You're just snooping around, aren't you? What are you, some sort of burglarizer or some such? Why, you little ratbag!' As she came round the counter towards Hugo, her voice grew louder and more piercing.

Sensing he was about to be forcibly ejected from the building, Hugo scooped Savage out of his pocket.

'Time for plan B,' he muttered.

'Gotcha,' said Savage with a wink, before leaping to the floor.

'Oh my gosh!' Hugo exclaimed, pointing at the ground behind the innkeeper. 'What on earth is that?'

Savage was running round and round in a tight circle, scratching the floor with his little claws and trying to squeak like an ordinary mouse as loudly and as shrilly as he possibly could.

'AAAiiEEH! A MOUSE!' screamed the innkeeper, lifting the hem of her skirt off the floor. Savage responded by scampering towards her and executing a perfect figure of eight pattern about her feet, rooting her to the spot in terror.

Hugo took his opportunity to explore the inn.

He ran to the desk and tore the last page from the ledger before heading towards the staircase. As he climbed the stairs two at a time he glanced at the page in his hands.

Name: *J. Jafil* Room: *3* Signed: *Jadeajafil*

In the comments column the innkeeper had scrawled,

No turndown service required. Guest takes afternoon catnap.

Reaching the top of the stairs Hugo hurried along the landing, checking the numbers on the doors. When he found room number 3 he pushed the page from the guest book into his satchel before banging on the door. As he knocked, the door's hinges screeched like a scalded cat and it opened about an inch.

'Mr Jafil?' Hugo called meekly.

There was no reply.

His mind picturing all sorts of horrible scenarios, he stepped forward and tentatively eased the door open. What if the bandits had come and done something nasty to Jadea? Even worse, what if they were still there doing it?

But the room was deserted. The bed in the corner was unmade and a meal of bread and cheese sat uneaten on a plate on the floor. The opposite wall was adorned with a distressed-looking mirror and two tankards stood on a rickety table by the grimy window.

He wondered if the bandits had taken Jadea. There was no sign of a struggle but there hadn't been at home either and he was sure Uncle Walter had been kidnapped. Now the bandits had his uncle, he concluded their only reason to come after Jadea would be to kill the one person who might identify them. But as he surveyed the simple room he decided the most likely explanation was much less sinister – armed with Uncle Walter's solution to Marcello's code Jadea must have already set off for Demonica.

As he turned to leave Hugo noticed a brown leather glove lying on the floor by the door. Recognizing it, he picked it up and slipped it into his satchel before going back downstairs.

The sight that greeted Hugo in the hallway was one that caused him to stop and stare for a moment as a wide smile dimpled his cheeks.

The innkeeper had taken refuge from Savage by standing on a chair next to the wall. The blood had drained from her face, which had the pallor and sickly

sheen of a wax candle, and she was still clutching her skirt with one hand while the other covered her mouth, out of which was emanating a deep-throated, murderous shriek.

On the floor in the middle of the hallway, Savage was now sitting on his haunches, having tired of scampering around. With one thumb pressed to his little pink nose he was waggling his claws furiously at the innkeeper while flapping his ears and blowing an incredibly enthusiastic raspberry in her direction.

'What are you smiling at?' the woman screamed at Hugo. 'That mouse is crazy.'

Hugo crossed the hallway and opened the front door before turning back.

'If you think he's acting crazy now, you should see him when his egg is overcooked,' he giggled. 'Come on, Savage, we've got a boat to catch.'

Chapter 13

Hugo stood on the dockside staring up at *The Iron Fist* and took a deep breath. The stench of fish oil and brine filled his nostrils. He was scared and excited and his arms and legs felt weak, as if nothing more than fresh air was flowing through his veins.

'I haven't felt this nervous since I joined the crew of *El Tonto Perdido* behind Uncle Walter's back,' he said, with a wry smile. 'Luckily for me he discovered what I'd done and joined me on the expedition. I don't know if I'd have had the nerve to set sail on my own. And, what's more, I don't think I'm brave enough to go it alone now.'

'Well, I can think of two good reasons for you to walk up that gangplank,' said Savage softly. 'Number one, Uncle Walter is depending on you. You're the only person who knows what kind of trouble he's in.'

'You're right,' agreed Hugo with a note of resolve. 'What's number two?'

'Number two is that you're not going it alone anyway,' said Savage, playfully tugging Hugo's blonde hair. 'You are ably accompanied and supported by the strongest, toughest, bravest and, it has to be said, most handsome talking mouse-like creature in the whole of England.'

Hugo turned to look at Savage, who was now clasping his paws together above his head as if he were a victorious gladiator accepting the applause of a packed coliseum.

'But Savage, you're the *only* talking mouse in the whole of England.'

'Have you had any better offers?' enquired Savage, dropping his paws to his furry hips. 'Now, let's go aboard. I'll make myself scarce.' He darted down into Hugo's satchel.

At the top of the gangplank Hugo was met by Sebastian Tumbledown-Smythe himself, his arms folded resolutely across his barrel chest and his jaw jutting forward in an ugly grimace. Even though it was bitterly cold his face and arms were covered with perspiration and steam rose from his muscular body, as if he were a stallion recovering from a long gallop.

'Where do you think you're going, you little rascal?' he demanded, resting an elbow on one knee and leaning down so that his eyes were level with Hugo's.

Hugo cleared his throat. 'I have come to join your crew, sir,' he announced, as assertively as he could.

Sebastian's mouth twitched. 'Oh really? And what position does a scallywag like you intend to fill on my ship?'

'I am applying for the position of mapmaker, sir.' Hugo lifted his chin as his confidence grew. 'I have trained with the great Walter Bailey and I sailed with your cousin Rupert Lilywhite on his first . . . and last . . . voyage. With my navigational skills and . . .'

Sebastian held out one hand, giving Hugo an uncomfortably close view of its calloused palm.

'I've already got a mapmaker.'

'Oh.'

'Surely you're not surprised? Look, it'll be high tide in less than an hour,' said Sebastian with an air of derision. 'What sort of a cabbage-brain plans to set off on a voyage across the world without a mapmaker?'

Hugo smiled sheepishly. 'Your cousin did,' he said. 'He hadn't even considered having a mapmaker until I asked to join his crew.'

Sebastian threw his head back and guffawed. 'Rupert knows nothing about sailing and even less about exploring. If you thought I'd be anything like my cousin then you're badly mistaken.' Suddenly his menacing frown was back. 'Now, are you going to leave my ship or am I going to leave my bootprint on your bony behind?'

'Maybe I could keep a lookout, in the crow's nest?'

'Don't tell me my cousin didn't have a lookout either?'

'No, he did, actually,' stammered Hugo. 'But he only had one eye . . . and he was always drunk.'

'Well, mine is stone cold sober and has a full complement of eyes,' hollered Sebastian, his face growing more and more puce. 'So kindly sling your hook before I sling you into the water.'

'But I really need to get to France,' pleaded Hugo.

'Oh, I didn't realize you *really* needed to get there. Why didn't you say so? Come aboard and enjoy the ride. You can share my cabin.'

'Really?' said Hugo dubiously.

'No!' bellowed Sebastian, his face just inches from Hugo's. 'Of course not. What does this look like, some sort of pleasure boat? Now disembark immediately before I disembowel you!'

As Hugo turned and slunk down the gangplank, Sebastian shouted after him. 'How dare you insult me by comparing me to my good-for-nothing cousin! Do I need a mapmaker indeed! The only thing this ship is missing is a champion rat catcher and that's only down to unfortunate circumstances. It's certainly nothing to do with a lack of foresight on my part, I assure you.'

'Sorry?' said Hugo, stopping and turning back. 'Did you say, "rat catcher"?'

'Aye. There was something of a misunderstanding yesterday,' muttered Sebastian. 'I told Cook to feed the crew cat, and he thought I meant "feed the crew *the* cat". Anyway, to cut a long story short, last night's beef stew was served with a little extra ingredient – chopped *Ginger*. And it wasn't the fragrant spice, if you get my meaning.'

Hugo's mouth was contorted in disgust. 'You ate the ship's cat?' he said – louder than normal so as to drown out the muffled sound of devilish chuckling coming from his satchel.

'It was surprisingly tasty,' remarked Sebastian. 'So the upshot of it all is that we ain't got a cat, and with six months' worth of supplies on this ship we're going to be overrun with rats before you can say "disease-ridden vermin". Unless we find ourselves a trained rat catcher within the hour, which seems pretty darn unlikely.'

Hugo's eyes twinkled. 'So if I could find you an effective rat catcher, could I come aboard your ship?'

Sebastian Tumbledown-Smythe gave him a sideways look.

'Don't tell me you've got a savage moggy in that there satchel of yours?'

'Well, he is savage.' Hugo flipped his satchel open. 'But he's not a cat, *exactly*.'

Chapter 14

'Are you trying to be funny, boy?' screamed Sebastian, grinding his teeth and staring at Savage who was sitting upright on Hugo's palm. 'If you don't distance that vermin from my ship I'll distance your head from your shoulders – and that's a promise.'

With a fluid sweep of his arm, Sebastian's sword was drawn, its point tickling Hugo's Adam's apple.

'Its not a joke,' protested Hugo. 'This is Savage. He's the best rat catcher in the whole of England . . .'

Savage pinched Hugo's palm with one of his claws and gave him an indignant frown.

'. . . if not the whole of Europe,' added Hugo, wincing. 'In fact he's quite possibly the best rat catcher in the whole world.'

Sebastian threw back his head and laughed, making a noise like a donkey braying. Some of the sailors on the ship had noticed the little blonde boy with the big-eared mouse and had gathered round to see what was happening.

'Tell them I'm fearless,' prompted Savage, whispering through the corner of his mouth. Hugo ignored Savage's suggestion until he felt a row of tiny claws pressing painfully into his palm.

'And he is, er, fearless,' repeated Hugo to his amused audience.

Savage stood as tall as he could and purposefully crossed his arms.

The sailors nudged each other and chuckled at the performing mouse.

'Don't forget strong,' insisted Savage, this time utilizing the claws on his toes.

'Ouch! And he is *very* strong,' Hugo proclaimed.

Savage adopted the pose of a circus strongman showing off his muscles and the sailors cheered.

'All I ask is that you give this little fellow a chance,' announced Hugo. 'I will wager one sovereign with every man here that this little mouse will catch a rat on your ship within a minute.'

There was a collective murmur of interest from the crowd.

'Well, this should be good sport if nothing else,' said Sebastian with a glint in his eye. 'Bring the mouse aboard so that I can bring you down.'

Seaman Flutter was appointed as the official book-maker and he collected the sailors' stakes while Savage warmed up by scuttling back and forth along the deck. There was a short debate about how to measure whether he had completed his task within the allocated minute.

Master Hawkins, the ship's navigator, thought it made sense that Savage should have to catch sixty rats within the time it would take the sand to run through the ship's hourglass as this would equate to an average of one rat every minute. Hugo protested that catching sixty rats was an unfairly arduous task for a single mouse and his complaint was upheld after a ship's steward's enquiry.

It was then suggested that someone should count to sixty, at one-second intervals, and it seemed that the problem had been solved. But on a practice run it was discovered that no one on board dared count beyond twelve – because thirteen was deemed to bring bad luck to anyone who uttered it – except for Hugo, and he was thought to be unsuitable on account of his allegiance with the contestant.

Eventually, after much debate and various experiments, it was agreed by both parties that it would take approximately one minute for Seaman Lugger to complete one circuit of the main deck carrying two sacks of corn.

As Seaman Lugger hefted the sacks over his broad shoulders ready for the competition, Hugo massaged Savage's neck between his thumb and forefinger.

'Deep breaths,' he whispered. 'You can do this – don't worry.'

'Who's worried?' protested Savage, skipping from foot to foot. 'This is hardly my first time, you know. Who was it that single-pawedly stopped scores of rats eating the meagre supplies on board *El Tonto Perdido*?'

'You did,' Hugo replied dutifully.

'Thank you. I caught more rats on that voyage back to England than you've had boiled dinners. And that's saying nothing of the rodents I've apprehended in the pantry in Peppercorn Lane.' Savage's mouth curved into a crooked, self-satisfied smile. 'Yes indeed, the stories I could tell! I mean, if I had a sovereign for every rat I caught stealing food in that house . . .'

'OK, I get it – you've caught a lot of rats!' Hugo interrupted. 'Just keep your guard up and your chin down.'

'By the way, boy,' Sebastian growled in Hugo's ear, 'how do I know you can afford to pay off your bets when the rats tear your funny little mouse apart?'

Hugo smiled with as much confidence as he could muster and patted his satchel. 'I've got plenty of money in here,' he lied. 'I give you my word.'

'I don't want your word. But if you can't pay up you'll give me your tongue, followed by your heart and your liver. Then I'll cut you into little chunks and feed you to the fish myself. Do I make myself clear?'

'Crystal.' Hugo clenched his teeth and forced his mouth into a dry smile.

'OK, let's get this over with,' announced Sebastian. 'Seaman Lugger, are you ready?'

'Aye aye, sir,' puffed Seaman Lugger.

'Performing mouse, are you ready?'

'He's ready,' said Hugo, giving Savage a final good luck stroke.

'In that case, three, two, one, GO!'

A huge cheer erupted from the crew as Seaman Lugger set off on his lap of the ship, labouring painfully under the weight of his ballast. Sniffing the air, Savage scampered to the edge of the deck and disappeared through the doorway to the crew quarters. Seaman Flutter, enjoying a bird's-eye view of proceedings from halfway up the main mast, gave a running commentary.

The mouse has disappeared into the cabin while Lugger has set off at a steady pace – at this rate he's right on course for a one-minute lap. Lugger is reaching the end of the starboard bow already and rounding the helm – and still no sign of the mouse. Lugger is blowing hard now but he's on the port bow, which means he's halfway round . . .

Hugo bit his lip and glanced anxiously at the doorway. 'Come on, Savage.'

But wait – I think Lugger is tiring at last! He's definitely slowing down. I saw him stumble there and he's beginning to stagger. Where is that mouse? Lugger has reached the end of the port bow. All he has to do is round the helm and he will be the victor. There's still no sign of the mouse. Lugger is nearly at the finish line! He's just got to stumble another ten yards . . . nine . . . eight . . .

'Savage, where are you?' hissed Hugo, his eyes trained on the open doorway.

. . . Six . . . five . . . Surely Lugger has won this race? Four . . . three . . .

'Come on, Savage!' Hugo willed him on.

Lugger only has two yards to go . . .

WHUMP!

As one, everyone on the ship turned to see something small and grey rolling along the wooden deck.

Lugger dropped to his knees, exhausted and dejected, the sacks slumping on to the deck just a yard from the finish line. A hush settled over the crew and a broad, gap-toothed smile spread across Hugo's face.

A short distance from the open doorway to the crew's quarters lay a hairy grey rat, its two front teeth protruding from its slack mouth as its feet twitched sporadically. A moment later Savage emerged from the doorway brushing his palms together, his ears fanned out with pride and tinged purple with exertion. Picking up the worm-like tail and draping it over his shoulder, he dragged the rat's motionless body across the deck and laid it at Hugo's feet.

Sebastian stared in open-mouthed disbelief at the fat rat and the little black and white mouse that appeared to be posing with one foot on its motionless body like a great warrior standing over the body of a fallen opponent.

'Is it dead?' he stammered at last.

'Goodness me, no,' said Hugo, hurriedly scooping Savage into his pocket just as he was beginning a little victory dance around the rat. 'It's just stunned, I think. You said you wanted a rat catcher, not a rat killer.'

'And what do you propose I do with the vermin on the ship once your, er, mouse has caught them?'

'Keep them in a barrel,' suggested Hugo. 'And when we reach France you could liberate them.'

As Sebastian considered the idea a satisfied smile spread across his face. 'I suppose it would be like exporting them, wouldn't it?'

'Exactly,' agreed Hugo. 'A gift from England's sewers – nothing but the pest.'

'OK, here's the deal,' said Sebastian. 'You can sail with us so long as your mouse guards our food supplies. But as soon as we reach the French coast, you're on your own. Seaman Lugger! Show the boy to the crew quarters.'

'Thank you, sir,' said Hugo.

'Don't thank me. If so much as one rat finds its way

into our supplies you'll be finding your way to the bottom of the sea.'

As Hugo followed Seaman Lugger into the dark airless room that was to be the crew's living quarters for the next few days, Savage pushed his way out of his pocket and clambered up to his shoulder.

'What took you so long catching that rat?' demanded Hugo.

'Actually, I think the words you're searching for are *Well done, Savage, old buddy*. I mean, would it kill you to say thank you? It's not as if you could have earned your passage on this boat without me. I'd like to see you try and catch a rat in under a minute, yes siree! Besides, I'd caught that old rat in about ten seconds – found him sleeping under a blanket.'

'So what were you doing for the other forty-nine seconds while I was panicking about having my vital organs removed from my body?'

'Snacking.'

'Snacking!' exclaimed Hugo.

'Snacking,' confirmed Savage.

CHapter 15

It was a moonless night and Hugo sat on the deck of *The Iron Fist* listening to the trickling sound of the sea lapping at its hull. The sky was clear and the stars, pinpoints of light in the black sheet overhead, reminded him of Uncle Walter. He had taught Hugo about the constellations during their last voyage together while the two of them had sat on deck admiring the sky, just as he was doing now. He felt suddenly lonely and wondered if Uncle Walter was looking at the same stars from wherever he was. If the bandits had set sail as soon as they'd kidnapped Walter they would already be making good progress across the French plains. Hugo pictured the bandits flying through the night on horseback and wondered how he would ever catch them up.

Six miles outside Dieppe, five men were shambling along a dirt track.

'Where's this bloomin' stable then?' demanded one. 'We've been wandering down this road for two hours and I ain't seen so much as a horseshoe.'

'Beats me,' shrugged another. 'Pierre just said we

should head south-east from the dock. You can't miss it, apparently.'

'Oi, you! Mr Navigator.' The first man drew his sword and held it against a third man's chest. 'Are you sure we been travelling south-east?'

The third man held his hands up. One was clad in a brown leather glove, the other was bare.

'South-*east*? Good heavens no – I thought you said south-west,' he exclaimed. 'I find it very hard to understand you all when you mumble so terribly. You really must speak more clearly. Well, I think the only thing we can do is head back to the docks and start again, don't you?'

The other four men ground their teeth and eyed their navigator angrily, before turning and traipsing wearily back along the track.

Only the occasional muffled sound of the sailors calling instructions across *The Iron Fist* disturbed the hush of the night. A keen wind held Hugo's hair off his face and filled the mainsail and the boat rose and fell with the swell of the sea as it skipped on its course. Soon they would reach the French coast and Hugo's thoughts turned to the journey ahead.

He took the copy of Marcello's map out of his satchel, unfolded it and anchored it to the deck with a lantern. Then he slid out the map from Uncle Walter's study and unfurled it on the oak floor, holding down the corners with various assorted objects. First he studied Marcello's code.

He tried saying the letters out loud in case they were phonetic clues, but found the first line meaningless and the second unpronounceable. Perhaps it was a foreign language spoken by an ancient African civilization Marcello had encountered on his travels, or possibly an acronym, each letter being the initial to a series of instructions.

Hugo screwed his eyes shut and combed his hands through his hair. He would have been surprised to see just how closely he resembled his uncle at that moment.

A shuffling, scratching sound made Hugo open his eyes. Savage was dragging a rather skinny rat by the tail towards an open barrel just a few yards away. At the base of the keg lay about five or six comatose rats, piled up in a flea-ridden heap.

'Savage, you startled me.'

Savage tilted his head up and twitched his whiskers, his beady little eyes staring hard.

'Sorry about that,' he whispered. 'How inconsiderate of me to disturb your lolling around with my frivolous hard labour. I really must try not to make so much noise humping these fat hairy vermin around. Perhaps I should douse them in oil to stop their coarse fur from rubbing so noisily on the deck or even shave them altogether.'

'There's no need for that,' smirked Hugo. 'Just try not to breathe so loudly.'

'I consider it an honour that you permit me to breathe at all, Your Highness,' said Savage, placing one foot behind the other and sinking into a deep curtsy.

Smiling, Hugo turned his attention back to Marcello's map. He pictured a panorama of craggy, angular mountains clad in crisp white armour before a backdrop of clean, cobalt sky. Running his finger along the ragged ridge he imagined the snow-covered peaks they described then he turned his attention to Uncle Walter's map.

They were due to dock at Dieppe harbour sometime the following day.

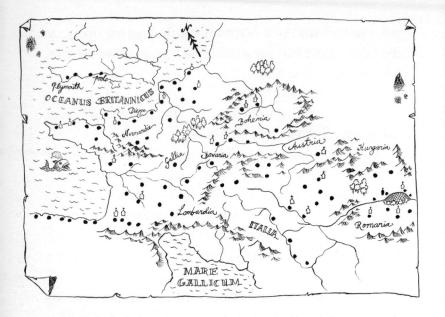

He pointed to the French port on the chart then traced his forefinger slowly across the continent, meandering through whole countries and gliding over hills and forests. In a few seconds his finger had traversed France and journeyed between Bavaria and Bohemia, crossing the border into Austria and negotiating Hungary before sliding effortlessly into Romania. If only the journey itself would be that simple!

His first task was to identify Lovdiv, the village from whence his expedition would begin in earnest. Lying on his belly he lowered his face close to the map and slid the lantern nearer, throwing an amber glow across the parchment. He knew that Lovdiv lay on the edge of the Transylvanian Alps, close to the Demonican border.

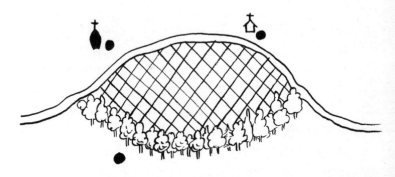

Three villages, denoted by small orange circles, lay close enough to the border to be considered possibilities but, due to the immense scale of the chart, none of them was labelled. Hugo's eyes darted from one to the other as he tried to assess which one might be Lovdiv. Two of them lay on a river or stream while the third was situated near the forest that marked the southern border. He remembered Jadea saying that the merchants had been following a stream when they discovered Marcello's satchel.

'You look pleased with yourself,' said Savage, sidling on to the map and sniffing at the inky lines under Hugo's finger. 'I thought I'd take a break to help you with the exhausting task of looking at a map.'

'I'm trying to find Lovdiv,' said Hugo. 'The good news is that I've narrowed it down to one of these two villages. The bad news is that they're about twenty miles apart.'

'I see,' said Savage, his nose darting from one to the other.

'This must denote a church.' Hugo pointed to the small pointed rectangle topped with a tiny cross that had been marked next to one of the towns when Walter had originally drawn the map.

Savage snapped his fingers. 'Jadea said the people of Lovdiv had built their village around an ancient Roman church to help protect them from evil,' he said eagerly. 'So that must be Lovdiv, right?'

'I'm not sure.' Hugo frowned. 'I'm still baffled by this other symbol.' He tapped a small black shape next to the circle of the other village.

'I don't remember seeing one like it before. It looks like a black arch or something. But the fact that it has a cross on top of it makes me think this is also some kind of church.'

'So which town is Lovdiv?' Savage sighed.

Hugo smiled. 'That, as Uncle Walter would say, is the sixty-four-thousand sovereign question.'

Savage peered closely at the symbols, his claws scratching on the paper as he darted between the towns. 'So we've got the normal rectangular church symbol,' he muttered to himself, 'or we've got this black arch, which actually looks more like a bishop's hat when you look at it up close.'

'Does it? Let me see,' Hugo exclaimed, peering closely at the symbol. 'Savage, that's it!'

'Is it?'

'Uncle Walter *was* leaving us a clue with his open bishop. The ancient Roman church in Lovdiv is marked with a symbol shaped like a mitre with a cross on top!'

'Ancient Roman church in spooky Transylvanian village, here we come,' said Savage. He turned his head sharply and sniffed the air. 'Listen I can't stand around solving your problems all night – I've got rats to catch.'

Darting across the deck he disappeared behind a coiled rope, reappearing a moment later with a hairy carcass in tow.

'Those rats just don't stand a chance with you on the job,' marvelled Hugo.

Savage gave a short, snappy salute. 'Just call me the Verminator.'

Chapter 16

Hugo stood on the dockside in Dieppe surveying the scene with *Savage* perched on his shoulder, his whiskers twitching furiously.

The crew of *The Iron Fist* were busily carrying crates and sacks and kegs down the gangplank and loading them on to a line of horse-drawn carts that were waiting on the shiny cobbles below.

'Come on, Seaman Flutter,' yelled Sebastian from the dockside. 'Are you going to step on it or am I going to have to step on you?'

The ship's captain turned and flung a cloth purse to Hugo, who caught it against his stomach with a grunt.

'That's your winnings,' said Sebastian. 'You and your peculiar little mouse did a good job controlling those rats. There should be enough money there to keep you both in food for some considerable time.'

Hugo hefted the purse in his hands then, nodding over Sebastian's shoulder, he said, 'Enough for a horse and cart?'

'You've got a lot of nerve, sonny,' growled Sebastian, drawing his sword.

Hugo gulped.

'I like that in a boy. You remind me of a young me.'

Hugo smiled.

Gesturing with his sword Sebastian pointed at the last horse and cart in his convoy. 'That pony and trap are all yours in exchange for the contents of the purse. The cart's a bit rickety but the horse is strong and he'll get you where you're going.'

'Fully loaded with provisions for our journey, I presume?' said Hugo.

Sebastian laughed. 'Why not? In for a groat, in for a sovereign, that's what I always say.'

'It's a deal,' said Hugo, tossing the purse back to Sebastian.

'Good. But listen,' whispered Sebastian, scratching his face to hide the movement of his mouth from any would-be lip-readers. 'This is strictly between you and me, OK? I don't want my crew to think I'm some sort of softie now, do I? If any of that lot got wind of my sympathetic nature I'd have the devil's own job getting them to lift a finger on board. My whole crew is driven by fear and fear alone.

'But the truth is . . . I like you, Hugo. You've got real courage and a great spirit of adventure. We could do with more of your sort in this world, that's for sure.'

'Thank you.'

The cart consisted of an open wooden box mounted on four solid wooden wheels. Two long timber shafts, which projected forward from either side of the wagon, were tied to the saddle of a grumpy, dumpy Shetland pony. Slinging his satchel into the back of the cart, Hugo climbed on to the wooden bench seat and took up the reins.

'Good luck on your expedition, Captain Tumbledown-Smythe,' he said. 'I hope you reach China safely – and discover the land full of silks and spices that I've heard about. Just think – you might even find a whole new continent beyond China. You're so determined I know you'll succeed.'

'The same to you, laddie,' said Sebastian with a wink. Then he yelled at the top of his lungs, 'Now then, you horrible little oik, are you going to head off or am I going to take your head off?'

'OK, I'm going,' said Hugo, cowering for the benefit of the other sailors. 'I know when I've outstayed my welcome.'

'Do you know how to drive a horse and cart?' asked Savage.

'Sort of,' Hugo replied, taking up the reins. 'A long time ago I used to work at the local stables to help my parents pay the rent. Occasionally I was allowed to ride a horse round the paddock. Here goes!'

With a flick of his wrists he snapped the reins and

clucked his tongue loudly. Without moving its hoofs the pony swung its head round lazily and gave Hugo a long, disdainful stare.

'I think he likes you,' said Savage. 'Good to see you haven't lost your touch.'

'Very funny.'

'Hello, Mr Horse,' said Savage, waving. 'My name's Savage, and this is Hugo.'

The pony stared back blankly, its long chocolate mane fluttering against its toffee-coloured neck.

'What's your name?' Savage persisted.

Hugo laughed and ruffled Savage's fur with one finger. 'When are you going to get used to the fact that you are the only talking animal around here?'

'Well, we should at least give him a name,' said Savage. 'How about Stilton?'

'If you insist. Come on, Stilton, let's go.' Hugo clicked his tongue and flicked his wrists again.

Outside the town, the countryside was flat and green, peppered with cows chewing the grass with a slow, circular motion. Hugo had steered the cart on to a dirt track heading east-southeast, towards Bavaria, and Savage sat alongside him, his ears pricked up eagerly.

'So I'm finally in France,' marvelled Savage.

'Oui,' said Hugo.

'I'm ever so sorry – *we* are finally in France.'

'No, silly, "oui" is French for "yes".'

'I see,' said Savage. 'And what's French for "nobody likes a smarty-pants"?'

Hugo flicked the reins and Stilton responded by striding into a canter. The dull thud of his hoofs on dry mud drummed a snappy rhythm, his tail bobbing to mark time.

It soon became clear that the cart's wheels weren't centred on their axle so the vehicle travelled with a combined bucking and rolling motion. The faster the cart went, the more its wobbling was exaggerated.

'Tumbledown-Smythe wasn't joking when he said this cart's a bit rickety, was he?' said Hugo, steadying himself with one hand.

'Something of an understatement, if you ask me,' replied Savage, his ears flapping as he was bounced out of his seat like a child on a seesaw. 'I'm beginning to feel rather seasick actually.'

'Don't worry – just another three months of this and we'll be there.'

'You're joking! Tell me it's not going to take three months.'

'It's not going to take three months,' Hugo turned up his collar. 'It'll be more like four.'

'So let me get the plan straight,' said Savage. 'We're going to follow Uncle Walter's map to Demonica, decipher Marcello's coded map to find Lifereaper's impossibly secret castle – avoiding the numerous life-threatening dangers (which may or may not be the stuff of legends) that lurk within the mountains as we go, kill him with his own sword in order to release Marcello from his evil power, and somewhere along the way we're going free Walter and possibly Jadea from a group of mercenary bandits who will stop at nothing to get the sword before we do?'

'That's about it,' said Hugo tentatively.

'Phew!' said Savage. 'For a moment there I thought this was going to get complicated.'

Chapter 17

The days grew shorter and the nights colder. Hugo and Savage saw few people on the road and even fewer places to stay. Most nights were spent in the open cart huddled under blankets, but occasionally a derelict cottage or an empty stable provided them with the luxury of four walls to contain the heat of their campfire.

Every day Hugo thought about Uncle Walter. He missed seeing his smile and hearing him talk about his adventures, and the vast empty terrain served only to magnify his loneliness. This was a world away from his last expedition where he had been constantly entertained by the antics of the sailors on board ship and had his uncle's reassuring presence for all but a couple of days when Walter had been missing on a small island. Even then he'd had the company of a group of wonderful creatures to keep his spirits up.

He and Savage passed the time talking about Walter and reminiscing about the friends they'd left behind on that island. Hugo often tested Savage with puzzles his father had taught him, sometimes letting his little friend sweat for days before revealing the solution.

'I've got one,' announced Hugo as the cart bounced along one morning. 'This was one of my father's favourites.'

'Hit me with it,' said Savage, who was lying on his back watching the clouds pass overhead.

'So, a long time ago there was a boy called Aquarius who lived with his mother, Andromeda, in a town called Saggitaria. What little money they had was taken by the evil mayor who demanded payments every week, threatening Andromeda with violence if she refused. Aquarius and his mother were so broke they lived on scraps of food and their tiny house was so cold that icicles hung from the ceiling.

'One dark night the Mayor visited, demanding more money. When Andromeda pleaded that she had none left, the mayor threatened to execute her on the spot for disobedience. As the mayor drew his sword, Aquarius lunged at him. There was a struggle and soon the mayor lay face down in a pool of blood – dead.

'The mayor's guards, who were waiting outside, heard the commotion and entered the house. Aquarius was arrested on the spot on suspicion of murder and taken to the dungeons.

'The coroner examined the evil mayor's body and concluded that he had died from a single stab wound to the chest. However, after searching Aquarius's house from top to bottom, the guards couldn't find the weapon he had used. According to Saggitarian law no one could be convicted of murder unless the murder weapon was produced in court.

'So Aquarius was released and he and his mother lived happily without the evil mayor's menacing visits.'

'So where did he hide the weapon?' demanded Savage.

'That's the riddle,' Hugo laughed. 'The coroner's report contained the crucial clue. It said the pool of blood beneath the mayor contained an unusually large proportion of water.'

'Water?' Savage frowned quizzically.

Hugo nodded and smiled. 'The mayor's warm blood melted the icicle Aquarius had stabbed him with.'

'Exactly. The icicle. That's what I meant when I said "water",' said Savage.

'Really?' asked Hugo. 'To me it sounded like you were sort of confused. Clueless, even.'

'No, no. I'd sussed it all out as soon as the mayor went down.'

Hugo tallied the passing days in his notebook and plotted their weekly progress on Uncle Walter's map. On every seventh day at noon he would measure their latitude using the backstaff and mark the chart with a horizontal index intercepting their planned route.

Then, relating the features of the surrounding terrain to the map, he would pinpoint their exact location.

Sometimes their progress was swift, Stilton's hoofs skipping across mile after mile of hard, worn track for days on end, and Hugo was encouraged by the distance they had covered in a week. Other times, they spent endless days hampered by thick forests or battling hard rain that came down in sheets, turning acres of pasture into an impassable quagmire. After seven days of such arduous travelling Hugo's plot would reveal that they had covered a pitiful distance and his spirits would plummet.

Their progress was slowed even further by the occasional need to retrace their steps. In Bavaria, Hugo's impatience led them into a forest that he would normally have circumvented. After a day spent forcing their way into the wood, Hugo was forced to admit what he had known, deep down, all along. The trees were too densely packed to get through so another day was spent on the retreat.

As time passed, the sun peaked lower in the sky each day and the rain turned to snow. The churned-up mud froze into solid, rutted, wasteland that jolted and jarred the cart and slowed it down even more.

One bitterly cold night, when the days had been drawing out for some weeks, Hugo lit a fire in the shelter provided by a solid cartwheel. Stilton whinnied with pleasure and sidled closer to the flames.

'How long have we been travelling?' asked Savage, holding his paws up to the flames. 'Forever?'

Hugo flipped open his notebook and ran his finger down his tally of sunrises, counting to himself in a whisper. 'Three months and twenty-five days,' he said with a note of concern. 'Which means we have to find the Diamond Sword and execute Lifereaper in the next six days if we're going to save Marcello.'

'What about Uncle Walter?' asked Savage.

'I was hoping we would have caught up with him, or even Jadea, weeks ago,' sighed Hugo. 'If we don't find them before we reach Lovdiv we'll have to enter Demonica alone. Assuming they follow Marcello's directions, we'll have to solve his clues to find them.'

'It would be great to have Walter around to help solve those clues, wouldn't it?' noted Savage.

'It would be great to have him around full stop.' Hugo smiled sadly.

'Don't be sad,' said Savage, clutching his paws into fists. 'Walter could easily be much closer than you think.'

'I appreciate the sentiment, Savage, but take a look around,' replied Hugo, spreading his arms out wide. 'There's no one else on this wasteland as far as the eye can see.'

Two hundred yards away to the south, the ground began to rise up, like the gentle billowing of a freshly thrown tablecloth. On top of this shallow hump sat three men on horseback – plotting their ambush as they watched a horse, a campfire, and a boy who seemed to be gesticulating to himself.

CHApter 18

'I think I've just seen where our next meal is coming from,' said the first horseman. He was a small chubby man, bald on top but with long straggly curls growing from a hairline just above his ears.

'I'm getting hungry just watching him cook,' said the second, a giant of a man with thick whiskers and a mop of bushy hair. His pony looked like a child's toy beneath him and his feet would have dragged on the ground were he not keeping his legs tucked up.

'So here's the plan,' said the small, bald man. 'We'll ride down the hillside screaming like banshees, kill them all and steal their cart and supplies.'

'How about we try not to kill anyone, just for once?' suggested the hairy giant. 'Killing everybody becomes a bit – I don't know – mundane after a while. Sometimes I think just the threat of violence can be so much classier than the violence itself.'

The bald man shrugged. 'All right then, what if we ride down screaming like banshees, just kill the horse and steal the food?'

'I don't know,' said the giant. 'Even killing the horse

is a bit obvious. Why don't we just ride down and steal the horse and cart and all the supplies?'

'Screaming like banshees,' insisted the bald man. 'I'm going to put my foot down on the screaming.'

'If you insist,' said the hairy giant. 'Although, personally, I'd rather not. I just find the screaming so cliché.'

The bald man turned to the third horseman and rolled his eyes. 'My younger brother – the *sensitive* bandit!'

The third man shrugged as best he could, given that his hands were bound tightly to the pommel of his saddle. 'I didn't realize you two were brothers,' he said. 'Yet we've been travelling together for months. We really should chat more often.'

'We're twins actually,' said the hairy giant.

The man looked from the bald midget to the hairy giant with astonishment. 'Twins?'

Both men nodded proudly.

'Although we're not identical,' added the midget, for clarity.

'You don't say?'

'No, it's true. I've got blue eyes, but my brother's are brown.'

'Not to mention that one of you is short and bald while the other is as big and hairy as a bear.'

The twins frowned.

'Come to think of it, I don't even know your names, which doesn't seem fair. You both know mine.'

'Don't tell him, Jake,' ordered the midget.

'Pleased to meet you, Jake,' said the man with a nod. 'I'd shake your hand if you'd only untie me.'

'Don't listen to him, Jake – it's a trick,' said the hairy giant.

'So you're both called Jake? How very unusual for brothers to have the same name,' smiled the man. 'I suppose your parents called you Big Jake and Little Jake?'

The hairy giant nodded. 'I was Big Jake,' he explained rather unnecessarily.

'Really? I take it Jake was your parents' favourite name?'

'Actually they preferred Gregory,' said Little Jake. 'But we've got an older cousin called Gregory.'

'I see,' said the man, raising his eyebrows.

Little Jake made a sound like an owl and soon two more horses, ridden by mean-looking ruffians, mounted the brow of the hill and joined the group.

'Are these two called Jake as well?' asked the man.

'He's William Blood,' said Little Jake, pointing at the bandit with lank black hair. Then he pointed at the one with a fresh, young face. 'And he's Tommy Guts.'

'Well, their names are certainly appropriate to their chosen profession,' said the man.

The others exchanged glances. 'What?' said Little Jake. 'Billy and Tommy?'

'Never mind,' said the man. 'Listen – if you want to get yourselves a reputation you need to have a really threatening group name. How about calling yourselves *The Four Horsemen of the Apocalypse*?'

Muttering behind cupped hands the bandits conducted a short debate and agreed that they rather liked this proposal.

'Of course,' added the man casually, 'if you keep killing all your victims then nobody will be able to spread the word of your fearsome banditry.'

'I hadn't thought of that,' said Little Jake thoughtfully.

'OK – here's the deal,' said Big Jake, gesturing down the hill with his chin. 'We're going to ambush that traveller. We can make as much noise as we like, but we won't kill anyone.'

'Unless they resist,' said Little Jake.

'Or run away?' offered Tommy.

'No,' insisted Big Jake. 'Only kill them if they resist.'

Billy gagged the man with a rag, tied a kerchief over his nose and mouth and pushed a wide-brimmed hat on to his head. Then the bandits covered their own faces with scarves and pulled hats down low over their eyes. Tommy grabbed the reins of the man's horse and the bandits galloped over the brow of the hill towards the glow of Hugo's campfire, screaming at the top of their lungs.

Instinctively Hugo leaped to his feet, grabbed his satchel, and mounted the cart where he laid the bag at his feet. Drawing his sword from his belt, he placed it in the hay behind his satchel. Savage scampered up the wheel and leaped into the hay, reappearing a moment later brandishing his trusty cactus spine, which he swiped through the air like a master swordsman.

Peering into the night, Hugo could just make out five murky silhouettes galloping down the hillside accompanied by a cacophony of whoops and yelps.

'Bandits!' said Savage. 'Do you suppose . . . ?'

'Stay calm,' whispered Hugo. 'We'll find out soon enough.'

The horses approached at speed and began circling the cart, their masked riders wielding swords and continuing their maniacal chorus – except for one who was unarmed and seemed considerably less enthusiastic than the others about the whole performance.

Finally the horses came to a standstill surrounding Hugo's cart. The short, tubby bandit spoke.

'Hand over your food and drink,' he ordered. 'And while you're at it, give us your horse and cart.'

Three others grunted their support.

'Why should I?' asked Hugo as boldly as he could.

'Because otherwise we will heap death, misery . . .

and . . . and . . . other horrible stuff on you. Soon the whole of Europe will live in fear of us, for we are the . . . the . . . Four Norsemen of the Acropolis.'

The giant bandit whose feet nearly touched the floor cleared his throat. 'He means we are the Four Horsemen of the Apocalypse.'

'So how come there are five of you?' asked Hugo.

The bandits looked at each other for a moment.

'He's just along for the ride,' said one of them, pointing at the one who wasn't carrying a sword.

Hugo could only see the unarmed bandit's eyes but he recognized his uncle immediately. He grabbed the side of his cart, ready to leap to the floor and run towards him, but Walter's eyes narrowed sternly and he shook his head curtly.

Even though his heart was thundering with the thrill of seeing his uncle, Hugo straightened up casually and considered his options. The thieves outnumbered him, but if he gave up his cart and provisions he would be stranded in the middle of nowhere. If that happened he had no chance of rescuing Uncle Walter or getting to Demonica in time – if at all.

'So what's it to be, boy? We asked nicely for your food and your cart,' snarled the bald midget. 'Are we going to heap death etcetera on you or are you going to let us have it?'

Taking a deep breath, Hugo glanced down at Savage

and winked. 'Oh, I'm going to let you have it all right,' he replied, bending down as if retrieving his satchel.

His fingers closed around the hilt of his sword.

Suddenly Uncle Walter let out an incredibly piercing – although muffled – scream and dug his heels into his horse's ribs. The startled animal reared up and bolted into the darkness dragging away a second horseman who was clinging desperately to its reins.

'Control those horses, Tommy!' screamed the bald midget, his eyes flickering over his shoulder for a moment.

In that instant Hugo sprang up and swung his sword over his head, bringing the flat face of its blade down on to the midget with a resounding clang. The thug's eyes crossed, then rolled back as he slumped unconscious over his saddle with a groan. With a firm slap on its rump, Hugo sent the horse galloping into the night.

The giant bandit whipped his horse and charged towards the cart, twirling his sword. Hugo raised his weapon to defend himself. The thief was approaching fast, flashing his blade, with fury in his eyes.

Meanwhile, unseen by the outlaws, Savage had leaped from the cart and scampered up the giant bandit's leg, up his coat and on to the brim of his hat.

Now Savage gripped the brim of the robber's hat with his rear claws and, grinning, toppled forward, flopping in front of the bandit's face.

'BOO!'

The bandit's eyes bulged in surprise and, startled, he lost his balance momentarily, dropping his sword. Instantly Savage jumped on to the horse's back and scampered towards its tail. Just before leaping to the dirt he jabbed his cactus spine into the stallion's behind, sending it bolting far into the night – and in a completely different direction to the other horses.

'Right!' said Hugo, sizing up the last thug. 'Now it's one against one.'

Without hesitating the remaining bandit pulled his horse round and rode back up the hillside as fast as his steed would carry him.

'Chicken!' Hugo called.

'I don't wish to be pedantic,' said Savage, 'but I'm pretty sure that's a horse.'

'We'd better get moving in case they regroup,' said Hugo, throwing Stilton's tack over his back. 'Savage, did you happen to think any of the bandits looked familiar?'

'Of course,' grinned Savage. 'I would have recognized those eyes anywhere.'

Hugo nodded eagerly.

'I wasn't sure if you'd noticed,' chattered Savage, 'but that little tubby guy was the spitting image of the fishmonger in Market Square!'

Hugo frowned. 'The fishmonger in Market Square?'

'Yes. Although to be honest,' said Savage, scampering on to Hugo's shoulder and looking him in the eye, 'I'd have thought you'd be much more interested in the one who was quite obviously Uncle Walter.'

'Hey, that's not funny!' laughed Hugo. 'I was beginning to think I was seeing things.'

'Well, you weren't,' exclaimed Savage. 'Uncle Walter is alive and well and riding a runaway horse not very far from here. Although at the speed he was going he soon will be a considerable distance away.'

Hugo felt his spirits slide. 'There's no way we'll catch him, is there? Not at the speed his horse was going.'

'Nonsense,' said Savage assuredly. 'Once your uncle's horse calms down I bet it'll take those bandits at least half a day to regroup, and at least we know we're on the right track. We'll catch them up all right – you'll see.'

Hugo glanced at the map on the bench by his side. By his reckoning they were a hundred miles from Demonica. Barring any major complications – and encounters with any more groups of bandits – they would reach Lovdiv within three or four days. If they hadn't caught up with Uncle Walter by then, they'd have had to follow the trail to Lifreaper's castle themselves.

'I hope you're right,' he muttered.

'Of course I'm right,' said Savage. 'I'm always right.'

CHapter 19

Stars peeped from behind patches of low, flat clouds as Hugo and Savage rode their cart into Lovdiv. Even Stilton seemed to sense their apprehension and slowed to a lazy walk.

There seemed to be no pattern to the way the small stone houses were laid out. It was as if they'd been slopped on to the hillside from a giant bucket. Coming from the far side of the village, Hugo could hear the shushing sound of flowing water – the river that separates Lovdiv from Demonica, he thought. Just above the low wooden roofs of the buildings he could see the tip of a modest church steeple.

'That must be the church on Uncle Walter's map,' whispered Hugo. 'Let's go.'

'This place is spooky,' said Savage, his ears perking up. 'I don't like it – it's too quiet. Listen to that – nothing. Absolute silence and that's not right. There's no light in any of the windows and not a sound from anywhere, which can only mean trouble if you ask me. *Eerie.* That's what it is – eerie. Can you hear that defeaning silence?'

'Actually, all I can hear is you babbling,' whispered

Hugo, then something made him shiver. He clenched his teeth to stop them chattering. 'But I agree, this place is a bit creepy. It's like a ghost town.'

Hugo stopped the cart outside the church, jumped to the ground and lashed Stilton's reins to a tree. Savage leaped on to his shoulder and they studied the building before them. It was a simple rectangular shape with a pitched roof and a small square steeple at one end, adorned with a short iron spire.

'It doesn't look much,' observed Savage.

'No,' agreed Hugo. 'But I'm sure Uncle Walter moved that chess piece as a clue and for some reason the symbol for this church on his map is just like a bishop's mitre.'

'So he was telling us to come here,' Savage surmised. 'I wonder why?'

Hugo took a deep breath. 'There's only one way to find out.'

The church's arched double doors were barricaded from the outside by a thick wooden plank slotted through iron brackets. Hugo slid out the plank and as he pulled open the heavy wooden door its hinges screeched in protest. He felt Savage's grip on his shoulder tighten.

The church smelt musty, like overdue laundry, and an eerie mist filled the damp air. It was even colder inside than it had been out and Hugo pulled his coat tightly around himself. The only light came from the moon shining sporadically through the sole window – an archway in the far wall, behind the altar.

'Hello?' called Hugo, squinting into the gloom. 'Anybody here?'

Silence.

He took another step. Something scraped on the rough surface of the cold stone floor. 'Hello?'

Nothing.

He turned slowly on the spot, taking in the bare walls and the few simple wooden pews. Then he proceeded tentatively to the altar. Noticing the font he took a soft leather bottle from his satchel and plunged it into the clear water. When the bubbles stopped escaping from the neck of his bottle he lifted it out of the water and took a long drink. Wiping his mouth, he corked the swollen pouch and slung it across his shoulder.

A figure in the corner made him jump. Immediately realizing it was an old statue carved out of a piece of black granite, he smiled at his own edginess. The statue was of a man wearing long robes. He was carrying a sceptre and on his head he wore a tall hat that curved to a point – like a bishop's mitre.

'The black bishop,' whispered Hugo.

'*That*'s why the symbol on Walter's map is like a bishop's hat,' said Savage. 'Who *is* that guy?'

Hugo noticed an inscription on the statue's plinth.

'Look – a name.'

Savage peered at the engraving. 'Who's that?'

'Claudius. Jadea said this place was built in honour of him – remember?'

'Ah yes, the famous Roman saint of spooky churches. Er, Hugo? This place gives me the creeps.'

'I know what you mean. And is it me or did it just get even colder in here?'

As Hugo spoke something grabbed his shoulder. Instinctively he spun round, drawing his sword and stepping back to distance himself from his assailant.

His heart was already galloping in his chest but as he stared into the mist it slowed to a trot. Standing little over five feet tall and wearing a black robe that brushed the floor was a grey-haired priest, smiling kindly at him.

'Hello, my child,' he said. 'Welcome to my chapel. I am Father Nikolai Romanov. What brings you to these parts?'

'Hello, Father,' Hugo breathed, sliding his sword into his belt. 'My name is Hugo. I'm looking for my uncle – Walter Bailey. He was kidnapped by bandits who want him to lead them to Lifereaper's castle.'

Hugo saw the priest's pale blue eyes flicker at the

mention of the name. Briefly they rolled skywards and just for an instant they seemed to glow blood red, then he blinked and regained his composure.

'Did you see that?' hissed Savage.

Hugo took a step back.

'Come with me to my chambers, Hugo,' coaxed Father Romanov. 'Tell me all about your troubles.'

Cold fear pumped through Hugo. 'Oh, it's nothing serious really – I should be going.'

'Look at the font!' urged Savage, digging his claws into Hugo's shoulder.

Hugo glanced down into the stone bowl. Now the surface of the water was completely still, like a mirror, and he could clearly see his reflection and the image of Savage gripping his shoulder.

But that was all.

Father Romanov had no reflection!

Violently twisting his torso to release the priest's grip on him, Hugo ducked under Father Romanov's arm and raced for the door.

'HUGO!'

The priest's furious cry echoed round the vaulted ceiling. Hugo kept running. He was nearly at the doorway and could see Stilton waiting outside, nibbling at the leaves on the tree. He couldn't hear any footsteps behind him. When he looked back, Father Romanov had gone.

Outside Hugo swung the church doors closed and slotted the thick plank through the iron brackets.

'Something's bothering me about this place,' he said thoughtfully, backing away from the church.

'You mean apart from the priest having blood-red eyes and no reflection?' asked Savage. 'And quite frankly I thought his people skills left a lot to be desired.'

'Precisely.' Hugo sucked on the night air. 'I'd never have taken the water from the font if I'd known he'd get so angry about it.'

Someone spoke behind them.

'Go to the windowless house. Ask for Crystal. She'll tell you all you need to know.'

Hugo spun around but could see no one.

The night was silent except for Stilton chewing leaves and the distant miaow of a cat.

'Who said that?' asked Savage. 'And why on earth would we want to go to a windowless house?'

Hugo frowned as he untied Stilton's reins. 'I have a strange feeling it might just be the next symbol on Marcello's map.'

Chapter 20

The house stood on a grassy hump on the eastern edge of the village. It was a small cottage built of rough bricks and its roof was clad in thick terracotta tiles. It was remarkable not only because of its total lack of windows but also because of the way its exterior walls had been decorated.

They were festooned with countless crosses of all sizes, nailed to the stonework of the walls or dangling from the overhang of the roof, intricately carved out of oak, hastily knocked together out of pieces of driftwood or fashioned out of copper or iron. Nailed on to the front door, about ten inches long, was a crucifix of pure silver.

Hugo unfolded his copy of Marcello's map and touched the black house-shaped silhouette. 'The windowless house,' he muttered. He walked Stilton to the side of the house and lashed his reins to a branch then, with Savage sitting up eagerly on his shoulder, he returned and rapped on the front door.

'Come in.' The voice within was soft and slow.

Drawing his sword, Hugo pushed the heavy door, which opened with a piercing squeak.

Savage jumped. 'Doesn't anybody oil their hinges round here?' he whispered irritably.

As Hugo stepped inside his senses were immediately assaulted by an overpowering stench.

Savage pinched the end of his snout with one paw. 'Now I like garlic as buch as the dext bouse,' he whispered. 'But you can definitely have too buch of a good thig.'

Hugo held one sleeve across his face and nodded.

A small fire glowed in a rustic hearth, casting a meagre orange light across the sparsely furnished room. There was a small dresser against one wall and a round table in front of a doorway in the far corner. A sleek silver-blue cat sat on the table, its thick tail curving elegantly upwards like the neck of a swan.

'Hello? Is anybody home?' called Hugo. 'I'm looking for Crystal.'

'Then your search is over.' The cat purred and slowly blinked its big amber eyes.

Hugo and Savage exchanged looks of amazement.

'You're Crystal? And you can *talk*,' exclaimed Hugo.

Savage nodded. 'And you're a *cat*.'

'Goodness me, who's a clever little mouse!' Crystal exclaimed. 'Your powers of observation are truly astounding.'

'Oh great. A sarcastic cat – even better.' Savage

scampered down Hugo's arm and leaped on to the table. Holding his two front paws up in little fists he squared up to Crystal, swaying his shoulders like a prizefighter. 'You may think you're clever just because you can talk but now I'm going to teach you a lesson.'

Crystal sprang to her feet. Straightening her legs and arching her back she hissed at the shadowboxing mouse, her fur bristling down the length of her spine.

'That's enough!' cried Hugo, scooping Savage off the table and spooning him back on to his shoulder. 'Say sorry to Crystal and let's hear what she has to say.'

Rolling his eyes, Savage mumbled an apology.

'Well, I'm not exactly bowled over by your sincerity but I suppose it's a start,' said Hugo. He leaned over the small pot on the fire and sniffed. His head snapped back and tears filled his eyes. 'Wow! That garlic soup is really potent,' he said, blinking.

'That's not just garlic soup,' said Crystal, 'that's a protective potage.'

'Protection from what?' asked Savage.

'You really don't know?'

'Well, we just met a very strange priest in the church,' said Hugo. 'He had no reflection and these weird eyes that flickered bright red.'

Crystal nodded. 'When I sensed his evil spirit stirring I knew he had company. That's why I went to lead you here to safety. He's one of *them*, you see.'

'One of who?' asked Savage.

Crystal looked lazily from Hugo to Savage and back to Hugo.

'You don't know?'

'I have an idea,' said Hugo, while Savage shook his head.

'Oh, dear me, don't rodents these days ever pay attention to ancient legends and myths?' Crystal leaped silently to the floor and slunk over to the fireside. Her eyes glowed like two torches as she spoke. 'Lifereaper preys on travellers who wander innocently into his kingdom of Demonica. That creature in the church would have been such a traveller some time ago but is now doomed to spend eternity haunted by the same unquenchable thirst for blood that drives his Evil Lord.'

'When you say "thirst for blood",' clarified Savage, 'that's just a figure of speech, right?'

'I've got it!' yelped Hugo. 'I know what kind of creature Lifereaper is! It's so obvious when you think about it, Savage. What has no reflection, is repelled by garlic, and has an unquenchable thirst for blood?'

'I give in.'

'Think, Savage, think – it's easy,' urged Hugo. 'OK, I'll tell you. Lifereaper is a *vampire*.' Looking at Crystal he smiled proudly. 'I'm right, aren't I?'

Crystal blinked slowly then answered, 'No.'

'Ha!' exclaimed Savage, punching the air.

Hugo's smile withered.

'You're only half right, Hugo,' added Crystal. 'The situation is much worse than you can imagine. Lifereaper *is* the evil, violent Lord of all vampires but he himself is no ordinary vampire.'

'Ordinary vampire,' repeated Savage. 'Now there are two words I wouldn't normally put together.'

Hugo's mouth was so dry he could barely speak. 'If he's not a vampire, what is he then?'

Crystal's eyes narrowed. 'A *vampanther*. Lifereaper is a *vampanther*.'

CHapter 21

'A vampanther?' echoed Hugo.

'As in a . . . vampire panther?' mumbled Savage.

'Very good.' Crystal nodded slowly. 'I shall relate to you the legend of how the vampanther was created, but before I do so I would recommend that you huddle close to the fire, for the story of Lifereaper's origin will surely chill you to the bone.'

Hugo dragged a stool to the fireside and let the flames toast his cheeks and Savage peeked out of his pocket as Crystal began her tale.

'Many years ago, a formidable black panther patrolled the deepest jungles of the Indies, preying on all who crossed its path. The local villagers named the cat Jaidev, believing it to be the incarnation of the ancient god of victory. Many brave hunters tried to slay Jaidev but none survived. The panther was too agile to be caught and too powerful to be out-fought.

'One day Jaidev ambushed a family as they trekked through the jungle on the way back to their village from a sacred watering hole. The father was attacked first and perished before he'd even drawn his sword.

Soon the whole family had been slaughtered except for a young boy by the name of Vikram.

'He knew he was too weak to overpower the ferocious panther and too slow to outrun it, but he refused to accept defeat and faced the beast down.

'As the black cat lunged, Vikram dropped to the floor, rolling beneath his attacker. Although he avoided the panther's clutches one of its fearsome claws swiped him as he passed. Standing to face the black cat, Vikram realized he was bleeding from his shoulder.

'The panther charged a second time. As it leaped, Vikram picked up a clay urn full of holy water that his mother had left behind before attempting to flee. Gripping the pot by its rim he tossed the water into the lunging panther's face. Jaidev spluttered to a standstill, momentarily blinded.

'Instantly the boy grabbed his dead father's sword – a rough, stubby blade with a hilt fashioned from granite. Leaping on to the panther's back he drove the sword between its shoulder blades, skewering its heart and pinning it to the ground. As the panther writhed on the ground it is said that a single drop of Vikram's blood dripped into its nostril. The scent drove the panther wild with desire, leaving it to die with an unquenchable thirst for blood on its tongue.'

'So the cat kicked the bucket,' smiled Savage. 'I love a story with a happy ending.'

'That is not the end of the tale,' said Crystal gravely.

Hugo and Savage huddled closer to the fire as she continued.

'Terrified and disorientated, Vikram trekked for days until at last he reached the safety of a small village. He told how he had killed Jaidev, claiming the execution had turned the panther's body to stone and the hilt of his sword into a single diamond. Although some were sceptical, none of the townsfolk dared enter the jungle to verify the boy's account and Vikram himself was too traumatized to return to the site of his family's massacre. As years passed, the location of the petrified black cat and the diamond sword fell into obscurity.

'Centuries later adventurers penetrated the jungle searching for the mythical sword, but none succeeded. Either they returned empty handed or they were swallowed by the immense forest for good.

'Then one day a fearsome warrior from the land south of Constantinople travelled to the region. Known only as Lifereaper, he was the most brutal warlord ever to rampage the earth. For years he had roamed the world, stealing from the wealthy and killing anyone who crossed his path. He could effortlessly slay a whole platoon of foreign soldiers single-handedly but he commanded a small band of thugs who thought nothing of murdering an entire village of innocent people.

'Lifereaper would cut his foes down with his sword or simply tear them apart with his bare hands. He had stolen gold from emperors and jewels from kings, always leaving a river of blood in his wake, but the one treasure he desired more than any other was the legendary Diamond Sword.

'Lifereaper went into the jungle with his mob of ruffians. After months of searching it is said they finally discovered Jaidev's body, still pinned to the ground by Vikram's father's sword. Sure enough, the panther's carcass had turned to granite and the weapon's handle was one enormous diamond.

'Consumed by greed, Lifereaper grabbed the hilt and drew out the sword, raising it triumphantly above his head.

'What he could not have known was that Jaidev's soul had been trapped – pinned down by the sword and encased within the stone corpse. Withdrawing the sword freed the evil spirit and left an open crack in the stone tomb through which it escaped, immediately entering Lifereaper's body. Suddenly possessed by this savage panther spirit, he became part murderous human, part bloodsucking monster.'

'A vampanther,' whispered Savage.

'Very good,' Crystal said. 'I'm so glad you're keeping

up. Anyway, according to folklore, Lifereaper went into a frenzied rage and savaged all of his henchmen on the spot then travelled home to run amok through his palace, killing all his subjects and even drinking the blood of his own family, turning each of them into a vampire.

'The sword he carried had skewered the panther spirit to the ground, controlling its evil for centuries, and he quickly discovered that it empowered him to control the spirit of every monster he created.

'The vampanther's victims roam the earth as vampires looking for their own victims but it is believed that Lifereaper came to settle in Demonica where, beholden to the power of the diamond sword, an army of soulless servants have built him a secret castle from where he conducts his vicious reign.'

'If the vampires are all over the world, how do you know Lifereaper lives in Demonica?' asked Hugo, confused and appalled by all he was hearing.

'There have been countless vampire attacks across the continent – some unspeakably horrific,' conceded Crystal. 'But for many, many years Demonica has been a consistently perilous region.'

She licked a paw lazily and shook her head. 'As the Vampire Lord, the vampanther will send most of his underlings out to terrorize the outside world but he will keep a core close to him to guard his castle and patrol his chosen kingdom. Not to mention his dungeon full of mezzaghouls.'

Hugo remembered what Uncle Walter had told him about Lifereaper's victims. 'So it's true! When a vampire attacks someone, he sucks their blood dry and they become a mezzaghoul for a year before being condemned to eternal vampirehood?'

'Precisely,' agreed Crystal. 'A vampire's victim will fall instantly under the spell of the Diamond Sword, following it wherever it goes and worshipping whoever possesses it.'

'Lifereaper must find it pretty tricky sneaking up on a hapless traveller with a throng of mezzaghouls shuffling along behind him,' observed Savage.

'That is why it is believed he keeps his victims locked up in his dungeons until their soul has withered completely,' Crystal explained. 'And the only way to rescue a mezzaghoul is to kill Lifereaper. If the vampanther were executed, all the mezzaghouls' hearts would come alive and reenergize their bodies with fresh new blood, returning them to healthy life.'

'So the only way to rescue Marcello is to destroy Lifereaper,' stated Hugo, clenching his fists.

'You know of Marcello?' asked Crystal.

Hugo nodded. 'He was an old friend of my uncle's. We believe he discovered Lifereaper's castle before he was killed and left this coded map of its location.'

Unfolding the map he held it up and Crystal studied it in silence.

'Let's go to the vampanther's castle and drive a wooden stake through his heart,' said Savage, stabbing the air with an invisible weapon.

'You can't kill a vampire with a stake,' said Crystal. 'That's an old wives' tale.'

'I'd heard you have to decapitate them with a silver sword,' said Hugo.

'Yeah, that's right,' agreed Savage, swiping the air with an imaginary blade. 'Off with their heads!'

'Quite right,' said Crystal. 'The best way of killing an ordinary vampire is to take its head off with a silver sword. Alternatively you could drive the blade into its heart, or submerge it in holy water.'

'Holy water?' said Hugo, cocking his head.

Crystal nodded slowly. 'Just a squirt of holy water feels like acid on a vampire's skin. Immersed in holy water, a monster would dissolve completely.'

'OK, so we'll find Lifereaper, cut off his head, stab him in the heart and plunge him into holy water,' said Savage, acting out the scene with gusto.

'But you forget, my sweet little mouse,' said Crystal, 'Lifereaper is no ordinary vampire. Killing him is so much more complicated.'

Savage sighed. 'This stuff is never simple, is it?'

'The diamond sword gives Lifreaper his ultimate

power but it is also believed to be his ultimate weakness,' continued Crystal. The only way to kill the vampanther is to drive the Diamond Sword into his heart, and in doing so, kill every other vampire he has created.'

'But if the vampanther is the original vampire, then aren't all vampires created by him?' asked Hugo.

Crystal stroked her whiskers with one paw. 'Exactly,' she said.

'So killing Lifereaper would completely rid the world of vampires?' said Hugo, his eyes twinkling. 'Imagine if we were responsible for eradicating vampires altogether! I mean, stories of vampires – and it seems vampires themselves – have been going around for centuries, but if we succeed we'll put an end to them once and for all.'

'Once and for all,' confirmed Crystal. 'But do not start planning your victory parade just yet. Countless others before you have tried and failed, most driven by greed but some, like Marcello, wanting to make the world safer. Even if you manage to get your hands on the fabled weapon you face an epic struggle to defeat the vampanther.'

'Then it only seems fair to warn you,' smirked Savage, 'epic struggles are our speciality.'

CHapter 22

'If you say so,' sighed Crystal. 'But don't forget – vampires are lethal creatures. Before you risk your lives battling them, you must understand their strengths and their weaknesses.'

'Fine. But how come you're such an expert?' asked Savage. 'Perhaps you have some *inside* information?'

'What are you suggesting, Savage?' asked Hugo.

'I'm just saying that cats and panthers are closely related. That's all.'

'If you are expecting Lifreaper to look like me then you have a terrifying shock in store,' Crystal said with a smile. 'But if it will ease your teeny mind, take a look at my reflection in this mirror.'

With one paw she slid an oval mirror into the centre of the table and stood over it. Hugo leaned forward to observe her reflection. Satisfied with what he had seen, he sat back and smiled apologetically.

'Now we have all seen each other's reflections I hope we consider ourselves amongst friends,' suggested Crystal.

Savage shrugged and Hugo nodded politely.

'Any more vampire-hunting tips?' he asked, leaning

his elbows on the table and cupping his chin in his hands. Savage perched on Hugo's shoulder, keeping his distance from the cat but listening no less intently as she spoke.

'The sign of the cross and the smell of raw garlic will repel them, but only momentarily. Their effect is to cause temporary blindness but recovery is relatively quick. In the same way that you would become accustomed to sudden exposure to bright light, so vampires quickly get used to these simple deterrents. And some, shall we say, *experienced* vampires wouldn't even flinch at their presence.'

'So the crosses on this house won't necessarily keep us safe?' asked Hugo.

Crystal shook her head. 'Crosses are merely a momentary defence. My garlic broth offers much more effective protection. Whole garlic cloves are more limited because their fragrance is so confined, but if a bulb around your neck causes a vampire to hesitate for even a second that could mean the difference between life and death.'

'Or life and eternal vampirehood,' said Savage.

'Precisely. Now, as you have deduced, vampires have no reflection. Your reflection is an image of your soul and they have no such inner spirit. Although, interestingly, mezzaghouls maintain their reflection throughout their time in limbo, but as soon as that year is up, their soul withers and their reflection evaporates.'

'That's what made me suspicious of the priest – he had no reflection.'

'And they are skilled shapeshifters,' said Crystal.

'Shapeshifters?' echoed Savage.

'It means they can take on the form of any other living being,' explained Crystal. 'Their skin and bones will expand or contract to replicate another creature almost perfectly.'

'*Almost?*' repeated Hugo, squinting.

'Their imitation has one basic flaw. Vampires can only shapeshift to represent a mirror image of their subject. All their features will be transposed.'

'Are there any warning signs to look out for?' asked Hugo. 'Anything that might let us know if a vampire is nearby?'

'Well, they have no smell and can move without making a sound,' said Crystal. 'But their blood is ice cold and they suck the warmth from their surroundings so you will feel an icy gust as they approach.'

'Your experiences have taught you a lot,' said Hugo sympathetically. 'How many vampires came to prey on the people of Lovdiv?'

Crystal looked into the fire and shook her head sorrowfully. 'It has been several months since so many of our townsfolk were slaughtered. Soon they will transcend from mezzaghouls to fully fledged vampires and all hope of rescuing them will be gone. They were hunted down by a single monster – a vampire possessed of such evil that it can only have been the vampanther himself.'

No one spoke for a while. The fire hissed gently and the garlic stew simmered.

'Your task is great but I have faith in your ability to succeed,' said Crystal at last. 'I have been expecting you for some time and I believe in you, Hugo.'

'What do you mean, "you've been expecting us"?' asked Hugo.

'My mistress was a witch.'

'Now, now,' said Savage, wagging a claw. 'There's no need to be catty.'

'I mean that I am a witch's cat,' sighed Crystal. 'My mistress was the talented sorceress and fortune-teller Margery Ickspel, who was the last in a long line of mediums and spell-casters. For generations her ancestors travelled across Europe trying to use their powers to help locate the vampanther.

'Some time ago Margery's grandfather had a premonition that the Diamond Sword was on the move and he followed his instincts here to Lovdiv. Soon after his arrival he was killed by vampires, leaving Margery to fend for herself. Determined to defeat the evil that had ruined her family, Margery immersed herself in the study of vampires and collated her findings in that volume.' Crystal nodded to a leather-bound tome lying flat on the dresser.

'After the vampanther rampaged through our village last year, Margery herself had a powerful vision of the Diamond Sword's whereabouts. Marcello came to see her, asking for her help in finding the vampanther's castle. She described her vision to him and gave him some guidance about the monsters' strengths and weaknesses.'

'Savage, that's why his map tells us to start our search here!' cried Hugo. 'Marcello wanted us to speak to Margery.'

Crystal nodded sadly as she continued, 'Margery foresaw that her own death was imminent and, fearing that her family's legacy would be lost forever, she set about passing her gifts on to me. Alas her premonition was to come true and she was killed by a vampire on the outskirts of Lovdiv some months later.

'Because of a spell she cast over me I am able to speak, and as a result of her tutelage I have developed considerable psychic powers.'

'You can see into the future?' said Hugo, wide-eyed.

'What a load of rubbish!' spluttered Savage.

'Well, I must be psychic because I knew you were going to say that,' said Crystal.

'What can you tell me about my future? Are we

going to catch up with Uncle Walter so that we can find the vampanther's castle together?' asked Hugo.

'Your uncle is missing?' said Crystal.

Savage snorted. 'What kind of psychic are you? Hugo's uncle has been kidnapped by bandits intent on stealing the diamond from Lifereaper's sword and selling it on the black market where, I'll have you know, it will not only be valuable, it will be invaluable.'

'I see,' said Crystal. 'So there are others trying to get to the sword before you. How many bandits were there?'

'Four, we think. Plus Uncle Walter.'

'Forgive me for stating the obvious,' said Savage, 'but if your powers are so great, shouldn't you know all this already?'

Ignoring Savage, Crystal closed her eyes and purred softly. 'I am sensing a stranger,' she announced at last. 'He is tall, suave and handsome.'

'Well, that's hardly psychic,' said Savage. 'I'm standing right here in front of you.'

Crystal ignored him and continued, 'He brings misery and despair to your doorstep.'

'She means Jadea Jafil,' said Hugo excitedly. 'He came to tell us the terrible news that Marcello had been killed and ask for Uncle Walter's help to find the Diamond Sword. We think he left England just ahead of us – and we could really do with his help.'

Crystal closed her eyes more tightly and was quiet for a moment. 'It's no good,' she said with a sigh. 'The vision has gone.'

'Great,' said Savage. 'I thought psychics were supposed to predict the future, not tell us what's already happened. Anybody can do that.' He closed his eyes and imitated Crystal's low tones. 'I see a silver cat. She pretends to be clairvoyant but she is a complete fraud.'

'Can you tell us anything else?' asked Hugo, pinching Savage's snout closed.

'Maybe, but I'll need to get some equipment.' Silently Crystal leaped from the table and trotted towards the doorway at the back of the room. 'I'll just be a couple of minutes – you won't go away, will you?'

'You tell us,' said Savage.

'Don't be so rude,' whispered Hugo when Crystal had gone. 'She's trying to help.'

'Don't tell me you believe this phoney feline?'

'It doesn't hurt to listen.'

While they waited for Crystal to return, they idly studied the room.

'It's a tiny house, isn't it?' remarked Hugo. 'You couldn't even swing a cat in here.'

'Probably not,' agreed Savage, 'but it'd be great fun to try.'

Chapter 23

Crystal appeared in the doorway a few minutes later, wearing a bright red silk scarf on her head like a bandanna and holding a deck of large cards in her mouth. She sprang up on to the table without making a sound and laid the stack of cards down in front of her.

'I don't want to be a killjoy but I'm not sure we've got time for a game of whist,' said Savage.

Ignoring the facetious mouse Crystal placed one paw on the top card and slid it off the pack, face down. Then she dealt the next card and the next until the whole deck had been spread across the tabletop, arranged in four rows of ten.

'Hugo,' she said softly, 'I want you to choose one card from each row and turn it face up. Do not touch any other cards but those you have selected.'

Hugo nodded solemnly.

Savage sniggered.

When Hugo had done as he'd been instructed he surveyed the cards he had chosen. They bore four pictures – a silver coin, a nettle, a snarling bear and a diamond.

Crystal placed one paw flat on the card showing the silver coin and shut her eyes. Then she started humming softly and shaking her head gently.

'Er, Hugo . . .' whispered Savage urgently, 'you do realize that while we're sitting here with this fur-brain, those bandits are out there actually searching for Lifereaper's castle?'

Hugo hushed him with a frown.

Eventually Crystal spoke. 'I sense some sort of betrayal. Someone close to you is not who they profess to be.'

'It's not a cat who claims to possess supernatural powers, is it?' asked Savage.

Crystal dismissed the comment with a heavy sigh then continued with the premonition. 'You will see an ally or a close friend upside down and you will realize that they are in fact your greatest enemy.'

'Who is it?' asked Hugo.

Crystal opened her big eyes and shook her head. 'I'm sorry, Hugo,' she said, 'I cannot interpret my visions. It is up to you to understand the wisdom I am giving you.'

'I think *wisdom* is overstating the facts just a little, don't you?' said Savage. 'How about gobbledegook?'

'What does the next card tell you?' asked Hugo.

Crystal placed her paw on the nettle card, closed her eyes and began humming.

'I sense poison – a lethal dose of it.' She closed her eyes more tightly. 'I see Hugo's face . . . Is he being poisoned? No . . . he is poisoning a friend.'

Hugo's heart was thumping. 'Why would I do that?'

Crystal pawed the next card – the one showing a snarling bear.

'This vision is a little hazy,' she muttered.

'Now there's a shocker,' remarked Savage.

'There is some sort of battle. I sense a bear's jaws. Your brave gang enters the fray, ready to fight. I see trails of footprints in the snow. Now I sense the group retreating from the fray, but one set of footprints is missing.' Crystal fixed Hugo with her almond-shaped eyes. 'I'm sorry, Hugo. They're yours.'

'It's not true,' insisted Savage, trying to disguise the quaver in his voice.

Crystal was already pressing her paw against the card bearing the picture of the diamond. Her velvety mouth curved up into a smile. 'Ah, this vision is much less muddled. I can see precisely what's happening.'

'Maybe soon you'll even see sense,' mumbled Savage.

'I can see a man with kind, smiling eyes,' said Crystal. 'He has tangled white hair and a thick, bristling moustache.'

'That's Uncle Walter!' yelped Hugo. 'What's he doing?'

Crystal's whiskers drooped and she gasped.

'What is it?' demanded Hugo. 'What's happening?'

'He has blood on his hands – his own blood. Hugo, your uncle is bleeding profusely. He's fading. No, don't go . . .'

Hugo was gripping the table with both hands.

'Tell me what you saw.' Tears welled in Hugo's eyes and spilled down his freckled cheeks. 'What happened?'

'I'm sorry, Hugo.' Crystal gently placed one paw on the back of Hugo's hand. 'I think I saw your uncle die.'

CHapter 24

Hugo lay on the hard mattress in the small room at the back of the windowless house and stared into the darkness. The night lay across his eyes like a blindfold, confining him to his thoughts.

Crystal's last vision haunted him, dancing in his imagination. He had quizzed her about what she had seen but he'd found no comfort in her replies.

'What's the point, Savage?' Hugo's whispered words filled the blackness.

Savage's claws scratched on the mattress by Hugo's head. 'I don't believe a word she says. She's a kook.'

'Her vision of Jadea coming to Uncle Walter's house was pretty accurate.'

'Big deal,' said Savage dismissively. 'So she saw a tall, handsome stranger – that could describe any number of people.'

'Maybe you're right,' Hugo whispered thoughtfully. 'If only I knew what to do next.'

In the black silence that followed he remembered being alone in a cave on a remote island, having watched his uncle being snatched by giant flying rats. He felt the same knot of despair in his stomach and the tide of hopelessness washing over him. But as he recalled the trials he had endured to rescue Walter on that occasion he felt his despondency give way to defiance.

'You know what,' he said suddenly, 'if we can survive Tanglefoot Forest and scores of hungry buffalogres then what's so scary about going into Demonica to take on one miserable vampanther?'

'That's more like the Hugo I know,' smiled Savage. 'So, do you have any ideas about Marcello's clue?'

'Well, we know the portcullis and the black cat tell us it's a map to the vampanther's castle. The third symbol must relate to this windowless house so the next riddle is to work out what on earth SIXEXIV means.'

'Wait – if we were right about the chess game, why was Walter giving us a clue to send us to a church inhabited by a vampire? What is it about the Roman church we're missing?'

'Not a lot really,' sighed Savage. 'The townsfolk used to think it would protect them from vampires – which seemed to work until the vampanther killed half the villagers and scared away the rest. Now it's home to one of Lifereaper's bloodsuckers!'

'What else?'

'Nothing, except that it was built for that saint guy – Claudius Icks.'

'Sorry?' giggled Hugo. 'Did you say Claudius Icks?'

'Y-e-s,' replied Savage warily. 'That was his name, wasn't it? We saw it carved into the statue in the church. Claudius Icks.'

'Oh, Savage, you funny little mouse! It didn't say Claudius Icks, it said Claudius the Ninth.'

'Well, my eyes may be small – some might even describe them as beady,' said Savage, 'but they saw the inscription quite clearly. It said Claudius IX. Icks!'

'But ix isn't a surname, it's a number – a Roman numeral. The I is one and the X is ten. Because the one is before the ten it means one less than ten.'

'And I thought the Romans were supposed to have made life *easier*,' said Savage, clambering up to sit on Hugo's chest. 'So the letters IX are Roman numerals for the number nine?'

'Exactly,' muttered Hugo.

There was a brief silence.

'EXACTLY!' yelped Hugo, springing suddenly upright on the bed. His exclamation was accompanied by a small squeak, followed by a faint thud in the dark.

'Savage?' he enquired, gently patting his chest but not feeling his little furry companion.

Near his feet Hugo heard the scrabbling sound of small claws clambering up the wooden bed, then he felt Savage dart up his leg and on to his shoulder.

'Next time you decide to sit up with such vigour, is there any chance of some advance notice?' asked

Savage. 'That way I'd be able to cling to your shirt rather than being catapulted across the room like a furry pea being flicked from a fork. Luckily I was able to spread my ears to slow my fall, allowing me to land with comparative safety.'

'Of course,' said Hugo. 'I'm sorry. I just hit on something all of a sudden.'

'So did I – the floor.'

'Listen,' said Hugo, stroking Savage's tummy with one knuckle. 'I've solved the next part of Marcello's clue.'

'I'm prepared to be amazed.'

'OK, SIXEXIV isn't a word at all. As we've just discussed, IX is the Roman numeral for nine. Similarly, XIV is how the Romans would have written fourteen. If we replace those letters with numbers we get S9 E14.'

'Directions!' chirped Savage.

'Precisely.' Hugo's voice trembled with excitement. 'I presume they're in miles. From here we must travel south nine miles and east fourteen.'

'What then? Do you think Walter will leave us any more clues?'

Hugo beamed into the blackness. 'I think he'll be with us every step of the way.'

CHapter 25

The following morning brought a cloudless sky and crisp cold air. Hugo woke early and walked Stilton to the farmhouse at the western edge of the village.

Entering the stables he found five horses enjoying the shelter. His pulse quickened as he realized these were the horses belonging to the bandits and Uncle Walter. When had they arrived? And where were they now?

Feeling a mixture of relief and impatience he unharnessed Stilton and left plenty of hay and oats to keep him going while he ventured into the mountains. Before leaving the cart he loaded his satchel with cheese and bread for the journey ahead.

On his way back to the windowless house he spotted a clutch of wild mushrooms growing in the shade at the base of an elm. They had plump mustard-yellow heads dappled with red blotches. With his mind still on provisions, Hugo picked a few and tucked them into his bag. When he arrived at the cottage Savage was waiting outside for him, his arms crossed angrily.

'What's up with you?' asked Hugo.

'She says she's coming with us.'

'Who does?' asked Hugo, scanning the grassy ridge immediately south of the river.

'That cat. Crystal. She says she wants to *help* us defeat the vampanther and save Margery from eternal doom.'

'Great news. The more the merrier,' said Hugo firmly. 'And listen – the bandits are here! Their horses are in the farmhouse stables. I reckon they've continued on foot so we'd better get going.'

'Just for argument's sake,' ventured Savage, 'couldn't we just wait by the stables for the bandits to return?'

'If they manage to get the Diamond Sword they'll have no further use for Uncle Walter.' Hugo clenched his teeth. 'So we need to we reach them before they reach their prize.'

'You're right.' Savage nodded his approval. 'And once we've rescued Walter we'll carry on and slay that overgrown, bloodsucking pussycat, right?'

'We'll see,' said Hugo. He checked his compass and identified a stony outcrop on top of the ridge on a southerly bearing from the house. 'We'll head for that rock, then take another bearing. Let's go. Crystal, we're ready!'

Crystal snaked around the door and strutted towards them. She had a bulb of garlic tied around her neck and a small silver cross hanging from one ear.

'There's plenty more garlic inside,' she announced lazily.

Hugo and Savage exchanged a momentary glance before darting into the cottage. When they reappeared a short time later, Hugo had a whole string of garlic tied round his neck like a garland, while a single peeled clove swayed at Savage's throat. As Hugo closed the door, Crystal suggested he should take its silver cross for added protection. Gratefully he slotted it into his burgeoning satchel and led the way out of town.

Earlier that morning, Hugo had laid his measuring rope straight on the ground and marched its twenty-yard length in thirty paces. Knowing from his training in Uncle Walter's study that there were nearly eighteen hundred yards in a mile, he calculated that to be equivalent to two thousand, seven hundred paces.

'Wait,' said Crystal. 'Before we go there's one more thing to do.' As she spoke she produced the silk scarf she had worn the previous night.

'For heaven's sake!' exclaimed Savage. 'I think we can do without any more mumbo-jumbo fortune-telling for the time being, don't you?'

'Do pipe down, little mouse,' said Crystal, tearing a strip of silk from the scarf with her teeth and handing it to Hugo. 'Tie this around your right arm.'

'What for?' asked Hugo.

'Recognition. If any vampire was to take your shape

they would appear as your mirror image. If the real Hugo has red silk tied round his right arm . . .'

'. . . the vampire me would have red silk tied round his left.'

'Exactly.'

Crystal tore off a tiny strip of silk for Savage and tied a strip round her own right paw.

'OK, we'd better get going,' announced Hugo. 'According to my calculations we only have until tomorrow night to rescue Marcello. Otherwise he's . . .' He paused, thinking of a delicate way of describing the fate awaiting Uncle Walter's friend.

'Otherwise he'll start getting a bit long in the tooth?' suggested Savage.

'Exactly.'

Hugo led the way south from the house, counting his strides. At the edge of the stream he stopped and scooped up a handful of small smooth stones, slipping them into his right-hand coat pocket. With Crystal under one arm and Savage on his shoulder he waded through the wide, shallow river.

'Ninety-eight, ninety-nine.'

Still counting his paces, he scaled the gentle slope to the top of the ridge, his satchel bouncing against one hip, his leather water bottle on the other.

Every time he reached a hundred he would slip a stone into his hand. When he had ten stones in his palm he planned to drop one into his left pocket and return the others to his right pocket.

As he neared the top of the ridge his heart began beating faster, not from the exertion of the climb but because of what was coming into sight.

At first Hugo could see just angular white tips peeking over the ridge like shy icebergs. But with each step he took, the mountains rose further from their cover, revealing their precipitous peaks, perilous slopes and sheer, monstrous expanse. It felt as if the sky had been squashed.

'One hundred.' Hugo perched on the rock he had been aiming for and surveyed the scene in awe.

'How far is that?' asked Crystal.

Hugo paused for a moment as he counted up his collection of pebbles – nine in his palm and one in his left pocket.

'Roll up, ladies and gentlemen!' Savage joked. 'Come and see the world's first human abacus. And believe me, you can *count* on him to entertain you.'

'One thousand, nine hundred paces,' announced Hugo.

'Over half a mile – that's great going,' said Crystal. 'I've never been outside the village before but I must say I'm finding this climb quite invigorating.'

'I think it's about to get decidedly tougher,' said

Hugo, looking from his compass to the rugged peaks ahead. 'Come on – we'll head for the edge of that swathe of trees.'

The slope was steep and the going was slow. A fresh snowfall overnight had quilted the mountains in fluffy powder that swallowed Hugo's legs as far as his knees. Crystal made less impression on the snow, managing to trot light-footedly behind him.

After a few hours they stopped to rest. Leaning on one knee Hugo surveyed the valley they had left behind and sketched it into his notebook.

'What's the purpose of your map?' enquired Crystal.

'If we need to retrace our steps we could easily get lost without a map,' explained Hugo. 'It's easy to get disorientated in the mountains and one wrong step could prove fatal.'

'I see you have been schooled well.'

'Besides,' Hugo grinned, 'no one has ever mapped Demonica before. When my chart is complete, the map of the world will be one step closer to completion.'

He recorded the lazy sweep of the river and the low ridge they had quickly surmounted. Then he drew the featureless snowy hillside they were currently scaling and the craggy, angular peak that stretched above the swathe of trees. Refreshed and re-energized, he trudged on.

The sun was low in the sky when they reached the edge of the forest.

'One hundred.' Hugo leaned on a tree to catch his breath, pressing one palm against the trunk. The buildings of Lovdiv were like a small patch of gravel in the valley far away. He counted seven pebbles in his palm and two in his left pocket.

'That's another mile,' he said, puffing as he opened his notebook to add another mark to his tally. 'We've come six miles already.'

'I'm exhausted,' gasped Savage. 'The air is getting very thin.'

Hugo turned his chin to his shoulder and peered down at his passenger. 'It must be really hard work, being carried up this steep mountain.'

'I'll be OK,' said Savage with a grin. 'But do you think you could possibly try not to breathe quite so loud?'

'Well, as someone once said to me, I'm honoured that you let me breathe at all.'

'Touché.' Perched on Hugo's shoulder, Savage peeked out from behind the tree. 'I can see some strange creatures peering curiously at us,' he said.

A wry smile twitched Crystal's whiskers as she trotted up the hill towards the others. 'Oh, very funny,' she said sarcastically. 'Are you ever going to get tired of mocking my psychic powers?'

'I see long floppy ears, thick white fur,' Savage continued.

'Still not funny,' said Crystal primly.

'They're about my height but much bulkier,' added Hugo. 'They're bounding along on powerful hind legs, using their long tails for balance, and they have stumpy little arms.'

Crystal glanced at the pair of them, her silver–blue coat prickling along the length of her rigid spine. 'You're not joking?' she gasped.

'No,' said Savage. 'And *two* of the creatures are about thirty yards behind you.'

Chapter 26

Crystal scarpered to join Hugo and Savage behind the tree. Curling herself around Hugo's calves, she peered down the mountain.

'Just beyond the shadow of the trees,' whispered Hugo. 'You see them?'

'Let's keep calm,' purred Crystal, nodding. 'They probably heard our footsteps and came to investigate.'

'What are they?' asked Hugo.

'They look a bit like a cross between a rabbit and a kangaroo,' suggested Crystal. 'Hopefully they're not dangerous.'

'Hopefully?' repeated Savage. '*Hopefully?* Is that the most accurate prediction you can give us? It would be a lot more helpful if you could actually foresee something *before* it happens – or is that too much to ask?'

'OK,' said Crystal. 'I see a small mouse-shaped hole appearing in the snow.'

'Where?' demanded Savage scornfully, scanning the pristine white carpet.

As he turned away from her, Crystal leaped on to the tree trunk and, gripping the bark with three claws, nudged the mouse with her spare paw.

Caught unawares, Savage toppled off Hugo's shoulder, landing with a muffled plop and punching a crisp silhouette in the deep snow.

'There it is!' said Crystal with mock amazement.

'That's enough!' Hugo delved into the snow and retrieved Savage. 'Any more sniping from either of you and you can find your way back to Lovdiv on your own. We have to work together, as a team. I've got plenty to deal with already without you two fighting like cat and, well . . . mouse.'

Hugo peered curiously round the tree. The two long-eared kangaroos had come a few yards further uphill. Their velvety white snouts twitched inquisitively and their long elliptical ears hung like pigtails either side of their heads. Thick soft fur and fluffy tummies completed their cuddly appearance.

Catching a whiff of something, one of the kangaroos began bouncing up the steep hillside. Propelling itself with its powerful haunches, it kept its front paws tucked into its chest while using its thick tail for balance. The other animal followed, its ears flopping up and down as it hopped.

'Aw, look how cute they are!' cooed Hugo.

'I know,' whispered Crystal. 'They're gorgeous.'

'I wouldn't say they're *gorgeous*,' countered Savage, 'or even all that cute for that matter. If you ask me they're just a couple of mangy marsupials.'

168

Peering around the tree trunk the three friends watched the animals approaching. The closest was about ten yards away when it spotted Hugo, cocking its head on one side and twitching its nostrils.

Hugo edged tentatively into the open, his palms held up, and waited. The kangaroo hopped closer.

'There, there,' whispered Hugo. 'Who's a handsome boy then?'

'Sorry, are you talking to me?' asked Savage.

'Nice kangaroo,' Hugo coaxed, reaching out to stroke the animal's velvety muzzle. The kangaroo purred.

'Listen to that,' said Savage. 'He's just a big softy!'

Hugo nodded and smiled, his pulse settling as he began to relax. Then his hand paused on the kangaroo's snout. 'He *is* purring, isn't he? It *almost* sounds a bit more like a growl.'

Savage froze. 'Actually, now you come to mention it . . .'

Suddenly the kangaroo lunged, emitting a frightening roar as it knocked Hugo on to his back and pinned him down with its front paws. Just inches from Hugo's face the animal's snout curled into a snarl, baring two rows of pointed teeth – each punctuated by two ferocious fangs dripping with gastric juices.

'This is no cuddly snow creature,' whimpered Savage, jabbing ineffectually at the animal's thick fur with his cactus spine. 'It's some kind of vampire kangaroo.'

'Margery told me about these!' cried Crystal, remembering too late. 'Fearsome fangaroos!'

'And I thought the vampire beetles on the island were ugly,' gasped Savage. 'Where's Snowdon with his bow and arrow when you need him?'

As the fangaroo's jaws pushed closer to Hugo's neck, its sharp fangs thirstily snapped a hair's breadth from his skin. Drawing his knees up to his chest, he pressed the soles of his feet against the monster's tummy and with all his might kicked his legs out straight, throwing the beast backwards into a heap. Clambering to his feet he scooped Savage back on to his shoulder and began to run for all he was worth, pushing his hands on to his thighs with each step.

Frantically Hugo hauled on low branches and pushed off sturdy trunks to propel himself uphill more quickly, but it was no use. Both monsters were gaining on him.

'Those fangaroos are seriously quick,' said Savage. 'It's not fair – with their stumpy front legs and muscular hindquarters they're perfectly designed for bounding up steep snowy hills.'

'Savage, that's it!' Hugo darted behind a tree, leaning his back against its bark as he sucked in some clear air.

'Uh, Hugo,' said Savage, watching the animals approach, 'I don't wish to interrupt your leisurely breather but those fangaroos are about to drink our blood like a flagon of ale.'

Crystal noticed Hugo waiting behind the tree and turned back to hunker down by his feet.

'What are you waiting for?' she demanded.

But Hugo didn't have time to respond.

Just then a large velvety snout appeared next to his head. Twitching hungrily, its nose was just a V-shaped fold in its soft muzzle. Its pearly fangs glinted at the side of its half-open mouth and, its eyes were like orbs of onyx.

With that Hugo bounded down the steep slope towards another tree, his feet sinking deep into the snow. Leaning back against the trunk he listened for the other fangaroo. Sensing movement on his right, he sidled round the tree to the left, keeping the trunk between him and his enemy.

Peering round the tree, Hugo watched the two fluffy white animals bobbing away up the mountain.

'Well done,' said Crystal. 'You lost them.'

'The're not lost though, are they?' said Savage. 'They're bound to double back in a little while. At least before we had the advantage of being uphill.'

'Just wait here,' said Hugo. Then he leaped out from behind the tree, jumping up and down, waving his arms and shouting. 'Hey! Big ears! Over here you buck-toothed fleabags!'

172

'What are you doing?' hissed Savage.

Further up the mountain both fangaroos turned back and, seeing Hugo's performance, began to hop down the mountainside towards him.

He watched them for a moment, then turned and charged down the hillside. Leaping and sliding in the thick snow, he belted out of the forest and on to the wide-open space beyond.

Glancing over his shoulder, Hugo slammed into something solid and covered in soft fur, punching the air out of his lungs. He staggered back a couple of paces, his chest heaving, and turned to see what had arrested his escape.

The third fangaroo had only popped out of its warren for some fresh air, but it reacted quickly to its good fortune and threw a short sharp punch straight at the boy's chin.

Hugo's head snapped back with the force of the blow and the hot salty taste of blood trickled under his tongue. He shook his head and tried to focus. Bobbing under the next punch, he sprang upright again and threw a punch of his own, catching the monster on its nose.

'Attaboy, Hugo!' whispered Savage, boxing his very own imaginary fangaroo further uphill.

As the fangaroo prepared to throw its next jab, Hugo grabbed a bulb of garlic from around his neck and shoved it into the animal's snout. Instantly the monster's head recoiled in horror and Hugo continued his escape down the mountain.

A second or two later the monster turned and gave chase, its tail swishing furiously.

The other two fangaroos pelted past Savage and Crystal, their bulbous eyes fixed on their target further away.

'They're gaining on him,' observed Crystal. 'I do hope he's got a plan.'

'He'll have one, I'm sure of it,' said Savage confidently.

As the trees came to an end, the ground fell away steeply. As Hugo slid downhill on his bottom, the monsters, leaning forward at an extreme angle, struggled not to topple over. They sat back on their haunches to regain control of their descent, but it was no good. Their weight was too far forward and their momentum was too great.

First one, then another, and finally the third fangaroo lost its balance. All three beasts toppled forward, somersaulting on to their backs and rolling head over heels down the mountain, snow sticking to their fluffy fleeces as they careered away. Completely out of control they accelerated, growing with each revolution as they picked up more and more snow until they were unrecognizable as anything other than giant snowballs.

Just as one of the spheres threatened to engulf him, Hugo threw himself to one side, allowing the snowball to bounce harmlessly past him. Getting to his feet he watched the three balls thundering down the hillside, leaving parallel tracks in the pristine snow.

'Everyone OK?' he asked when he had climbed back to the tree where he'd left Savage and Crystal.

'Fine,' said Crystal. 'Do you think they'll survive and come after us?'

Hugo looked back at the rocky terrain awaiting the fangaroos in the valley. He shook his head. 'Not a snowball in hell's chance.'

'Great boxing, Hugo,' said Savage. 'You must be bowled over.'

'Pleased as Punch.' Hugo dabbed his cut lip with his sleeve and smiled. 'Now we'd better get a move on. And we'd better hope those fangaroos delayed the bandits as well or we're never going to catch up with Uncle Walter.'

Chapter 27

'I can't believe he's gone,' sobbed Tommy, shaking his head. 'Poor Billy Blood.'

'I know,' said Big Jake softly.

'One minute he was next to me and the next . . .'

'I know.'

'And did you see what they did to him? It was horrible.'

'I know.'

'Having the blood sucked from his body – that's no way for a man to die.'

'At least he died with the sound of screaming in his ears,' said Big Jake with a wistful smile. 'He loved to hear screaming, didn't he?'

'Not his own screaming though, Jake. No one likes the sound of their own screams.'

'No. You're probably right.' Big Jake tightened his grip around his friend's shoulders. 'Your partner in crime was a bad man, Tommy. A really despicable human being – one of the nastiest I ever met.'

Tommy looked up at Big Jake and gave him a grateful smile. 'Thank you, Jake. It's nice of you to say so.'

Inside the cave Little Jake sighed and shook his head.

'That business with those vampire kangaroos has really shaken the boys up,' he said. 'I mean, fancy dragging a dying man underground like that.'

'Lifereaper's vampires have ensured Demonica is dominated by evil and violence,' said Walter, without looking up from his map. 'I dare say we'll have to face worse than a few angry kangaroos if we're to wrest the Diamond Sword from his devilish grasp.'

Little Jake studied Walter for a moment, then he snorted. 'You're bluffing. You don't know what you're talking about.'

'You're right.' Walter looked up and smiled at him. 'I don't *know* anything. But what I've heard since arriving is that Lifreaper is in fact a vile, vicious . . . well, you don't want to worry about such tittle-tattle.'

'I'll be the judge of that,' snapped Little Jake. 'Finish what you were saying – he's a vile, vicious what?'

Walter fixed Jake with a grim stare. Then he took a long breath and whispered, '*Vampanther.*'

Little Jake gasped and flinched then, regaining his composure, he managed a derisory laugh. 'A vampanther?' he scoffed. 'I ain't never heard anything so ludicrous in my entire life.'

'I mean, I presume you have planned how you're

going to disarm the most fearsome beast ever to terrorize the globe?'

A frown creased little Jake's forehead and his eyes shifted nervously.

Walter continued, 'I mean, only a complete fool would take on the vampanther without preparing every detail of their assault.'

Little Jake flung out a hand, pressing a dagger against Walter's cheek. 'You just worry about leading us safely to Lifereaper's castle, or you'll suffer a death so ghastly you'll wish those kangaroos had taken you in the forest rather than Billy Blood.'

Without flinching, Walter smiled. 'All I can do is follow this map.'

Little Jake lowered his blade and ran a hand over his face. 'How does it work then – that magic *map*?' He spat the last word out as though it were poison.

Walter placed the map on the ground, smoothing it flat.

'It shows a small section of the mountains here in Demonica.' He pointed to the legend containing the code. 'And this tells us where to find the castle.'

'But if it's that simple, why did we travel all the way to England to kidnap you? We could follow those directions ourselves, couldn't we?'

'Have you read the directions?'

'No, I haven't read the bloomin' directions!' snapped

Little Jake. 'I've got far too much killin' and stealin' to do to be bothered about learnin' me alphabet.'

'So you can't read?'

'Course I can't read! What do I look like – some sort of genius?'

'Then allow me to explain the basic principles of map reading.' Walter pulled a long twig from the pile of sticks they had collected for their fire. He laid it on the ground at the mouth of the cave and, snapping a small twig into six, arranged its pieces into a triple-headed arrow at one end. 'Every map has an arrow on it like this, indicating which way is north.' He pointed to the arrow on Marcello's map. 'These twigs point north so all we have to do is turn the map so both arrows line up and Bob's your uncle. Although in your case I expect someone called Jake is your uncle.'

Walter snapped up another twig and arranged its pieces into a letter next to the arrow's head. 'There we go,' he said. 'N for north.'

'N for north,' repeated Little Jake.

'Once you know which way is north, it's easy to work out every other direction.'

'Really?'

Walter laid another long twig accross the first, making a large cross. Snapping up some more small twigs, he made three more letters. 'These are the cardinal points,' he said, sitting back to admire his work. 'E for east, S for south and W for west.'

'It all seems a bit clever for me,' said Little Jake. 'I think I'll probably stick to robbing and let you do the map stuff.'

'Very well,' said Walter.

'Can I stop waving this torch about yet?' whined Big Jake. 'My arm is killing me.'

'Actually you can,' said Walter. 'This cross on the ground should deter vampires long enough for you to gather your weapons.'

'What are those symbols round it?' asked Tommy Guts, frowning at the twigs as he stepped over them.

'Them's the carnival points,' said Little Jake snootily. 'They'll lead us to Lifereaper's castle and the Diamond Sword.'

Big Jake's eyes swelled with greed. 'And then we'll be richer than King Henry himself.'

Tommy Guts nodded eagerly, blinking away his tears.

Big Jake was on first watch so he stood guard outside the cavern. As the other two bandits settled down, Walter took one last glance at his handiwork, then curled up for the night.

Chapter 28

Some way down the hillside Hugo, Savage and Crystal had made camp at the southern edge of the forest. A small potage of garlic and melted snow simmered on their campfire.

Hugo, who had been studying the mountainside ahead for some time, sat up straight.

'That flickering light's gone,' he said. 'I think it was a signal.'

'From your uncle?' asked Crystal.

Hugo checked his compass. 'The light was on a southerly bearing from here,' he said. 'It must be Uncle Walter. He's still alive!'

'Of course he is,' said Savage. 'Haven't you realized yet that Crystal's premonitions are total fantasy? No offence, Mystic Moggy.'

'You know, Savage, I see a large slice of humble pie in your future,' said Crystal.

'Great,' said Savage. 'I love pie.'

While Savage and Crystal slept curled up by their little campfire, Hugo unfolded his copy of Marcello's map. Intrigued by its code and eager to see how their journey might develop, he studied the next message in its legend.

KNNJHMRHCDLNTSGNEBQXRSZKEZMFR

He was sure it was some sort of code but its solution was still a mystery. He tried reading the letters backwards and rearranging them. Gripping his fists with frustration, he lay back and stared at the night sky.

'It's no good,' he whispered to himself. 'I need to solve the code to follow Uncle Walter and find the castle, but I need Uncle Walter to help me solve the code. If he weren't leaving me clues along the way I'd be completely lost.'

A couple of hours later Crystal woke with a start, her fur bristling as she stared into the blackness.

'Hugo! Savage! Wake up,' she hissed. 'We've got company.'

Hugo was on his feet in a flash, drawing his sword from his belt and brandishing it blindly at the night. Savage scrambled up to his shoulder, where he thrashed his cactus spine sleepily.

The three of them waited, and watched, and listened.

For a couple of minutes they saw nothing but the edges of tree trunks highlighted by the moon and heard nothing but their own breathing, shallow and fast.

'What did you see?' Hugo whispered at last.

'I didn't *see* anything,' said Crystal.

'Well, what did you hear then?' asked Savage.

'I didn't *hear* anything either.'

'Let me get this straight,' said Savage, lowering his weapon. 'You didn't hear or see anything, and yet you decide to wake us up and scare us half to death by claiming we'd got company?'

'I just had a feeling – a sort of sixth sense.'

'Well, I've heard of cats having nine lives but I've never met a cat with six senses.' Savage scampered down to the ground and curled back up in his little snow hole. 'Goodnight, folks. If you "sense" any more monsters in the night please don't bother to wake me. I'll take my chances.'

'Are you sure there's something out there?' asked Hugo, keeping his eyes on the trees.

Crystal peered into the night for a moment. 'Well, I suppose I might have been mistaken,' she conceded, sounding surprised. Her fur was smooth and sleek once again. 'I'm sorry.'

'That's OK,' said Hugo lowering his sword. 'Better safe than . . .'

Before he could finish, a terrible sound echoed down the hill – part scream and part howl. Spinning round and raising his sword, he took a few strides to the edge of the forest and surveyed the mountainside.

Standing out against the cool-blue moonlit snow, a

tall figure was approaching at speed. As it got closer Hugo could see the man's hunched, broad shoulders and a torso tapering into narrow hips. His coarse cotton shirt barely covered his hairy midriff and a pair of brown britches exposed long skinny calves and huge flat feet clad in thick black hair. Tangled hair flew from his head – and his face, which was wrinkled into a grimace, was almost hidden behind a matted, straggly beard.

As the man charged down the snowy slope he seemed awkward and gangly, occasionally stumbling forward and lolloping a few strides on all fours, yet closing in at an alarming rate.

'What on earth is that?' gasped Hugo.

'It's hard to say,' replied Crystal. 'Is he even human?'

'Either way you were right about us having company.'

'You don't know the half of it,' sighed Crystal.

'What do you mean?' Hugo glanced over his shoulder to see Crystal backing towards him, her legs and tail rigid and her fur spiky once again. Ten yards beyond her about twenty eyes seemed to be floating in the blackness just above the ground, like small luminous planets. They were moving in pairs and edging ever closer.

'What are they?' Hugo demanded.

'Wolves,' hissed Crystal. 'And they don't seem particularly friendly.'

Hugo glanced back up the mountain. The lone marauder was nearly upon him, his wild steel-blue eyes glinting and his gangly arms thrashing the air.

'Is *this* Lifereaper?' wondered Hugo.

Crystal allowed herself another glance up the mountainside. 'Somehow I doubt it,' she said dryly. 'Speaking as a feline, I think we can safely assume the vampanther would make an altogether more *elegant* entrance.'

Hugo's head snapped from side to side as he gauged the danger approaching from uphill and down. The wolves had emerged from the cover of the trees, their heads hanging low and their tongues lolling hungrily.

Up the hill the figure was just yards away, hurtling towards him.

Hugo gripped his sword tightly.

Panting and snarling, the wolves broke into a run.

The wild man accelerated.

Two of the wolves yowled as they leaped at Hugo, their claws stretched out in front of them, jaws agape.

The man took a running jump. Planting one foot on a fallen tree trunk, he sprang high into the air, snarling angrily and flailing his long, scrawny limbs.

Chapter 29

Everything seemed to move in slow motion as Hugo watched the wolves and the wild man sailing towards him through the night sky. The man pedalled his hairy legs in mid-air and threw his long arms forward. The wolves thrust out their claws and let their tongues flail.

This is it, thought Hugo. There's no escape. As he cowered, praying for a miracle, he glanced up . . . and saw the wild man sail headlong over his head.

Stretching both arms out wide the wild man grabbed both lunging wolves, intercepting them just before their claws and teeth turned Hugo's soft skin into ribbons. Gripping them by the scruff of the neck he halted both wolves and all three crashed to the ground, tumbling down the snowy slope in a howling tangle of hair and teeth.

The wild man was first to his feet, spreading his long arms out wide and bellowing a hideous roar. Skulking low to the ground, the two wolves sidled around him while the rest of the pack closed ranks behind them.

The two sides eyed each other for a moment, then a single wolf bolted out of the pack and pounced. The

man's reactions were too quick. With one swipe of his rangy arm he slapped the wolf across its snout, sending it sprawling and whimpering across the ground.

The man growled, eyeballing each of the wolves as if daring it to attack. The stalemate continued for another few seconds before the pack turned tail and were swallowed silently up by the night.

The man watched the blackness for a moment, his menacing snarl subsiding with each breath. Long, messy hair completely masked his low forehead and straggly tufts grew from his cheeks and jowls. Only his nose and two patches around his eyes were unadorned by this wiry beard. The man turned to see Hugo and Crystal staring at him, frozen with amazement.

'Don't come any closer!' commanded Hugo with as much authority as he could muster.

The wild man paused a few feet from Hugo. Stooping so that his ice-blue eyes were level with his, he curled his lips back to show the ragged teeth lining his mouth.

'One more step and I'll chop off your ugly head, you horrible hairy monster.'

Much to Hugo's astonishment, his warning stopped the wild man in his tracks.

Hanging his head, his bottom lip stuck out and quivered. 'There's no need to be quite so personal,' he complained in a surprisingly posh voice. 'I know I'm not the prettiest fellow in the world but none of us can help the way we look. I try not to let it bother me but it really doesn't help my confidence being called "ugly" and a "horrible hairy monster".'

'Oh,' said Hugo, feeling a mixture of surprise and shame. 'I'm really sorry. I didn't mean to offend you, I just thought you were about to, you know . . . kill me.'

'Why would you think that?' The man shrugged, turning his hands up in a gesture of innocence.

Hugo shuffled his feet. 'Oh, I don't know,' he said softly, trying not to stare at the man's hairy palms. 'It was probably just the way you were charging towards me, flashing your teeth and waving your arms about.'

'*And* you were howling,' added Crystal. 'Quite scarily, I might add.'

'But not at you,' said the man sorrowfully, 'just at those wolves.' He slumped down in the snow, wrapping his long arms around his legs and resting his forehead on his knees.

As Hugo and Crystal looked at each other in bemused silence the man began whining quietly, occasionally stopping to inhale a long gurgling sniff.

Hugo stepped towards him. 'Oh, don't cry,' he said, tentatively reaching a hand out to stroke the thick mane of hair on his head. 'We're actually incredibly pleased that you turned up when you did.'

'Really?' The man looked up. His eyes were rimmed

with red and two lines of snot streaked from his nose. 'I didn't mean to scare anybody. It's so hard to make friends when you look as frightful as I do. Everyone runs a mile as soon as they see me – that's why I just hide up here in the mountains alone.'

'You're not *that* scary,' said Hugo kindly. 'In fact, now I can see you properly, you're really quite . . . distinctive.'

'Really? You're just saying that . . . *Distinctive*, you say?'

'And thank you again for scaring off that pack of wolves,' said Crystal. 'You saved our lives.'

'Oh, that was nothing really,' said the man. 'Besides, they probably wouldn't have harmed you.'

'Well, I'm glad you didn't wait to test that theory out anyway. I'm Hugo, by the way.'

'I'm Lupus.'

'This is Crystal,' said Hugo.

'Who are you talking to?' asked Savage, who had heard the commotion and wandered, still half asleep, on to Hugo's shoulder to investigate.

Hugo nodded in Lupus's direction.

Dozily Savage turned his head until his eyes locked on to Lupus.

'Yikes!' he cried, his ears shooting up with surprise. 'Who is *that*? More to the point, *what* is that? Talk about ugly! Hang on – that's not the vampanther, is it?'

'Look at him,' urged Crystal wearily. 'Does he have any feline traits whatsoever?'

'Let me see,' said Savage, scratching his chin. 'Well, he doesn't strut about, he doesn't have an infuriating air of superiority, and he has obviously never preened himself in his whole life.'

'What's that supposed to mean?' demanded Crystal.

Savage sighed and rolled his eyes. 'It means that cats are smug and irritatingly sleek and he's got nothing to be smug about, and what's more he looks like he's been dragged through every hedge in Europe – backwards and forwards.'

'I'm just over here,' Lupus pointed out politely. 'I can hear every word.'

'So, how did you come to be . . . you know . . . ?' Hugo couldn't think quite how to phrase his question.

'What?' asked Lupus. 'You mean how am I so scary looking?' As he spoke an ear popped up out of the coarse hair on the side of his head. It was pink and bald, just like a large human ear but strangely pointed at the top.

'Whoa!' exclaimed Savage. 'How come you've got such poin—'

Hugo grabbed Savage's snout to shut him up. 'Like I said, you're not scary, you're distinctive,' he said.

Hurriedly Lupus scratched the side of his head,

covering the ear with his hair, and smiled gratefully. 'Some time ago I was walking through these mountains when I was attacked by a ferocious vampire. He tried to sink his teeth into my neck but I managed to wriggle free and escaped with just a couple of flesh wounds. I thought I'd be fine once my cuts had healed, but within a few hours I realized that some of the vampire's evil had infected my blood. I began to change.'

'Change?' whispered Crystal. 'How?'

'I didn't always look like this,' moaned Lupus, 'but after that bite everything started to stretch. It felt as if my muscles were being wrung out and my bones forced apart. It was agony. Then my hair started to change and my ears . . . Oh dear lord, my ears!'

Sobbing, Lupus wrapped his arms over his head.

'Ears?' asked Savage, trying to compensate for his earlier rudeness. 'What's wrong with your ears? They look perfectly fine to us. We hadn't noticed your ears at all, in fact.'

'Sometimes I think I'd have been better off if the vampire had killed me there and then,' blubbed Lupus into his knees. 'At least I would have become a fully fledged vampire rather than the strange misfit that I am. I would have belonged somewhere instead of having to hide in the mountains. I can't go home looking like this and yet I haven't taken on a single vampire trait. I'm neither fish nor fowl.'

As Lupus lifted his head, a string of snot stretched from his nose to his knee.

'Right now I'd have to say he's pretty foul,' whispered Savage.

Crystal strutted around Lupus, scrutinizing his attire. 'Are those your own clothes?' she enquired.

'Goodness me, no!' insisted Lupus, tugging at the hem of his shirt self-consciously. 'Mummy would have a fit if she saw me in this get-up.'

'My mother always made me tuck my shirt in and wear a jacket on Sundays,' remembered Hugo, smiling fondly. 'Was yours like that?'

'Gracious no!' blustered Lupus. 'Mummy hated me wearing any clothes at all. My brothers and I always used to play in the forest naked.'

Hugo, Savage and Crystal exchanged astounded looks.

'That's one way of cutting down on the laundry, I suppose,' noted Hugo.

'So where did these undersized garments come from?' asked Crystal.

'I'm ashamed to say I stole them from a washing line in a nearby village,' confessed Lupus. 'Ever since my encounter with that bloodsucker I've really started to feel the cold.'

'How long ago did you say you were attacked?' asked Hugo.

Lupus shrugged. 'My life was ruined a little under a year ago.'

'That's brilliant news!' Beaming, Hugo put his arm round Lupus's shoulders and gave him a squeeze.

'I beg your pardon?' asked Lupus.

'No,' laughed Hugo. 'Not that your life was ruined – it's brilliant news that it was less than a year ago.'

'The vampires' evil doesn't take permanent hold of your body until a year after the attack,' explained Savage. 'All we have to do is destroy Lifereaper before twelve months is up and you will be returned to normal.'

'We're on our way to find his castle right now,' said Crystal. 'We've got a coded map and we think Hugo's uncle is up ahead, leaving us clues. When we find Lifereaper's castle we'll kill him with his own sword and set all the mezzaghouls free.'

'And I'd be willing to bet,' added Hugo, 'that killing the vampanther will reverse the effects his vampire's bite had on you.'

'Really?' Lupus wiped his long hairy forearm across his snotty snout. 'Is that possible?'

'Of course it is,' said Hugo. 'Anything is possible.'

'Even a talking cat,' said Savage.

CHApter 30

Cool peach-coloured sunlight washed the sky behind the icy ridges to the east. The north face of the mountain was still clad in deep blue and black, but it wouldn't be long before pale gold sunlight seeped over the peaks like fingers.

Hugo, Savage and Crystal had spent the last hour filling Lupus in on the details of Marcello's map and Uncle Walter's kidnapping and the disappearance of Jadea Jafil. Now they were preparing to continue their ascent.

Hugo passed around a loaf and some cheese from his satchel. Savage perched on his shoulder and nibbled at a chunk of Cheddar.

'I don't suppose you've got any Stilton in that satchel of yours?' he enquired.

'No,' laughed Hugo. 'No Stilton on the menu today, sir, but I do have some rather delicious-looking mushrooms that I picked in Lovdiv.'

Hugo took one of the wide, flat mushrooms out of his satchel. It smelled rich and flavoursome so he dangled it in front of his face and took a large bite.

'Help yourself, Lupus,' urged Hugo, his cheeks

bulging. 'You look like you haven't had a decent meal in weeks – your ribs are like a xylophone!'

Suddenly Lupus leaped over the campfire and lunged at Hugo with both arms outstretched. He knocked him to the ground, sending Savage somersaulting into the air. 'Talk about touchy!' cried the mouse.

Crystal watched in horror as the hairy figure straddled Hugo on all fours, pinning down his limp body and gnawing his face.

With a ferocious screech she leaped on to Lupus's back, clawing through his shirt and into his coarse hair. An instant later Savage had regained his composure, and his bearings, and joined in the fray. Scampering up Lupus's britches, he began jabbing his cactus spine repeatedly into Lupus's bottom.

'OK, OK,' he yelped, releasing Hugo from his grip. 'I give in.'

Savage and Crystal jumped to the ground, circling Lupus to stand between him and Hugo.

'I knew all along you couldn't be trusted,' hissed Crystal.

'Actually, I was the one who suspected he might be the vampanther,' said Savage.

'Didn't you conclude that he couldn't possibly be part of the cat family because he was too scruffy?'

'There's been a terrible mistake,' interrupted Lupus.

'I know, us trusting you,' said Crystal.

'Take one step and we'll all be eating wild-man kebabs for breakfast,' warned Savage.

'Savage? Crystal? What's going on?' Hugo demanded groggily, shaking his head as he sat upright.

'Lupus was attacking you,' said Crystal.

'I wasn't attacking him, honestly. I didn't even scratch him,' implored Lupus. Savage glanced at Hugo, who shook his head to confirm the claim. Lupus continued, 'I was trying to save his life.'

'Ha!' Savage snorted. 'What exactly were you saving him from? I don't see any vampires or fearsome fangaroos around here. Do you?'

'This.' Lupus stuck out his unusually long, pink tongue, upon which sat a small morsel. He picked it off and held it out in the palm of his bony, hairy hand. One edge was curved, the other scalloped in the shape of tooth marks and it was mustard-yellow, dappled with red blotches.

'The mushroom?' said Hugo.

'The Terribly Toxic Toadstool,' corrected Lupus. 'If you'd consumed even this small piece it would have poisoned your entire bloodstream almost immediately. You would have been paralysed within five minutes and dead within ten. You'd already swallowed it so I hit you in the stomach to make you cough it back up again. Then I had to suck the mushroom, and its venomous juices, out of your mouth.'

'Thank you,' said Hugo bewilderedly.

'I should think so too,' said Savage, awkwardly hiding his cactus spine behind his back.

'Hang on a minute,' said Crystal. 'If the mushroom juice is so toxic, why hasn't it poisoned you?'

'Well, I'm much bigger than Hugo so it will have less effect on me,' said Lupus. 'But my tongue will probably swell up soon and become paral-la-la-la.' As he spoke his tongue suddenly ballooned to many times its usual size, filling his mouth and jamming it open as if he were chewing a big pink sponge.

'Oh dear,' said Hugo shakily. 'That mushroom really was poisonous.' He got up and placed a hand on Lupus's shoulder. 'Are you OK?'

Lupus nodded. A long string of drool bounced from the corner of his mouth.

'Is there anything I can do?'

Lupus shook his head. The drool wrapped itself round his wild beard.

'Will the poison wear off?'

Lupus nodded vigorously and gave Hugo two hairy thumbs up.

'Come on, guys,' said Hugo, tearing a strip of silk from Crystal's scarf and tying it around Lupus's right arm. 'The sun's almost up – let's get going.'

Hugo began to lead the way out of the forest on to

the craggy slope that lay ahead. Crystal and Lupus followed.

'HA!'

They turned to see Savage grinning at them, his big pink ears flapping with excitement.

'Ha what?' asked Crystal wearily.

'It's just occurred to me,' said Savage. 'In your second prediction you said Hugo would be poisoned or he would poison a friend.'

'What's your point?'

'My point is that you were wrong. Hugo wasn't poisoned at all and he hardly poisoned Lupus. If anything Lupus bravely poisoned himself in order to save Hugo's life.'

'I can't explain my visions,' said Crystal firmly, 'but I certainly was right about Hugo encountering poison.'

'Encountering it, yes. Swallowing a lethal dose of it, no. That's quite a significant difference if you ask me.'

'Well, I didn't ask you.'

'Maybe in future you should!'

'Enough!' yelled Hugo. 'I'm going to set off now because Uncle Walter's life is in danger. If those bandits get to Lifereaper's Diamond Sword, they'll have no more use for Uncle Walter. They'll probably kill him and every mezzaghoul, including Marcello, will be doomed to spend eternity as a blood-crazed vampire. But if your petty quarrel is more important, feel free to continue bickering.' He turned and continued climbing the mountain, followed by Lupus.

Savage and Crystal exchanged guilty looks.

'Maybe we should call a truce,' suggested Crystal.

'OK,' agreed Savage. 'I'll try not to mention your laughably inaccurate predictions again.'

'And I'll do my very best not to make fun of you for being a tiny rodent with ridiculously big, flappy ears.'

The pair eyed each other suspiciously for a moment.

Chapter 31

The mountain was too steep and rugged to head straight for the top so Hugo led the team on a meandering path towards the ledge where he'd seen the flashing light the night before. The sun passed overhead and glistened on the snow but did little to warm up the day. Icy air rasped in Hugo's throat as he picked his way between snow-clad boulders and lumps of ice and clambered up sheer passageways. Savage clung precariously to his coat while Crystal leaped from rock to rock with elegant agility. Lupus used his lanky limbs to good effect, easily reaching footholds and handholds that were out of Hugo's reach. Every now and then he would scoop a handful of snow and hold it against his tongue, which was gradually recovering from its temporary paralysis.

Dusk was beginning to settle when, hearing a scuffling sound, Hugo stopped sharply. About twenty yards up the mountain a beautiful stag was traversing a ledge around a sheer rock face.

'Look at that,' he whispered, touching Lupus's arm and nodding uphill. 'Aren't its horns amazing?'

Without a word Lupus nodded.

'It could, of course, be a vampire stag,' suggested Savage softly.

Crystal shook her head. 'You can see its reflection in the icy cliff face. It's harmless all right.'

For a few seconds the four companions admired the handsome deer negotiating the ledge with elegant calmness. But suddenly it froze then scrabbled backwards a couple of steps, its hoofs slipping as its poise deserted it.

'Something's spooked it,' whispered Hugo, scanning the mountain.

'There!' hissed Savage, 'Directly above it.'

Now Hugo saw it too. Long and low, it was covered in sleek black fur from its smooth crown to its huge paws, which gripped the snow with surprising precision. Even through the black cloak draped over its body Hugo could make out its muscles and its shoulder blades sawing as it stalked the stag.

'Great ears,' remarked Savage.

'I know,' said Lupus. 'They're almost like bat's wings.'

Hugo swallowed and tried to lick his lips. 'Is that who I think it is?'

'It must be.' Crystal nodded gravely. 'Check out its feline grace. I think we're about to witness our very first vampanther attack.'

The gang gasped as the vampanther pounced,

spreading its arms wide as it sailed gracefully towards its startled prey below. Landing square on the stag's back it wrapped its muscular limbs around its victim, which collapsed immediately under the immense burden. There was just a flash of ivory fangs and lascivious tongue before the vampanther buried its velvety black snout into the deer's soft neck, the monster's body convulsing with pleasure as it drank thirstily.

When it had finished its meal it stood upright over the stag's limp carcass, which appeared to shrivel up and disintegrate on the spot. Cupping one paw over the hilt of the sword hanging from its hip it wiped its thick whiskers clean with the back of the other. It scanned the terrain from left to right, its powerful jaws set in an imperious sneer. Then it bounded nimbly along the ledge, its cloak rippling behind it as it disappeared into the twilight.

For a moment no one spoke.

'Golly,' said Lupus at last. 'Talk about clinical . . . I wouldn't want to meet him on a dark night.'

'Or indeed at dusk,' added Hugo.

'Yes, Crystal,' said Savage accusingly. 'I thought you said vampires only attack at night.'

'I've told you – a different set of rules apply to Lifereaper. It appears he's not too shy to conduct his business in daylight,' retorted Crystal.

'What if he's waiting for us further along that ledge?' asked Lupus.

'All the better,' said Hugo, managing a brave laugh. 'It'll save us having to go all the way to his secret castle to get his sword and kill him.'

As the four companions continued their ascent an uneasy silence settled over them. Try as he might Hugo couldn't shake the image of the vampanther's brutal attack from his mind and he guessed the others were similarly daunted by the scene they had witnessed. He had no idea how they would begin to take on such a fearsome opponent – assuming they ever managed to find Lifereaper's secret castle – and he could feel his hopes dwindling. Concentrating on the thought of seeing Uncle Walter again, he trudged on through the snow.

'By the way,' said Savage eventually, 'did anyone else notice any resemblance between the vampanther and one of us – suggesting, possibly, some sort of ancestry?'

'Now you mention it, I did,' said Hugo, 'but just because you've both got strange ears and appalling table manners I don't think for a moment that you're related to the vampanther.'

'Oh, please!' exclaimed Savage, throwing his little arms up. 'Not ME! Her! Crystal! How do we know she's not a vampussycat – sent by Lifereaper to derail our quest?'

'Oh dear me,' teased Crystal. 'I think someone's getting just a little vamparanoid.'

'Oh, I'm vamparanoid, am I?' sneered Savage. 'Well, if I'm vamparanoid what does that make you?'

Crystal shrugged. 'An ordinary cat?'

'She's right, Savage,' said Hugo. 'I don't want to hear any more of your fangtasy.'

CHapter 32

Night hung like a black curtain drawn across the sky as the gang inched along the narrow ledge that rimmed the mountainside in a shallow zigzag. As they rounded an outcrop of rock the ledge widened and the hillside receded into a shallow cave.

A large stick, charred black at one end, lay in the snow outside the cave.

'The flashing light from last night!' exclaimed Hugo.

'So we're definitely following your uncle's route?' asked Lupus.

Hugo nodded. 'I just hope he keeps leaving us signs because so far I'm no closer to solving the next part of Marcello's code.'

He turned and surveyed the valley. 'The forest is due north from here,' he announced. 'So we have travelled generally in a southerly direction. And I would estimate the trees to be about two-thirds along the way from Lovdiv to here.'

'Lovdiv to the edge of the forest was six miles, wasn't it?' confirmed Crystal.

Hugo nodded. 'Which means Lovdiv to here must be about nine!'

'So Lifereaper's castle is fourteen miles east of here,' said Savage.

'According to Marcello's map it is.' Hugo nodded. 'Let's build a campfire and rest here for a while. Lupus, can you guard the entrance and let us know if you see any living creature at all? Even a butterfly could be a vampire in disguise.'

'Hugo!' called Crystal from inside the shallow cavern. 'Come and look at this.'

Hugo lit the torch and went to investigate. Crystal was studying the floor where a selection of twigs had been arranged in the shape of a large cross with a different letter at each point.

'What does it mean?' she asked, prowling around the mysterious message.

'I'm not sure.' Hugo frowned and crouched down to examine the twigs. 'The letters don't spell anything and it's unlikely to be an anagram because there aren't any vowels.'

'Could they be initials?' asked Crystal.

'They could be. But of what, I haven't a clue.'

'What about that strange cross?'

'I know. It's like the symbol mapmakers use to denote the cardinal points of the compass, except they usually use a double-headed arrow for north, not triple.' Suddenly Hugo's eyes lit up. Leaning the torch against a cave wall and swinging his satchel round he delved inside and pulled out a piece of folded parchment. Hurriedly he unfolded it and his eager gaze immediately fell on the symbol at the top of the page.

'Marcello drew the compass rose with a triple-headed arrow pointing north!' he exclaimed, tapping the map in his hands. 'This must be a clue from Uncle Walter about the map.'

Hugo's hands moved nimbly as he studied his compass, comparing its readings to the symbol on the ground.

'That triple-headed arrow is aligned with north,' he confirmed. 'But why on earth has Uncle Walter labelled it with the letter M, not N?'

'And why has he used a D for east, an R for south and a V to indicate west?' asked Crystal, brushing past Hugo's shins.

'Why label them at all?' puzzled Hugo. 'He of all people knows I'm familiar with the points of a compass already.'

Hugo took his notebook from his bag and wrote the letters from Walter's clue in a column. Next to them he wrote the initials they represented.

$$M - N$$
$$D - E$$
$$R - S$$
$$V - W$$

'They're all pairs of letters that come side by side in the alphabet,' said Hugo.

Crystal leaped on to Hugo's lap and perused his notes. 'I wonder why he did that? Why not just use the actual letters for the cardinal points?'

'Because the compass points aren't the message!' said Hugo excitedly. 'I know that north is over there without Uncle Walter leaving me a clue. I'd bet a sovereign to a pinch of salt that it's the same code Marcello used on his map!'

'So to *decode* Marcello's message you swap each letter for the letter that *follows* it in the alphabet?' suggested Crystal.

Hugo clicked his fingers. 'Exactly!'

His hands trembled as he copied the message from Marcello's map into his notebook. Underneath each letter he wrote the subsequent letter in the alphabet.

KNNJHMRHCDSGDLNTSGNEBQXRSZKEZMFR

LOOKINSIDETHEMOUTHOFCRYSTALFANGS

'Loo kinsid et hemout hof cryst alfangs?' pondered Crystal, resting her paws on Hugo's knees so she could see his notebook. 'That doesn't make any sense. Is it French?'

'Lookinsidethemouthofcrystalfangs,' read Hugo, stumbling over the pronunciation. Finally understanding the message, he beamed. 'Look inside the mouth of crystal fangs!'

'Well, that actually makes much more sense,' conceded Crystal then her ears pricked up. 'I wonder what the mouth of crystal fangs could be though?'

'Yes, I wonder,' agreed Savage drumming his fingers on his chin. 'If only we knew someone called Crystal whose teeth might be referred to as fangs.' Suddenly he stared at Crystal and let his mouth fall open in mock shock. 'Hang on a minute – *you're* called Crystal . . .'

'Brilliant!' exclaimed Crystal. 'Are you saying that you think I've swallowed Lifereaper's secret castle?'

'Be fair, old chap,' Lupus called from outside the cave. 'That is a little far-fetched – even for this neck of the woods.'

'Mouth of crystal fangs,' murmured Hugo. He

scrutinized his notebook for a few more minutes then let out a frustrated sigh. 'Well, I'm stumped. Savage, do you have any other bright ideas? Savage?'

'He scurried out of the cave just now,' Lupus replied. 'He said he had to answer a call of nature. I'm sure he won't be long – in fact here he comes now.'

Savage scampered through Lupus's long legs into the cave and on to Hugo's shoulder. 'Sorry about that,' said Savage. 'But when a mouse has got to pee, a mouse has got to pee. Now, how are you getting on with the code? Where's the Diamond Sword hidden? I need to know.'

'OK, calm down,' Hugo laughed. 'Why are you so impatient all of a sudden?'

'Impatient? I'm not impatient!' snapped Savage. 'It's just, we've only been travelling for four months, concentrating our considerable efforts solely on locating this bloomin' sword and now you've finally worked out where it is, all of a sudden it's like some great big secret or something. Well, excuse me for thinking we were working as a team but I deserve to know, WHERE IS THE DIAMOND SWORD?'

Hugo and Crystal glanced quizzically at one another. 'Talk about tetchy,' murmured the cat.

Distracted by a commotion coming from the entrance to the cave, Hugo looked over to see Lupus talking to a small creature he was holding cupped in his hands.

'Oh dear me,' muttered Lupus anxiously. 'This really is most confusing.'

'Put me down, you dozy hairball!' said a voice that Hugo thought was eerily familiar.

'I'm terribly sorry, little fellow,' mumbled Lupus. 'Please don't take this personally but I really can't let you loose until I've double-checked your identity.'

'Well, take a second look. Who do I look like to you?'

'You look like Savage – but that is precisely my problem.' Lupus hoisted the big-eared white mouse by his tail until they were eye to eye. 'If you're Savage, who's that in the cave with Hugo?'

Chapter 33

Hugo's mouth fell open as he did a double take.

'Are you thinking what I'm thinking?' asked Crystal.

Hugo grimaced and nodded. 'I think so – one of these Savages is a horrible, despicable lowlife.'

'Yup,' Crystal nodded. 'And the other one must be a vampire.'

The mouse dangling from Lupus's grasp was now thrashing his little arms and legs in an attempt to break free, shouting, 'Let me at him! I'll show him who's Savage all right!'

'The only way to sort this out is to get them together,' said Hugo, gesturing for Lupus to release his Savage, who immediately scampered into the cave and squared up to his double.

'Listen, pal,' said the first, drawing his cactus spine. 'This cave ain't big enough for the both of us.'

'I couldn't agree more,' said the second Savage, brandishing his own identical weapon.

'One of us is going to have to leave.'

'Well, it's very gallant of you to offer. We'll all miss you terribly.'

'I'm going nowhere because I'm the real Savage.'

'On the contrary, my friend. *I* am the real Savage.'

'OK, OK,' Hugo interrupted. 'This could go on all night. Both of you, prove yourselves to me – in thirty words or less.'

The Savage who'd entered the cave first stepped forward and puffed out his chest. 'You can tell I am Savage because I am handsome and brave and I will stick with you through thick and thin, no matter what. You are my best buddy in the whole world and I know you will agree that such evidence is conclusive.'

With a derisive snort the second Savage stepped forward. 'You can tell *I* am Savage because I am handsomer and braver than this mangy impostor,' he said, jabbing a thumb at his double. 'I will stick by you because you are honest, undaunted, gallant and optimistic and I know you will agree that my evidence is not just conclusive, it's *in*conclusive.'

Hugo beamed broadly at the second Savage as the icy grip of doubt was flushed away by the warmth of friendship. Realizing his cover had been blown, the shapeshifting impostor charged at the real Savage, who reacted just in time to avoid being stabbed but was unable to escape being bowled over.

The two mice sprawled across the icy cave floor, pirouetting on their tummies as they came to a stop. Clambering to their feet they circled one another in silence, occasionally feinting or jabbing their weapons. Hugo and Crystal watched in stunned silence.

'I've lost track – which is the real one now?' asked Hugo frustratedly.

Crystal shrugged. 'Maybe we should get rid of them both – you know, just to be on the safe side.'

'The armbands!' shrieked Hugo. 'That's how we can tell!' He bobbed and jerked his head to try and get a clear view of the claw-to-claw combat.

There was a blur of black and white as the two mice rolled head over tail together across the cave like a ball of fluffy wool. They wrestled on the floor, rolling from side to side as first one then the other managed to get the upper paw. Crystal and Hugo edged closer, trying to decipher the tangle of limbs and tails.

One Savage used both feet to lever the other off him, sending his lookalike sprawling across the cave and bumping his head on a rock. They both tried to clamber to their feet, but the one who had bumped his head tottered about, lurching from side to side. Seizing his opportunity the other Savage picked up a pebble and scampered forward, hefting the stone over his head.

'That's the vampire!' shouted Hugo desperately. 'His armband's on his left arm. Savage, look out!'

Before Hugo had finished shouting his warning Crystal leaped across the cave in a flash of silver-blue. Hissing like a leopard she pounced on the mouse holding the pebble, pinning him to the floor with her front paws.

'Oh, leave me alone,' cried the impostor.

'You were going to kill my friend, you evil monster,' spat Crystal, squeezing the mouse's mouth shut with her paw.

Aware of his whereabouts at last, the real Savage approached his double.

'What have you got to say for yourself?' he demanded. 'What's the matter? Cat got your tongue?'

'Are you OK, Savage?' asked Hugo.

'Just fine.' Savage managed a smile as he looked his double in the eye. 'In fact I'm beside myself.'

'What are we going to do with this little vampire?' wondered Hugo.

'Actually, I don't think he's going to stay little for very long,' said Crystal. 'I can feel some very strange vibrations under my paws – I think he might be morphing back to his normal shape. Stand aside, Lupus.'

Deftly Crystal rolled the little mouse on to one paw and quickly tossed it into the air. As the rogue rodent reached the top of its flight she sprang off the ground and swatted it with a fat paw towards the mouth of the cave. Lupus stepped to one side just in time to let the mini monster fly past, screaming wildly as it sailed into the night.

Everyone ran to the edge of the ledge in time to witness the tiny silhouette tumbling past the sheer mountainside towards the rocky slopes hundreds of feet below. Silence settled upon them as they peered over the precipice and waited.

Seconds passed. Then came a sickening thump, accompanied by a horrible tortured scream that echoed chillingly through the valley.

'I'm sorry I let that vampire into the cave in the first place,' pleaded Lupus. 'I feel terrible about it. He was just identical to Savage in every way – he even had the clove of garlic round his neck.'

'So he did!' said Hugo, his eyes bulging at the realization.

'That doesn't make sense,' said Savage. 'The garlic didn't seem to bother him in the slightest. I thought any vampire would be repelled by the garlic, at least briefly – unless . . .'

'. . . Unless I have just tossed the vampanther over a cliff,' concluded Crystal nervously.

'Well, that's certainly one way of letting him know we mean business,' said Savage.

'We have to keep moving,' said Hugo. 'If that really was the vampanther he'll probably want to lick his wounds for a while but then he's going to do whatever he can to stop us getting his Diamond Sword.'

Hugo followed closely behind Lupus as he strode

carefully along the narrow ledge that rose gradually to join the ridge of the mountain. Crystal trotted at Hugo's heels, while Savage scampered along the icy path behind her.

'Thank you for getting rid of that other Savage, Crystal.'

'One of you is bad enough,' replied Crystal primly. 'Seeing two of you was unbearable.'

'That's not a very nice thing to say about your friend,' said Savage, feigning hurt.

'Friend?' Crystal laughed sarcastically.

Savage smiled coyly. 'Yes. You told that vampire mouse fellow off for trying to kill your friend.'

'I didn't say "friend".'

'Yes you did.'

'I'm sure I didn't.'

'I'm sure you did.'

'You're concussed.'

'I know what you said though. It's OK – I'll be your friend if you really want me to.'

'This is absurd. I think you're still delirrrious,' said Crystal, barely managing to disguise the purr in her throat.

CHapter 34

The band of friends cowered against the southerly wind that swirled powdery snow across the exposed ridge like smoke. When they stopped for a short break, huddling against the cold, Hugo added more details to his map of Demonica. He recorded the jagged line of the ridge that led back to the shallow cave, which he annotated with a sketch of two duelling Savages. From the ridge he could see most of the Kingdom, like the choppy peaks of a rough sea frozen for eternity, and he recorded the scene in his notebook.

They had covered five miles through the night so far and Hugo estimated they might travel another two before sunrise. That would mean they'd have to cover seven more before finding whatever Marcello had described as 'the mouth of crystal fangs' – and before time ran out. Hugo tried not to think about Crystal's predictions – about Uncle Walter dying and about him dying.

They resumed their journey and soon came upon a sheer lump of granite that protruded from the mountain blocking their route. The elliptical rock was about two hundred feet tall and covered in sheet ice. Time and the elements had cleaved it open down the middle like a huge mussel shell, leaving a narrow chasm through its centre.

'What do we do?' asked Hugo.

'We can't go round it,' said Crystal. 'The slope either side is almost vertical.'

'We'll have to go through it then,' stated Savage.

'Ursa's Jaws,' muttered Lupus, staring up at the giant obelisk. 'My father told me about it.'

'Where are your family now, Lupus?'

Lupus looked wistfully across the mountainous kingdom. 'Somewhere out there.'

'Have you tried to find them?' enquired Hugo.

Lupus shook his head. 'Look at me,' he said sadly. 'I can't possibly go home in this state.'

Hugo watched a pool of water swell around the rims of his friend's sad eyes. He reached out and gripped Lupus's long bony hand, squeezing his fingers gently.

'I miss my parents too,' whispered Hugo. 'When I feel most alone, I find it helpful to focus on a really happy memory of them. Why don't you try?'

Lupus nodded appreciatively and closed his eyes.

'OK – I'm coming home after playing in the forest with my friends. My father is sleeping and my mother is preparing my favourite supper.' A contented smile spread across Lupus's hairy face and his nostrils flared as he savoured the imaginary aroma.

'I used to love coming home for tea as well,' enthused Hugo. 'What are you having? One of my favourites was vegetable broth.'

Lupus shook his head and closed his eyes more tightly. 'We're having lamb.'

'Yum,' said Hugo. 'Is it grilled or roasted?'

'Neither.' Lupus licked his lips. 'It's raw.'

'Well, that sounds, er, *interesting*,' said Hugo dubiously.

'By *interesting* I suppose you mean *crazy*,' whispered Savage.

'Lupus, what else did your father tell you about Ursa's Jaws?' asked Crystal.

Lupus opened his pale opal-coloured eyes and sighed, dismayed to be brought back to the reality of the present. 'He used to warn me that any fool who entered that godforsaken valley would surely fall prey to the creature within – the beast they call the Abominable Orangufang. This vampire monkey is said to live high on the rock face,' said Lupus. 'Our best chance is to stay close to the cliff and hope it doesn't see us in the shadows.'

'Why is he called the Abominable Orangufang anyway?' asked Savage. 'Maybe he's really not that bad. Maybe he's been unfairly judged on appearances and should be called the Grouchy-Looking Orangufang or the Deceptively Stern-Faced Orangufang. Perhaps he's just a plain old Facially-Challenged Orangufang.'

'He guards this pass mercilessly,' explained Lupus. 'They say that if he catches anyone, he bites off their head and discards it, then he takes the corpse high on to the rock where he gorges himself on their blood until he is almost too full to move.'

'I stand corrected,' agreed Savage. 'He does sound pretty Abominable.'

'OK, let's go,' whispered Hugo.

'Wait!' hissed Crystal. 'My prediction! Remember, I saw a battle from which Hugo didn't emerge?'

'Correct me if I'm wrong,' argued Savage, 'but you sensed Hugo falling in a battle involving a bear's jaws, didn't you? If there is any kind of battle in there it'll be with a monkey, not a bear.'

'Now that you mention it,' Hugo said, 'Ursa *is* actually Latin for bear.'

'Since when are you a Boffinus Latinus?' demanded Savage.

'Uncle Walter taught me how to navigate using the constellations. Ursa Major is a group of stars all mapmakers recognize. Its name is Latin for Great Bear.'

'So that crevice is called the Bear's Jaws!' yelped Savage. 'You can't go in then. I'm not going to let you die. I forbid you to enter that pass.'

Hugo stroked Savage's tummy with his knuckle.

'I thought you didn't believe any of Crystal's psychic readings?'

Savage glanced at Crystal and shrugged. 'I don't. Not really. But it's better to be safe than sorry, isn't it?'

'Thank you for your concern,' said Hugo kindly. 'But we don't have any choice. If we're going to rescue Uncle Walter and find that Diamond Sword we have to take our chances with the Abominable Orangufang. And if I don't make it out the other side then the three of you will have to finish the job without me.'

'You can count on us,' said Savage, his beady eyes shining as he clambered on to Hugo's shoulder.

'We won't let you down,' said Lupus sadly.

Too upset to speak, Crystal rubbed herself against Hugo's legs.

'Don't worry about me, I'll be fine,' said Hugo. 'So let's stick together, and don't make a sound.'

Then he turned and crept into the crevasse.

CHapter 35

The still air was numbingly cold as Hugo led the way down through the icy jaws of the ravine. If he spread his arms out he could almost touch both sides of the narrow gorge and he had to fight the sensation that it was closing in on him. His breath rushed gently through his lips and his feet creaked quietly on the snow. Crouching as he edged his way along the base of one rock face he kept his eyes trained on the shadows dappling the opposite wall.

The V of night sky up ahead was gradually growing larger. Each precarious step brought the open ridge a little closer. A lump of ice rattled as it bounced down the rock face and landed at their feet with a soft whump, followed by two more. Hugo backed into the shadows as far as he could, followed immediately by Lupus and Crystal.

They waited for what felt like an eternity, scanning the empty rock face above. At last Hugo exhaled. 'False alarm,' he whispered. 'Must just be the glacier shifting or something.'

'There's nothing to worry about,' said Savage confi- dently. 'That cat and the weird hairy one have got us all wound up about nothing. I'd be willing to wager there's actually no such thing as an Abominable Oranguf—!'

A sudden shriek had filled the cavern. Then came another shriek overhead followed by a series of angry grunts, and a silhouette leaped across the chasm to the opposite cliff face where it clung on with both arms.

Letting go with one hand and casually scratching itself, the animal looked over its shoulder, studying the valley below. The size of a small elephant, it had a rotund body with long thick arms and short chunky legs. It was clad in shaggy white fur but for its hands, feet and face, which looked like they had been fashioned from some sort of blue rubber.

'OK,' conceded Savage. 'It's just possible I was wrong. But don't worry, it hasn't seen us ye—!'

Just then the monkey shrieked excitedly, its face stretched into a manic grin as it began to descend into the valley, deftly gripping the rock with its hands as it swung down the icy rock face.

'Savage, will you stop tempting fate!' yelled Hugo. 'Everybody run!'

Lupus led the way with his long stride carrying him swiftly through the craggy pass, closely followed by Crystal. Hugo ran as hard as he could but his progress was hampered by a lack of grip, and the faster he tried to run, the more his feet seemed to slip on the compacted snow.

The Orangufang had reached the bottom of the crevasse and was lumbering after the intruders, its square shoulders brushing the icy walls. With straight arms it was planting two fists on the ground and swinging its hind legs as it closed in on its prey.

'It's gaining on us!' cried Savage.

Hugo glanced over his shoulder to see the monkey's blunt silhouette looming large. As he turned back his foot caught on something and he tripped over, sprawling across the snow on his stomach. Savage was propelled off his shoulder, gathering snow as he tumbled head over heels. When he came to a stop he was almost entirely encased in a little snowball with just his head and paws sticking out.

As Hugo clambered to his feet he looked back instinctively to see what he'd caught his foot on. Lying in the snow a few yards back, looking at him with an expression of utter terror, was a human head. Boasting a mop of thick bushy hair, its skin was pale and its slack chin covered in coarse whiskers.

Hugo was rendered motionless with fear for just a moment but that was all the Abominable Orangufang needed. Grabbing a rubbery fistful of his collar the colossal creature lifted Hugo off the ground, sniffed him and cocked its head.

'Lupus!' called Savage, fighting his way out of his snowy tomb. 'It's got Hugo!'

Hugo watched the changing expression on the monkey's wrinkled face. It had gone from baring its lethal fangs angrily at Savage to jabbering excitedly. Now its eyes were wide and its lips puckered as if it was blowing a kiss. It wagged its head vigorously from side to side.

'Put him down, you big banana brain!' ordered Crystal.

'Take me instead,' implored Lupus, jumping up and down wildly to distract the monkey. The ruse worked momentarily but then the huge primate focused on Hugo once again.

It sat down to examine him, turning him upside down and this way and that, like a baby playing with a new toy. Then it grabbed him around the waist with two enormous rubbery hands, lifting him head first towards its gaping, fanged jaws.

'It's going to bite his head off!' exclaimed Crystal. 'We have to do something.'

Lupus charged at the monkey, yelling and waving his gangly arms above his head, but the ape simply kicked out a giant foot and sent him cartwheeling into the icy wall.

'Right! I've had quite enough of your monkey business, buster,' called Savage, but his threat made no impression.

The giant chimp grinned hungrily at Hugo. Its fingers tightened round his middle.

'This is it,' thought Hugo as his head passed into the monkey's mouth.

His friends watched powerlessly.

Two rows of fearsome fangs began to close around his neck.

An almighty growl echoed through the ravine.

Hugo held his breath.

It was a moment before he realized that the roar had not come from the ape's mouth . . . but from its stomach. Suddenly the monkey hiccupped, gasping down a lungful of air with an almighty *hic!* as its whole body convulsed violently.

A moment later the Orangufang's hungry smile withered, it pursed its lips and its cheeks ballooned. As it exhaled the odious product of its belch with an apathetic sigh, Hugo felt its hot stinky blast on his frosty skin.

The vampire monkey withdrew Hugo from its mouth and dangled him by his ankles. Rubbing its leathery belly with its free hand it looked like a bloated Roman emperor sizing up one last drumstick after gorging himself for days. Blowing a bilious raspberry, the

Orangufang dropped Hugo on to the snow and stood over him grunting.

'Quickly, Hugo,' urged Crystal. 'Run away.'

'I can't,' Hugo gasped, wiping at the sticky monkey saliva coating his face. 'I think I've twisted my ankle.'

'Hang on,' called Lupus, staying as low as he could as he loped towards the giant monkey. He was expecting to be swatted away at any moment but instead of defending its catch, the ape sat back patting its tummy.

Lupus lifted Hugo up and slung him across his shoulders like a sack of corn before beginning his hasty retreat. As they all scampered to safety, the occasional half-hearted grunt came from the ravine but the monkey gave no chase.

When they were all well clear of the crevasse, Lupus set Hugo down, propping his back against a rock.

'Thank you, Lupus,' whispered Hugo.

'That was lucky,' purred Crystal. 'For a moment I thought it was going to decapitate you there and then.'

Savage laughed. 'Hugo's much to cool to lose his head over something as trivial as an Abominable Orangufang.'

'That was really weird though,' said Lupus. 'I wonder why it let you go. Its meals must be so few and far between you'd think it would eat ravenously when food does come along.'

'That's just it,' said Hugo. 'Even as it put me to its lips it had this strangely nauseous look in its eyes – you know, like you might get after polishing off a dodgy ferret pie.'

'I don't think there are any ferrets in these mountains,' said Lupus.

'Well, maybe it wasn't a ferret pie,' smiled Hugo. 'But I definitely think that Abominable Orangufang had eaten something pretty unpleasant.'

Chapter 36

'That hairy monkey ate Big Jake and Tommy Guts,' sobbed Little Jake. 'I can't believe it.'

'I know,' said Walter sympathetically. 'It's terrible.'

'Tommy Guts was one of the worst friends I ever had – and as for Big Jake,' Little Jake sniffed and dragged his sleeve across his face, 'he was the meanest, nastiest brother anyone could wish for – that's why we were so close. Of course he had his good points but nobody's perfect. Besides, it doesn't do to speak well of the dead. I'll always remember him as ugly and violent and downright despicable.'

Walter nodded solemnly. 'That was a disgusting eulogy, Jake. I'm sure your brother would have spoken just as lowly of you.'

The two men were huddled in a snow hole they had dug into a drift on a steep slope.

'So it's just me and you now, Mapman,' snarled Jake with renewed defiance. 'And I'm beginning to wonder if you actually know what you're doing.'

'I can assure you I'm doing my very best,' insisted Walter.

'So how far is it to this secret castle? When am

I going to get my hands on that lovely Diamond Sword?'

'Soon enough,' Walter smiled easily. 'Soon enough.'

'What's with all those pebbles anyway?'

Walter gazed at the pattern of little stones he had laid out in the snow. 'I'm just plotting our course,' he lied. 'I wondered if there was some logical sequence to the legs of our journey. You see, this is where we started in Lovdiv, then this pebble is the point at which we entered Demonica and this is where we lost Billy Blood to that Fearsome Fangaroo.'

Jake frowned. 'If that's Lovdiv and that's where we entered Demonica, then didn't Billy die about here?' He pointed with a stubby finger to a position some distance from the third pebble.

Walter was surprised and alarmed to discover that Jake's grasp of basic geometry was considerably sharper than his literacy.

'Ah, yes. If I was using a *standard* scale then you'd be quite right,' he bluffed. 'However, we in the mapmaking trade often prefer to opt for the more complicated, er . . . Lyor-Heddov scale – named after the Bavarian mapmakers Klaus Von Lyor and Ludvig Heddov. It allows us to represent mountainous terrain on a flat surface. It's really very clever.'

Little Jake looked at Walter, his eyes narrowing suspiciously.

Walter swallowed hard and smiled.

'Well, whatever you're doing we ain't got time to cuddle up in a snow hole all night so let's get going.' Jake shoved Walter in the back with his boot.

As he stood, Walter pushed one final stone into the snow, then he stumbled out of the shelter and led the way down the treacherous slope.

CHAPTER 37

Lupus carried Hugo until dawn, when the gang rested and ate. Hugo sat hunched over his notebook, rotating his foot gingerly. He added Ursa's Jaws to his map and drew the Abominable Orangufang hanging from the rock face and a severed head in the valley.

'Five miles to go,' he announced, examining the pebbles in his palm. 'If we don't find Lifereaper by tonight Marcello will become a fully fledged vampire.'

'What are we waiting for?' asked Savage, jumping from foot to foot energetically. 'Let's go. I'll ride on your shoulder.'

'Hugo probably shouldn't carry any extra weight for the time being,' said Crystal.

'I'll carry his satchel and water bottle,' offered Lupus.

'What about me?' asked Savage.

'You're much too small to carry anything,' purred Crystal.

'I *meant*, who's going to carry me?'

'Poor baby,' said Crystal, nudging Savage with her paw. 'Why don't you ride along on my back?'

'Yours?' asked Savage, fanning his ears in a show of horror. 'I'd rather wade through whisker-deep snow.'

'Fine. Have it your way.'

'However,' added Savage hurriedly. 'I'm willing to put my own principles to one side – if it will make you feel safer to have me close by.'

'Oh, Savage!' said Crystal with mock admiration. 'You're my hero – thank you.'

Savage accepted Crystal's gratitude with a shallow bow, then scampered up her leg and nestled into the thick soft fur between her shoulder blades.

Hugo grinned at the unlikely pair. 'Don't you make a lovely couple?'

The ridge led the group down a shallow decline for a couple of miles, but before they knew it the path was climbing again – slowly at first then more aggressively. Soon they were picking their way along a razor-sharp ridge, clambering over icy rubble.

Hugo slipped and stumbled, wincing in pain as he clawed desperately at the crystalline snow. A mass of frozen scree bounced down the precipitous mountainside into silent oblivion. Lupus gripped his elbow and helped him up.

'I don't want to be a nuisance,' said Lupus, 'but I thought it might be a good idea if we tied ourselves together with the rope. Then if one of us should slip, or something, the other could anchor down and pull him to safety.'

Hugo knew he was the one struggling to keep his footing on the precarious path and he appreciated Lupus's tact. He smiled gratefully and nodded.

He and Lupus each tied one end of the rope round their waist and Lupus led on. When the rope grew taut between them he waited for Hugo to catch up, then continued.

Hugo looked back and smiled at Crystal trotting keenly behind him with Savage riding her like a knight. Then he felt a jerk on the rope.

When he turned back Lupus had disappeared.

Looking down he saw a hole had been punched in the ground. Powdery snow poured into the opening like sand through an hourglass.

The rope was slithering into the ground like a speeding snake. Loop after loop whipped from his shoulder.

Desperately Hugo looked around as the other two arrived on the scene.

'Hey! Where did Lupus go?' asked Savage.

Snap, snap, snap! The rope uncoiled.

There were just a few loops left. Hugo knew that Lupus's momentum would take him into the void as well. If he untied the rope he at least would be safe.

Snap, snap!

Hugo dived to the side and wrapped the rope twice round a boulder of broken ice. Pressing his feet against the frozen rock he straightened his legs and leaned back, as if he was in a tug of war.

The rope snapped taut with a twang. A high-pitched grunt came from the snow hole. The ice block shifted a few inches . . . then stopped.

Hugo could feel the rope creeping through his grasp. He watched helplessly as an inch of twine slid through his hands and snaked round the ice block. Then another and another.

Lupus hung upside down staring at the sheer ice face that plummeted to unseen depths. The rope had lodged itself round his skinny waist but he could feel it slipping steadily. Suddenly he was falling. The rope had worked its way over the widest part of his hips and he was plummeting into the dark chasm below.

Hugo fell back as the weight at the other end of the rope was released. A split second later the rope yanked him forward with such force that his feet left the snow and before he could react he was slammed against the ice block, thumping the air from his lungs.

Lupus was now dangling precariously by his ankles, the rope having slipped over his narrow hips only to catch again on his enormous feet.

Hugo had become embroiled in the rope and was trussed to the ice block like a joint of roast beef.

Savage leaped on to the snow and scampered over to Hugo.

'Don't worry, Hugo,' he called valiantly, digging his claws into the rope and pressing his feet against the ice block. 'I'll have you out of there in no time.'

Savage leaned back, hauling on the rope and screwing his face up, but in spite of his incredible efforts the rope didn't budge.

Crystal lay on her stomach and crawled forward until her paws just touched the lip of the crevasse. Tentatively she peered over the edge of the hole in the snow. 'He's hanging *upside down*,' she whispered back to Hugo. 'Remember my premonition about you being betrayed? I said you would see an ally or a close friend upside down and realize that they are in fact your greatest enemy.' She shrugged her slender shoulders. 'Perhaps during the night Lupus was replaced by a vampire lookalike.'

'Which arm is his red silk tied to?' asked Savage.

'I'll have a look,' said Crystal, slinking back towards the hole. 'Lupus, are you OK?' she shouted.

'I'm fine,' came the doleful reply. 'Don't worry about me.'

Crystal turned to Hugo and Savage. 'I can't make it out,' she reported. 'His arms are dangling down by his head.'

'I won't let him fall,' said Hugo, grimacing. 'We have to stick together.'

'But he could pull you both over with him. That's too much to risk for someone who might actually be your enemy.'

Savage relaxed his grip on the rope. 'I hope you'll forgive my bluntness, but seeing as we're friends now I feel it's my place to inform you that your predictions are about as accurate as a flying pig shooting arrows in a pitch black forest.'

'But what if this time I'm right?' whispered Crystal.

Just then Lupus's timid voice drifted up from the depths of the ravine. 'I'm really sorry to be such a nuisance, everyone. I think it would be best for all concerned if you just cut the rope and carried on without me.'

Savage snorted a scornful laugh. 'That's hardly the fighting talk of a dangerous and ferocious monster, is it, Crystal?'

'OK, maybe I was wrong,' admitted Crystal darting across the snow to join Savage on the rope. 'But I have a strong feeling that a dark power isn't very far away.'

For a while everyone was motionless, locked defiantly in their task, but eventually their resistance began to give way. Slowly but surely the rope started to snake through their grasp.

'It's no good,' said Savage. 'We can't hold him any longer.'

'Perhaps I can be of assistance,' said a deep voice behind them.

Struggling against the constriction of the rope, Hugo turned to see a tall figure wrapped in black, his long cloak billowing around him.

'Jadea Jafil?' he exclaimed with delight.

The figure bowed slightly. 'At your service.'

CHapter 38

With the rope draped over his shoulder and gripped firmly in his leather gauntlets, Jadea Jafil steadily heaved Lupus out of the cavernous crack in the mountain.

'That's incredible,' enthused Hugo. 'The three of us couldn't move him an inch.'

'Just a matter of technique,' replied Jadea with a token smile.

Lupus's long hairy feet appeared first, then his gangly legs, and soon his whole body lay spreadeagled on the snowy floor, shivering violently.

Hugo pulled off the loosened bindings and helped Lupus to his feet. As he did so he felt him stiffen.

'What's the matter?' he asked, following Lupus's gaze to Jadea's silhouette.

'Who is that?' Lupus growled, sniffing the air suspiciously.

'He is the man that saved your life. Lupus, I'd like you to meet Jadea Jafil.'

Jadea stepped forward and flashed a pearly smile. 'At your service,' he said with a nod.

'How long have you been in Demonica?' asked Hugo.

'Ten days, maybe twelve,' said Jadea. 'The day after I came to your uncle's house I left England and travelled here to search for Lifereaper's castle. I have been methodically scouring the mountains but in vain.'

Hugo noticed a bruise and a cut on Jadea's cheekbone and saw that he seemed to be holding one arm awkwardly.

'Are you hurt?' he asked.

Jadea waved his hand dismissively. 'It has been a long journey and these hills are rugged indeed.'

'What an incredible coincidence that we should meet,' marvelled Hugo. 'I mean, Demonica must cover hundreds of square miles and we just happen to bump into each other.'

Jadea Jafil smiled enigmatically. 'Incredible indeed,' he agreed. 'But tell me – what brings you here? When I saw your uncle last he gave me the distinct impression that he had no intention of travelling to these parts. Don't tell me you have run away from home?'

'Not exactly.' Hugo smiled sadly. 'The day after we met, Uncle Walter was kidnapped by bandits. They are using him to find the Diamond Sword and I think they are just a few hours ahead of us – we are on their trail.'

'Kidnapped!' Jadea raised one eyebrow in horror. 'Then we must hurry. I will teach those bandits not to interfere with my friends. And when we have rescued

Walter, we will continue the search for Lifereaper's castle together.'

Hugo nodded eagerly. 'Let's go.'

The crevasse Lupus had fallen into was about five feet wide and cleaved through the rock to an unfathomable depth. Jadea took a short run-up and leaped the chasm easily, followed by Lupus who made the jump with Crystal wrapped round his neck like a fur stole. Savage slipped into Hugo's satchel and closed the flap behind him and Hugo began his long run-up. Nearing the edge of the ravine he had to adjust his stride, losing a lot of his speed as he shuffled his feet. As he leaped into the air he cycled his feet then threw his arms forward and landed firmly, right on the far edge of the opening.

A smile of relief curved across his mouth. Then he rocked backwards on his heels. He windmilled his arms to propel himself to safety but it was no use – the weight of the satchel was pulling him back. He was toppling into the icy gorge like a tree being felled. Helplessly he clutched at the air. His eyes bulged in terror. He was falling.

Strong hands gripped his wrists, arresting his fall.

'I've got you,' said Jadea, pulling his right arm.

'*I've* got you,' insisted Lupus, tugging at his left.

Between them they dragged him to safety.

CHapter 39

Hugo led the party while Savage snoozed in his satchel. Lupus and Jadea followed in silence, Crystal's sleek silhouette gliding between them.

'Jadea, I was wondering . . .' started Hugo casually. 'When you reached Demonica, why didn't you just follow the directions on Marcello's map?'

Jadea laughed. 'That map is like a foreign script to me. It might as well be written in ancient Hebrew for all the sense I can make of it.'

'But the night you came to see us, Uncle Walter spent hours studying Marcello's map,' said Hugo, frowning. 'And the next morning he left the house early, saying he was going to share what he had deduced with you.'

'Well, he never made it as far as my guesthouse. I was waiting in all morning and I received no visitors. I suppose those bandits must have accosted him during his journey across town.'

'But he definitely came back to the house because his coat was left there.'

'The bandits might have escorted him there to collect the equipment he needed to lead their expedition.' Jadea placed a fatherly hand on Hugo's shoulder.

'So you didn't see my uncle again after the night you visited us?'

'Alas, no.'

'But . . .' Hugo shivered and decided not to finish his sentence.

'Don't worry, Hugo,' said Jadea warmly. 'Your uncle will soon be in safe hands.'

As with the rest of their trek so far, the descent into the steep-sided basin took longer than Hugo had expected. The ridge behind them had thrown a long shadow over the path ahead when Lupus spotted something unusual.

In a deep snowdrift under an overhang just off to the left, someone had excavated a sizeable snow cave.

Jadea volunteered to keep guard outside while the others examined the snow hole. It was surprisingly cosy inside, sheltered from the wind and small enough to be warmed up by their shared body heat. Crouching under the cave's arched roof they surveyed its walls but found nothing that could be construed as a clue.

'Let's go – we have to keep moving,' said Hugo.

As he turned, he felt Lupus grab his arm.

With a long bony finger Lupus pointed to the floor where nine pebbles lay scattered.

'That's strange,' said Crystal, rubbing one ear with the back of a paw. 'Do you think someone was stockpiling pebbles as ammunition?'

'Oh, definitely,' said Savage. 'I mean, nothing's going to protect you from a horde of vicious vampires like a pile of small stones. I'm sure there isn't a vampire alive – or dead – who isn't in fear of being on the receiving end of a handful of shingle.'

'At first glance the pebbles appear to be scattered randomly,' observed Hugo, clasping his hands behind his back as he peered at the stones. 'And yet there's something strangely familiar about their arrangement.'

'Is anyone else confused?' asked Savage, popping up from behind a chunk of ice.

'I just get the feeling there's some kind of pattern to them – that they've been placed very deliberately.'

'Do you mean it's some sort of sign – from your uncle?' said Crystal. 'What does it mean?'

'I haven't got the foggiest idea.'

'If you'd like I could try and take a psychic reading,' Crystal offered. 'It might take a few hours but I'm sure I could pick up some extrasensory evidence from their pattern.'

'No, no, *no*, **no!**' Savage leaped on top of one of the pebbles, waving his paws, and ears frantically.

'Do I take it from that little outburst that you have an objection to Crystal's idea?' asked Hugo.

'I don't have *an* objection,' Savage replied calmly, 'I have about *ten* objections. Firstly, after the abysmal inaccuracy of every one of her predictions so far, I think we should insist on no more prophecies. Secondly, we don't have time to sit here for hours while she sniffs around this scattering of gravel, strokes her whiskers and waits for answers from the afterlife. I mean she might as well ask you for Uncle Walter's star sign and read you his horoscope for all the good it'll do. Fifthly, I'm sure I'm not the only one—'

'That's enough,' said Hugo sternly.

'It's OK, Hugo,' said Crystal softly. 'I'm used to the likes of Savage deriding what they don't understand – but it's kind of you to stick up for me.'

'Actually, I wasn't sticking up for you, I'm afraid. To be honest, I rather agree with Savage. Your fortune-telling is a little hit and miss – mostly miss.' Hugo smoothed Crystal's fur to show there were no hard feelings. 'I was interrupting Savage because his rant about horoscopes and star signs made me realize something. These stones are laid out in a pattern that's similar to Aquarius – one of the astral constellations.'

Lupus frowned. Savage blinked.

Crystal licked a paw. 'What does that mean?' she asked eagerly.

Hugo felt his smile fade. 'Well, I'm not exactly sure, as such, at this moment in time. Maybe it's no more than a coincidence. We'll work it out.'

'Honestly,' tutted Savage. 'You're about as much use as Crystal.'

Chapter 40

'Well?' snapped Little Jake.

Walter frowned and shook his head. 'It must be round here somewhere.'

'Listen, Mapmaker, don't tell me you're lost because that just won't wash.' Little Jake lifted Walter's chin with the tip of his sword. 'Need I remind you that a lot of people have died following you on this journey to find the Diamond Sword?'

'No indeed. And we're not lost,' said Walter, trying not to move his jaw. 'I know exactly where we are. It's Lifereaper's castle that is lost.'

'Uncle Walter! Uncle Walter!'

Walter gasped, and spun round to see Hugo pelting towards him across the snow, pumping his fists. His blonde hair was held back by the cold air and a gappy smile was spread across his freckly face.

'Who's that?' hissed Little Jake.

'My nephew.' Walter dropped to one knee, beaming at Hugo as he considered how to protect him from his captor.

'Stop right there, boy, or I'll cut . . .' Jake was still in mid-threat when Hugo leaped at Walter, throwing his arms round his neck and nearly knocking him to the ground.

Walter clasped Hugo to his chest and stood up laughing. Squeezing Hugo's ribs with his bound hands he stepped back and swung his young nephew round.

'Hugo! I'm so happy to see you. I knew you'd decode Marcello's riddle. Did you come alone?'

'The others are just coming. They'll be here soon. I missed you so much, Uncle Walter.'

Walter lifted both hands and clasped Hugo's wavy hair. 'Oh Hugo, your cheeks are freezing!'

Without answering Hugo buried his face deep inside Walter's collar.

'Really, you feel like a block of ice. Are you all right?'

Suddenly Walter's eyes and mouth opened wide in agony and despair. He gripped Hugo's hair and yanked his head back. What he saw made his blood run cold.

The boy's skin was clammy and colourless, almost translucent. His eyes were blood red. A triumphant snarl had peeled back his lips and at either side of his gappy teeth, dripping scarlet spots into the snow, were two long fangs.

Walter tried to throw the vampire off him but it dug its claws into his shoulder blades, clinging to its prey like a wild cat. Tugging at its hair he held the monster's head back, averting his face from its lethal teeth and its rotten breath.

Suddenly Walter realized that his grip around the monster was growing tighter and tighter. He could hear muscles twang and sinews pop while the monster howled in terrifying agony. It grew beneath Walter until his feet left the ground and he felt like a small child in its immense grasp.

The creature's face contorted and twisted as Walter looked on in horror. Its forehead grew lower, its jaws jutted forward and its fangs grew longer.

Little Jake had staggered backwards in the snow. He wanted to scream for help but terror strangled any sound he tried to make. He wanted to turn and run but something made him stay and watch.

The mapmaker's feet kicked in the air as he struggled to break out of the monstrous grip. He grimaced in silent agony as the ropes around his wrist sliced through his skin before the strain finally loosened them enough for him to shake his hands free. Apparently too weary to fight, Walter tugged at something around his neck.

The vampire gripped the mapmaker by the throat and held him off the ground at arm's length. His long dark hair tangled around his shoulders like a mane, and a black cloak billowed from his neck.

'I am head guardian of the Lifereaper's castle,' hissed

the vampire. 'You will never locate his lair and you will never get your hands on the Diamond Sword.'

'I know what you are, and I know where he lives,' gasped Walter. 'Soon others will come and your precious lord will feel the blade of his own sword through what passes for his heart.'

'Let them come.' The vampire smiled evilly. 'I have a great thirst tonight.'

Then he pulled Walter towards him and clamped his jaws around his throat.

'HELP! IT'S A VAMPIRE!' Little Jake had finally found his voice. As he screamed the vampire turned his way and studied him with its wild scarlet eyes.

The monster's blood-smeared mouth curled into a threatening snarl, then it threw its head back and let out a spine-juddering howl of triumph and anger that echoed round the basin and up into the night.

Little Jake fainted.

Chapter 41

Crystal stopped in her tracks, her ears jutting forward. 'Can you hear that?' she asked urgently.

'What?' asked Hugo.

'That. It sounds like an animal – like some sort of howling.'

Everyone listened in silence. Savage popped out of Hugo's satchel and scurried up to his shoulder, fanning his ears out wide. 'I can hear something,' he whispered.

'It sounds like it's in pain,' Lupus agreed.

'Let's keep going,' instructed Hugo.

But the next cry brought a collective gasp from the group.

HELP! IT'S A VAMPIRE!

'Crystal, any predictions about the meaning of that?' asked Savage wryly. 'It's pretty cryptic but if we put our heads together I think we might crack it!'

Then came a murderous howl that made their hair and fur stand on end.

Hugo reacted first and charged off down the mountain towards the sound, lifting his knees as he bounded through the deep snow and clutching his sword at the ready. Crystal, Lupus and Jadea Jafil followed close on his heels.

'Faster, Hugo, faster!' urged Savage bouncing around on his shoulder.

The ridge fed into a steep, narrow valley, which opened out into the bottom of an icy basin. The group skidded to a halt, sucking hard on the cold night air.

'Who's that over there?' Crystal held out a paw. 'Someone's lying in the snow.'

Hugo jogged across and knelt by Little Jake, who was just coming to.

'What happened here?' demanded Hugo. 'And where's my uncle?'

Little Jake sat up and looked around at the faces peering at him. There was the blonde boy who had turned into a vampire, now with a strange flappy-eared mouse on his shoulder, a silver-blue cat, a dark stranger with a fearsome crescent-shaped sword and a skinny man with a mane of hair and a wild beard.

'Keep away from me!' Jake screamed. 'You won't get me, you 'orrible vampire!'

As Jake tried to scrabble backwards Jadea grabbed him firmly by the back of his collar.

'I'm not a vampire,' said Hugo. 'Would I be wearing this string of garlic if I were?'

'Wh-wh-who are you then?' Jake stammered.

'I'll ask the questions.' Hugo kicked away Jake's

weapon and brandished his own sword for emphasis. 'Now, I'll give you one more chance. Where is Walter Bailey?'

'He's dead,' whispered Little Jake. 'The vampire got him. Ran up to him lookin' just like you, it did, then it changed into a monster – clean lifted him off the floor, it did. I ain't never seen nothing so hideous in all my years.'

Hugo felt woozy, his strength suddenly draining to his boots. He staggered forward a step and stabbed his sword into the hard-packed snow for balance.

'He's not dead,' he said defiantly. 'He can't be.'

'Oh, believe me he's a goner,' chuckled Jake grimly. 'I never saw so much blood – and believe me I seen plenty in my time. Take a look over there.'

Hugo turned to where the bandit was pointing. A patch of snow about the size of a cartwheel was stained deep red. Blood red.

He ran across and dropped to his knees next to the stain, holding his face in his hands.

'Don't give up, Hugo,' whispered Savage. 'He's not gone yet, remember? This simply means that Walter is now a mezzaghoul.'

'But Crystal predicted Uncle Walter's death. She said he would never recover.'

Crystal had approached silently and sat next to Hugo. 'The vision I had of your uncle's death did not show him becoming a mezzaghoul. I cannot explain it but the death I sensed involved total destruction of body and spirit. It was death with no hope of salvation.'

Savage forced a dismissive chuckle. 'But the great news is that Crystal's predictions have been way off the mark. In fact for every one of her premonitions, the exact *opposite* has happened.'

Hugo looked up at his friends. His cheeks were glistening with tears but there was a flicker of hope in his eyes.

'It pains me greatly to admit it, but perhaps Savage is right,' conceded Crystal. 'My mystical powers are certainly yet to be proven on this adventure.'

'Thank you!' exclaimed Savage. 'At last you admit your attempts to see the future have been one big catastrophe.'

'Please, Savage, let me finish,' said Crystal icily. 'I agree that my premonitions have not yet been proven – I'm just confused because my gift of foresight has never let me down before.'

'Oh well. Maybe you've just lost the knack,' said Savage with a chuckle. 'Too bad.'

'Enough,' said Hugo. 'So let me get this straight. If Uncle Walter is a mezzaghoul then his soul is in limbo until he becomes a fully fledged vampire or Lifereaper is destroyed.'

'Exactly,' said Savage emphatically. 'Limbo must be about the safest place he could be.'

'Not necessarily.' Jadea's voice was deep and firm as he hauled Little Jake to his feet. 'The vampanther has ultimate power over every mezzaghoul. If Lifereaper considers one of his mezzaghouls a threat to his position he will terminate it by driving the Diamond Sword through its empty heart.'

For a moment they pondered Jadea's warning in stunned silence.

'Then we have no time to lose,' Hugo urged at last. As he spoke something caught his eye in the snow by his feet.

CHapter 42

Hugo picked the object off the bloodstained snow and held it up between his thumb and forefinger.

It was a small silver pendant, about two inches long, strung on a leather lace.

Lupus and Jadea approached with Little Jake firmly in their grasp.

'The old man pulled that necklace off when the vampire had him,' said Jake with a smirk. 'Silly old fool would have been better off trying to fight the monster, if you ask me.'

'Well, we didn't ask you, so keep it shut,' snarled Lupus with uncharacteristic hostility.

'I've had enough of this thief's insolence,' said Jadea. 'I'll tie him up somewhere where we won't have to listen to his lying tongue.' As he dragged Jake towards a wide cleft in the icy rock face, Hugo studied the pendant.

'What is it?' enquired Lupus.

'A silver dagger,' said Hugo quietly. 'Bartolomeu Dias gave one to every member of his crew for good luck on their famous voyage round the Cape. My father went with Uncle Walter on that voyage but he never returned. The daggers didn't protect my father but Uncle Walter still wears his as a reminder of the fragility of life and to encourage himself to make the most of every day. He always said that whenever he was feeling sorry for himself he would feel the cold dagger resting against his chest and it would make him appreciate his good fortune – for my father's sake. "We're lucky to be on this earth, Hugo," he used to say. "There are plenty of people who would love to be in our shoes and we owe it to them not to waste a moment."'

'Do you think he left it here as a gift for you?' asked Savage.

Hugo shrugged then nodded. 'I suppose so,' he said, brushing his cheeks with the back of his wrist.

Suddenly Crystal stiffened, her back arched and her fur bristled. 'My senses are telling me the Lifereaper is nearby.'

'And my senses are telling you to give it a rest,' said Savage.

'OK, let's be nice . . .'

Hugo's voice was drowned out by a hideous cry erupting from the crevice where Jadea had taken Jake. Little Jake's shriek was so gut-wrenching and terrifying in tone that everyone stiffened instantly with terror. But it was the actual – now familiar – words he screamed that chilled everyone to their very core.

'Help me!' he cried. 'It's a VAMPIRE!'

Chapter 43

The bandit was lying on his back, his face lifeless in ashen terror while a pool of deep red blood bloomed beneath his head.

A few yards beyond Jake stood Jadea Jafil, holding his scimitar at his side and breathing heavily as he stared into the black depths of the crevice.

'Jadea,' gasped Hugo. 'What happened?'

Startled, Jadea spun round and raised his sword in both hands – lowering it when he saw Hugo's face.

'I was just tying the bandit to that ice block when three vampires came out of nowhere.' As he spoke Jadea glanced nervously at the blackness behind him. 'They came at us in a flash, each one as strong and ferocious as the vampanther himself. Naturally I fought like a wildcat and managed to behead one of the despicable fiends but while I was dealing with it, the other one savaged the thief.'

'You mean "the other two",' corrected Lupus.

'Sorry?'

'You said there were three vampires,' Hugo pointed out. 'You killed one, so the other *two* must have attacked the bandit.'

'Correct,' said Jadea. 'That is what I intended to say. It all happened so fast the details are a little blurry. Anyway, there was nothing I could do.'

'Where is it?' asked Hugo, studying the chasm behind Jadea. 'The vampire you killed.'

'When a vampire is killed it dissolves instantly, like its victims,' explained Jadea, his headscarf covering all of his face but his eyes.'

'Look,' said Savage urgently. 'The bandit is dissolving now too.'

As they watched, Little Jake's body evaporated before their eyes. His clothes disappeared and his flesh shrivelled up and flaked away as if being dried up by some intense heat, until only his skeleton remained. Then his bones imploded into a thin layer of fine dust, which was absorbed by the snow on which he lay.

'He's gone,' said Lupus, unaware that one pink, pointed ear had popped up inquisitively through his scruffy hair.

'Not gone – just transported,' corrected Jadea. 'He's gone to the dungeons in Lifereaper's castle to join Walter and the other mezzaghouls.'

Realizing that what he had witnessed happening to the bandit was exactly the fate that must have befallen his uncle, Hugo felt his heart pumping with anger and determination.

'We have to find that castle,' he said resolutely. 'It must be around here somewhere.'

He led the others back out into the icy basin. 'But where do we start looking now that we have no more of Uncle Walter's clues to follow . . . or do we?'

As they all studied the sheer sides of the rocky bowl, clad in thick snow and icy tendrils, Hugo unfolded his copy of Marcello's map.

'Maybe this silver dagger isn't just a gift,' he muttered, clutching his uncle's pendant in his fist. 'Maybe it's some sort of clue. The bandit said Uncle Walter struggled to snap off this necklace rather than fight the vampire, so it must be pretty important. But what does it mean?'

'A silver blade is a common weapon used by vampire hunters,' said Jadea. 'Maybe your uncle was simply signalling that you should now have your sword at the ready.'

Hugo shook his head. 'Uncle Walter knows I always have my wits about me.'

'Perhaps the tip of the dagger was indicating which way we should proceed,' suggested Crystal. 'Which way was it pointing when you picked it up?'

'Walter dropped it while he was being throttled by a vampire,' said Savage. 'I doubt he would have had the chance to orientate it carefully in any particular direction.'

264

'I suppose not.'

'I'm still trying to work out what the constellation of pebbles meant,' mumbled Lupus, hanging his head shyly. 'I don't suppose there's any chance the two clues go together, is there? Maybe Aquarius had a dagger or something.'

'Lupus, you're right!' Hugo grabbed his friend's arm as he turned to walk away. 'I was so focused on this clue I'd forgotten all about the last one. In mythology Aquarius didn't have a dagger – he was the water-carrier, but in one of my father's favourite riddles he used an icicle to commit the perfect murder.'

'But Marcello's clue makes no mention of icicles, does it?' asked Lupus.

Hugo delved into his satchel for his notebook and flipped it open where he had decoded Marcello's message.

'It just says, "Look inside the mouth of crystal fangs,"' he said with a sigh.

'What could that mean?' pondered Savage, scratching his head.

'Icicles could be described as crystal fangs,' said Jadea.

'But what kind of creature has a mouth full of icicles?' asked Crystal, prowling thoughtfully around the group. 'Hugo?'

As if in a trance, Hugo wandered out into the open

bowl, staring across the frozen lake to the far side of the basin. His head was motionless but his eyes were darting eagerly between his copy of Marcello's map and the icy wall opposite.

Across the lake the rime- and ice-coated rock face parted around the arched entrance to a cave. From the upper rim of the mouth hung a row of ragged, glistening icicles. At either end of the row a huge icicle about ten feet long grew from the rock like a mighty icy stalactite. The giant icicles were thick at their base, each tapering to a sharp point like two immense fangs.

'The mouth of crystal fangs,' recited Hugo, blood pounding in his ears. His eyes darted to the next symbol on Marcello's map and he felt a sudden surge of inspiration.

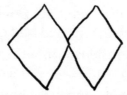

'All this time I thought this symbol was two diamonds. I thought it might represent a symbol on one of the doors inside the castle or something.'

'Doesn't it?' asked Savage, cocking his head.

'No,' said Hugo emphatically. 'I'm pretty sure it's made up of two letters – initials, in fact. Marcello always used to annotate his coded invitations to Uncle

Walter with a special symbol he'd designed to signify that they were perfect opposites.'

'M for Marcello and W for Walter,' whispered Savage.

'Exactly,' confirmed Hugo. 'And if I'm right, it tells me which part of the castle we must head for.'

'If you say so . . . and what about the last symbol?'

Hugo studied the final shape on Marcello's map.

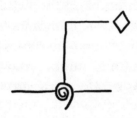

'I have a feeling it's . . .' he stopped abruptly just as Lupus, Crystal and Jadea arrived and gathered behind him.

'What is delaying you?' asked Jadea. 'Time is short and we must hurry.'

'Have you found something?' asked Crystal.

'I think it's fair to say we have struck vampire gold,' said Savage.

'Over there,' said Hugo, his hand shaking as he lifted a finger to point at the cave lined with icicles. 'That cave is the gateway to Lifereaper's castle.'

Chapter 44

Hugo studied the rock face as he hurried around the frozen lake, slipping and skidding in his haste. The more he stared the more he was convinced he could see a geometric pattern amongst the twisting veins of ice and the rugged rocks before him. Smooth rimy columns high on the cliff face suggested minarets positioned symmetrically about the entrance and clumps of snow protruded from the surface as if sitting atop conical towers.

'This isn't just a cave that will lead us to Lifereaper's castle,' Hugo panted when they reached the far side of the basin. 'It looks like Lifereaper had the mezzaghouls carve his castle into the solid rock. This is the very gateway to the castle itself.'

'So it does exist,' breathed Crystal. 'Margery's vision was right.'

Dry-mouthed, Hugo gazed at the stone towers and ramparts lurking behind its icy veil. 'I can't believe we've actually found it,' he marvelled.

'Beware! Wondrous though it is, it will be guarded by many vampires,' stated Jadea. 'Everyone must be ready to fight.'

Hugo drew his sword and side by side he and Jadea led the way beneath the icy teeth and into Lifereaper's castle.

Rather than the rugged cave-like interior he had been expecting Hugo found himself at the end of a corridor with flat stone floors and cold, smooth walls. The ceiling was carved into an arch and dancing orange light came from the flame of a single torch on the wall at the far end of the passage.

As they passed, Jadea lifted the torch from the wall and held it up to light their progress. Cautiously the gang followed the narrow corridor, breathing in the cold, dank air. No one spoke and the only sound was the soft tapping of their footsteps and the gentle rustle of Jadea's silk cloak.

The corridor opened out into a square hallway with high vaulted ceilings and a wide spiral staircase carved from stone that led to floors above and below. A torch on each wall threw an eerie light across the granite atrium.

'What, no welcoming party?' whispered Savage. 'I shan't be recommending this establishment to any of my friends.'

Suddenly the chamber echoed with piercing shrieking and a pair of shapes dropped from above. Two figures were crouched where they had landed, heads bowed and bodies draped in black cloaks. Two more shrieks signalled the arrival of another pair of monsters, this time cutting off any possible retreat through the corridor.

'Looks like you got your welcoming party,' muttered Hugo, turning slowly to assess the opposition.

He, Jadea and Lupus instinctively formed a triangle,each facing outwards. Crystal remained at the centre of the group, her claws out ready to fight.

The hallway was icy cold, as if the vampires had sucked all the warmth from the room.

'What do we do now?' asked Lupus. 'If that's not a silly question.'

For a second or two everyone was still.

Then the vampires attacked as one. Half running, half flying, they lunged at the group, barely skimming the ground. Their wide eyes oozed pus, their bloodless lips peeled open and their fangs glinted horribly.

Jadea reacted the quickest. With expert precision he stepped to one side, swiping his blade horizontally and slicing one vampire's head clean off its shoulders. Its face still wore an expression of murderous intent even as its head somersaulted backwards and bounced on the solid floor.

Without pausing to admire his handiwork, Jadea dropped deftly to his knees and swiped his blade in a wide arc, severing another vampire's legs just below the knees. As the beast fell, squealing in agony, he thrust his sword forward, driving its silver point through the monster's heart.

A moment later both of Jadea's victims had withered to piles of dust. Meanwhile Lupus and Hugo were fighting off their assailants with equal fervour but a good deal less finesse.

Lupus was standing his ground, thrashing his hands frantically. His attacker bore numerous parallel scars as proof of the sharpness of his fingernails but seemed unperturbed by the wounds.

Hugo had backed away from his assailant, swiping his sword to persuade it to keep its distance. Then he felt the wall against his heel. He had nowhere to go and the vampire was looming over him. It lunged. Desperately, Hugo extended his arm, stabbing his sword at its chest for all he was worth. The vampire pulled back and looked down at the silver hilt protruding from its body. With a dismissive smile it reached up for the handle and withdrew the sword. Hugo realized he must have missed the vampire's heart.

Then the monster's pallid skin began to darken like paper scorching over a naked flame. Its eyes shrivelled up like raisins, its face withered and its whole body disintegrated until there was nothing left but a pile of ashes.

'Good shot, Hugo,' said Savage. 'You got straight to the heart of the matter.'

'Thank you.' Hugo shrugged and retrieved his sword. 'It was just a stab in the dark really.'

Across the hallway Lupus was beginning to tire. A wave of demoralization sapped his resolve and his defensive blows started to slow. Seizing its chance the vampire lunged at him, gripping him by the throat and wrapping its cape round his whole body.

'Hang on, Lupus!' yelled Crystal and she leaped on to the monster's shoulders, sinking her claws into the waxy skin of its face.

Releasing its grip on Lupus, the vampire staggered backwards, twisting and turning. In its frantic efforts to throw Crystal off, the monster stumbled towards Jadea who stabbed it through the heart.

The gang gasped on the cold air and studied the four piles of dust that peppered the floor.

'We have to hurry,' said Jadea. 'They were Life-reaper's guards. When they don't return he will come looking for us and our only hope of disarming him is to take him by surprise.'

Hugo ran to the spiral staircase. 'We have to split up. Jadea, you go downstairs – we'll search upstairs.'

'Fine. If you find Lifereaper, try to stay hidden. Don't take him on – he's much too dangerous,' Jadea instructed. 'Come and find me. I will slaughter him for you.'

Hugo paused for a second. 'Thank you.'

272

Jadea bowed his head. 'At your service.'

Hugo snatched a torch from the wall at the foot of the stairs and held it above his head. With his back pressed against the cold stone wall he edged cautiously around the spiral steps, craning his neck in order to afford himself as much warning as possible of any oncoming danger.

Chapter 45

Hugo had lost count of the number of turns he had made climbing the staircase. Eight? Maybe nine. The icy black air compressed his torch so that it offered barely more light than the embers of a dying fire. All he could see above him was the darkness that filled the spiral passage.

Just as he was beginning to believe he was engaged in an eternal climb, he transferred his weight on to his front foot to find that there was no step to support him. As he stumbled forward he realized that the floor now opened out into a wide, circular hallway. Four straight corridors led off the landing at right angles to one another. Hugo could just make out the shadowy silhouettes of two cloaked sentries patrolling each passageway.

'What now?' asked Savage. 'Even if we knew which corridor to go down we'd be lucky to get past those chaps.'

'And it looks like there's about ten doorways down each corridor,' groaned Lupus. 'It could take us all night to find the Diamond Sword.'

Desperately casting his eyes around, Hugo noticed

a low doorway leading to what looked like a narrow spiral of stone steps. 'Bingo!' he whispered, ducking through the doorway and scurrying up the stairs. 'If I'm right about the initials on Marcello's map, we should start looking at the very top of the castle.'

Lupus and Crystal hunkered down behind Hugo and waited to hear his plan. As Hugo studied the gloomy corridors ahead, his hand felt inside his satchel and he pulled out his map of Demonica. Feverishly he began to sketch, glancing up only briefly to assess the layout of the castle.

'Come on, Hugo,' urged Savage. 'We don't have time for you to finish your map now.'

'Look!' Hugo stabbed his sketch with his forefinger.

He had drawn a small spiral to denote the staircase with two short horizontal lines to mark the corridors leading away to his left and right. A vertical line radiating from the spiral represented the passageway directly in front of them.

'Now look at this.' Hugo unfolded his copy of Marcello's map and pointed to the last symbol.

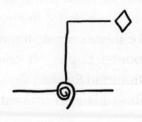

'You think Marcello's last symbol is some sort of floorplan?' asked Crystal.

'If I'm correct,' whispered Hugo breathlessly, 'the end of that corridor straight ahead it should bend to the right where – if the diamond shape on Marcello's final clue means what I think it means – we should find the Diamond Sword.'

'And the vampanther,' said Lupus solemnly.

Hugo nodded grimly. 'And the vampanther.'

Reaching a right-angled bend in the corridor, he crouched against the wall and peered round the corner. Then he gasped.

At the far end of the passageway was a heavy wooden door, in front of which stood a huge cloaked vampire. The figure's head was bowed and hooded, concealing its monstrous features in a shadowy veil.

In the gloom Hugo pictured its sleek coat, its square, sneering snout and its black lips peeling back to reveal its lethal fangs. Beneath the beast's cloak, he could just make out the rigid line of something hanging from its hip.

'The Diamond Sword,' he murmured.

The others peered out from behind him. Savage perched on top of his head, clutching two pawfuls of his blonde hair.

'Is that the vampanther?' asked Crystal.

'It must be,' breathed Hugo.

Success was within touching distance, utter defeat equally close.

'I'd love to take him out but it's not quite as simple as catching rats, is it?' sighed Savage.

Hugo's mind was suddenly filled with a vivid memory. He was watching his father placing pieces of cheese around the kitchen in the small house they'd lived in with his mother. When he'd asked his father what he was doing he'd said he was ridding the house of rats.

'Why are you feeding them good cheese if you want them to go away?'

His father had winked and said, 'Who said the cheese is good?'

'Actually,' whispered Hugo, scooping Savage off his head, 'I think it *is* precisely that simple.'

Chapter 46

'My father used to lace pieces of cheese with poison in order to kill rats,' explained Hugo, rummaging around in his satchel.

'I don't want to dampen your enthusiasm, but I'm not sure Lifereaper is much of a cheese connoisseur,' said Savage. 'Besides, we don't have any poison.'

'Actually, we do,' said Hugo producing two giant mushrooms from his bag with a triumphant smile. 'Luckily I forgot to throw these away in the woods.'

'I don't think vampires are very partial to mushrooms either,' said Lupus glumly.

'As far as I can work out the only substance to pass the vampanther's lips is fresh blood,' said Savage.

'Exactly,' said Hugo.

'S-surely we're not going to hide the mushrooms in some blood?' said Lupus.

'It's very simple,' explained Hugo. 'I'm going to eat the mushrooms and immediately bait the vampanther, before the poison has had a chance to paralyse me. Lifereaper will savage me and drink my blood, which will paralyse him and possibly even render him unconscious. You three will then snap into action, steal his sword and stab him through the heart with it. Simple.'

'What about you?' asked Savage, blinking rapidly with concern.

'Well, if you kill Lifereaper then I will be released from being a mezzaghoul.'

'True, but you'll still be poisoned,' Crystal pointed out.

'I hadn't thought of that.' Hugo's shoulders sagged.

'Wait!' said Savage, leaping off Hugo's head and punching the air. 'Crystal, the night we met you in the windowless house you told us that if the Vampire Lord were executed, every mezzaghoul's heart would come alive and reenergize their bodies with fresh new blood.'

'True,' confirmed Crystal.

'So my poisoned blood would be replaced by healthy blood.'

'We can't know that for sure. Don't do it, Hugo – it's too dangerous,' said Lupus with surprising authority.

'Yes, but it's our only chance.'

'Unless I swallow them,' said Lupus. 'You have much more to lose than I do. I don't even have a family to miss me if something were to happen.'

'No, Lupus,' argued Hugo. 'I refuse.'

Before Hugo realized what was happening Lupus

extended a hairy arm, tightly grasping his wrist with his long bony fingers.

'Let me do this,' pleaded Lupus, holding firm.

'No, I must do this.' But as Hugo protested Lupus pulled his hand towards his mouth. Hugo tried to resist but he was no match for Lupus's wiry strength.

Forcibly unfurling Hugo's fingers, Lupus snuffled the mushrooms from his palm and without pausing, stepped into the open corridor and charged towards the cloaked figure.

CHapter 47

The vampire saw Lupus coming and reacted with power and savagery in equal measure. Snatching Lupus from the air, it ravaged his throat before tossing his limp body aside.

Looking along the corridor, the vampire's gaze fell upon Hugo peering around the corner. Howling furiously it wiped its glove across its bloodied mouth and began marching towards him. Its huge cloak billowed behind it like a black ocean as it covered the ground with long, nimble strides.

Suddenly the vampire's body twisted in agony. Doubling over as if it had been punched in the stomach, it dropped to its knees, clutching its throat. Hissing like a caged tiger its head thrashed from side to side, sending bloodied saliva spraying on to the stone walls, then it collapsed forward, hitting its skull on the stone floor with a sickening thud.

Hugo cautiously circled the vampire's prone body, searching for any sign of movement. As he stepped over his enemy's hooded head, he noticed a trickle of slime running from its eye like a gooey yellow tear.

'Poor thing,' said Crystal sarcastically. 'All the emotion must be getting to him.'

'He probably doesn't get many surprise visitors,' noted Savage. 'I think he was rather choked to see us.'

But even as he smiled at Savage's comment, Hugo felt the fingers of panic tightening around his throat. 'Hang on a minute,' he muttered, grabbing two fistfuls of the vampire's sleeves, 'this doesn't look like . . .'

With immense effort he braced his heels against a wall and, using his body weight, he levered the monster on to its side then allowed it to topple on to its back. One limp arm slumped to the floor, dragging the vampire's cloak away from its side and uncovering its sword.

Hugo's eyes darted immediately to its handle. 'I don't believe it!' he gasped.

Savage and Crystal stared at the sword in silence.

Lying by the vampire's side was a long metal blade with an intricate handle, which had been elegantly tooled from a single piece of . . . wood.

Chapter 48

'This isn't the vampanther,' Hugo muttered. 'This is just another vampire guard.' He felt a stab of grief in his heart as he turned to look at the body of his friend lying at the end of the corridor. 'Oh Lupus, what have we done?'

As he spoke, a clattering sound came from beyond the wooden door. Without speaking Hugo stood and crept along the passageway to investigate.

Examining the door by the meagre light of his torch, Hugo realized that it had been pushed to, but not closed. Holding his breath he eased the door open an inch. The hinges turned without making a sound and he pressed one eye to the narrow opening. Clambering on to Hugo's head, Savage pushed his pointy snout through the gap and Crystal leaned over the top of both of them.

Beyond the door was a vast chamber with the same high, arched ceilings as the entrance hall. A few wall-mounted torches fought against the blackness, their weak orange halos flickering against the smooth walls. A single high-backed chair stood at the far end of the room and a stone plinth in the foreground supported a rectangular box, carved from stone and inscribed with an indecipherable script.

'Lifereaper's tomb,' whispered Hugo. 'That's probably where he sleeps.'

'It's open,' said Crystal.

Hugo jumped as a huge shadow came into view, stretching high across the stone wall. Standing about ten feet tall, it seemed to be cast by a figure wrapped in a long cloak with a high collar turned up about its pointed ears. It had a short snout and carried a long straight blade in two hands.

Tentatively Hugo stepped into the room, followed by Crystal.

'You!' A growling voice erupted from the far corner. 'How dare you enter my chamber! I am Lifereaper, lord of all vampires, and you will perish for your insolence unless you leave my castle immediately.'

Trembling, Hugo turned to face the shadow and felt Crystal's warm body pressing against his ankles.

'We've finally found him,' whispered Savage.

Hugo licked his dry lips and, summoning all his strength, raised his sword, which wobbled unsteadily in his grasp. Taking a deep breath, he said, 'We've come for your Diamond Sword.' He'd hoped to sound masterful and threatening but his voice came out squeaky and uncertain.

The chamber erupted with a malevolent laugh that

grew in a crescendo of evil glee: 'Mwah, ha, ha, ha, ha!'

While Hugo and Savage remained entranced by the sinister shadow, Crystal skulked silently across the chamber to a black silk curtain partitioning off a small corner of the room. After sniffing the silk a few times she started pawing at the curtain then trying to grab hold of it with her teeth.

Hugo gripped his sword tightly and edged towards the shadow's source. 'Y-you don't scare me,' he lied unconvincingly.

'I don't intend to scare you,' came the menacing reply. 'I intend to slaughter you.'

The shadow raised its sword above its head and snapped its jaws viciously. 'I can taste your blood already. Tonight I will feast on your corpse.' With that it threw back its head and let out another deep, devilish laugh that grew in volume with every peal.

At that moment Crystal, who now had a mouthful of the black silk, pranced sideways across the concrete floor, drawing back the curtain to reveal the hitherto veiled monster.

Backlit by a small flame which threw its impressive shadow across the chamber wall, and wrapped in a black cloak with a sword clutched in its two front paws was . . .

. . . a small woolly poodle.

Unaware that its cover had been blown, the dog was hamming up its fiendish cackle – throwing back its head and shaking its shoulders with relish.

Hugo waited patiently for the poodle's laughter to subside but its enthusiasm seemed only to swell.

'Excuse me!' Hugo called at last. 'Er . . . hello! We can see you.'

Suddenly the dog's laughter ceased and it opened its eyes, yelping with dismay when it saw the three visitors staring at it. 'Oh,' it said quietly. 'There you are.'

'You're not Lifereaper,' scorned Hugo.

'Ooooh yes I aaaam,' insisted the poodle in a strange, warbly voice. 'How dare yooooou question meeeeee! Whooooo do yooooou think you are?'

'Why's he talking like thaaaaat?' whispered Savage.

'You're not Lifereaper,' said Crystal. 'There's no way you are a vampanther.'

'I'm much more fearsome than a mere vampanther.'

'Let me guess,' said Savage. 'You're a vampuppy?'

'How dare you!' said the cloaked dog defiantly. It cleared its throat, 'I'll have you know I am actually a vampoodle.' Its attempt at a menacing growl petered away to a high-pitched yelp within a couple of seconds.

'Ah yes, *vampoodle*,' said Savage. 'A name to strike

fear into the hearts of all living creatures. Watch out – he might give you a nasty lick.'

'Where is the real Lifereaper?' demanded Hugo.

'Don't talk to me about Lifereaper,' muttered the vampoodle bitterly. 'I used to be his faithful pet, waiting patiently at home while he went off on his travels. When he returned I used to take him his slippers and lie at his feet while he regaled everyone with his tales of murder and pillage. For many years I did what I was told – fetch, sit, stay – and all without a word of thanks, I might add.'

Hugo found himself nodding sympathetically to the vampire dog's tale of woe.

'Then he returned from somewhere in the Indies and brought this Diamond Sword with him. The day he got back he was like a bear with a sore head – talk about a temper! I for one couldn't work out what had got into him.'

'Wasn't it the evil spirit of an Indian panther-god?' mumbled Savage.

The vampoodle continued, 'He was in such a foul mood, if anyone crossed his path he'd bite their head off – literally. That very night he dropped the pretence and rampaged through his palace as the vampanther, killing his whole family and yours truly. Then he kept us all cooped up in a dungeon for a year and expected our loyalty when he let us out. His wife and child just seemed to accept their fate but I wasn't quite so compliant, I can tell you. I played along initially but when the time came I vowed that man's best friend would become man's *worst fiend*.'

The vampoodle looked at its audience with a crooked, self-satisfied smirk.

Hugo, Savage and Crystal stared at it blankly.

'I said that man's best friend would become man's *worst fiend*,' repeated the vampire dog.

'We heard you,' said Hugo.

'Worst fiend, get it?' The dog waited expectantly, smiling cleverly at its audience.

'Brilliant,' said Savage. 'You've spent decades in this castle preparing for this moment and that's the best line you can come up with?'

'I suppose you think you could do better?' huffed the vampoodle.

Savage shrugged. 'Just off the top of my head, you could have said something like, "With *dogged* determination I vowed that I would em*bark* on a plan to one day take the sword from the lord."'

'Take the sword from the lord,' echoed the vampoodle. 'That's not bad.'

'So *anyway*,' said Hugo assertively, 'what happened next?'

The vampoodle paused to remember which part of its story it had reached, then continued. 'One dark and stormy night, when lightning cracked the sky and thund—'

'Sorry, excuse me,' interrupted Crystal. 'I know you've waited an awfully long time to recount this story to anyone who isn't actually already dead but we're really pushed for time so do you think you can just get to the point, please?'

'Fine,' said the vampoodle sulkily. 'One night Lifereaper leaves his sword outside his tomb when he goes to sleep. I steal the sword. All *his* vampires now worship me instead so they follow me here and build me this magnificent castle. *My* vampires roam Demonica looking for blood and every mezzaghoul in the world lives in my dungeons downstairs. I am lord of all vampires because I possess the all-powerful Diamond Sword.'

'Would that be this sword?' asked Hugo, grabbing the weapon just as the vampoodle was setting off on another burst of fiendish laughter.

Holding on tightly to its prize the dog growled and snarled as Hugo lifted it off the ground and waggled the sword from side to side as vigorously as he could. Crystal leaped on to the vampoodle's cloak to try and anchor it to the ground while Savage scampered down Hugo's arm and jabbed his cactus spine into the dog's paws.

The struggle lasted just a few seconds until the

vampoodle lost its grip and went tumbling into a heap in the corner of the chamber.

'Hey!' complained the small woolly dog, but Hugo was already at the doorway, with Crystal at his heels.

'Stay!' commanded Savage as they disappeared into the corridor. 'Good doggie.'

CHAPTER 49

Gripping the Diamond Sword, Hugo leaped down the steps four at a time, the curved wall pressed firmly against one shoulder. At the bottom of the staircase they all spilled out on to the hallway calling for Jadea.

A few moments later he arrived at the top of the staircase.

'What happened?' he asked. 'Where's Lupus?'

'A vampire got him,' said Hugo sadly. 'Lupus has become a mezzaghoul.'

'You have the sword.' Jadea's eyes widened gleefully. 'What about Lifereaper?'

Hugo glanced nervously around the hallway. 'He's not here,' he said with a note of despair. 'You'll never believe there was only his stupid dog upstairs.'

'He must be somewhere,' insisted Jadea, holding out an eager hand. 'Give me the Diamond Sword. I will track down and slaughter that beast and free Marcello and your uncle.'

'I know I'll sound crazy but I feel Lifreaper's presence close by,' said Crystal.

'You know, Crystal, for once I agree,' said Savage.

'You do sound crazy. Weren't you listening at all upstairs?'

Suddenly shivering Hugo held the sword out, but as Jadea went to take it from him he withdrew it from his reach and retreated two strides.

'Hugo, what are you doing?' demanded Jadea. 'Lifereaper must be here somewhere. If his pathetic poodle is here, he's bound to be here too.'

Hugo paused for a heartbeat.

'How did you know it was a poodle?' he asked. 'I only mentioned a dog.'

Jadea's eyes narrowed. 'I suppose you might call it a hunter's instinct,' he said patiently.

'Something's been bothering me,' said Hugo, holding Jadea's gaze.

'Perhaps I can settle your mind at a more *convenient* time?' suggested Jadea, bowing respectfully. As he stepped forward Hugo took another step back.

'Tell me again, Jadea,' he challenged him. 'Why *were* you wandering aimlessly around Demonica before you happened to find us? Uncle Walter decoded the directions on Marcello's map the night you visited our house and he came to see you the next day to report his findings.'

'I have already explained that the bandits must have captured your uncle on his way to see me.' Jadea's eyes narrowed and Hugo knew that his mouth was smiling behind his headscarf.

'And you had no visitors all morning?'

Jadea shook his head. 'I waited in until midday. When your uncle didn't come I deduced he had decided to refuse my plea for help. That's why I came to Demonica alone.'

'Then perhaps you can tell me why there were two empty tankards in your room at the Sailors' Inn.' Hugo flipped his satchel open. 'And perhaps you can explain how this came to be in your room that morning?' With a flourish Hugo produced a brown leather glove from his bag. 'This is my uncle's glove. He must have dropped it when he came to see you that morning.'

Jadea stammered but said nothing intelligible.

Hugo continued. 'So I'm wondering why you lied about Uncle Walter visiting you. Perhaps he came to see you but refused to tell you what he had learned from Marcello's map. Maybe Uncle Walter didn't trust you for some reason.'

'We don't have time for this nonsense.' Jadea laughed dismissively. 'Give me the weapon and I shall answer your childish questions when this business is over.'

Hugo shuffled uncertainly. Jadea stepped closer.

'Answer them now,' commanded Hugo, his body convulsing with cold.

'I will not tolerate this insolence,' said Jadea. 'You

are making a considerable mistake. You probably went into the wrong room at the inn.'

'There was no mistake,' said Hugo. Reaching to the bottom of his bag he dragged out a piece of paper. 'I tore this page from the guest book at the Sailors' Inn. According to this document you signed in to room number three and that is the room I searched.'

Hugo glanced down at Jadea's signature on the page in his hand.

His mouth was instantly parched, his heart fluttering in his chest.

'Give me the sword,' demanded Jadea.

'What's this all about?' enquired Savage.

'Are you OK, Hugo?' asked Crystal. 'You look like you've seen a ghost.'

Hugo's mind was racing. He remembered the icy blast of air he'd felt when he'd opened the door to Jadea at Walter's house four months ago, and again when Jadea had appeared in the mountains. He remembered Jadea's description of the night Lifereaper had massacred his family – *even my dog fell prey to his ferocious rage*.

Slowly Hugo turned his wrist, rotating the page in his hand until he was holding it upside down.

He drew in a long, laboured breath. He felt sick but he stood straight and looked Jadea in the eyes. 'You weren't attacked in Scandinavia, were you? You killed that botanist, didn't you, and that bandit too?'

'What are you talking about, Hugo?' whispered Savage.

'And all those poor people in Lovdiv! You had such perfect cover being a vampire hunter. And what about your family? How dare you allow me to sympathize with you over their deaths, when you had murdered them yourself!'

Jadea said nothing.

'Tell me,' said Hugo. 'How *did* you injure your arm and cut your face? Were you perhaps thrown over a very steep cliff?'

'Hugo! Tell me what you are talking about right now,' instructed Crystal.

Hugo glanced down at the inverted signature on the page in his hand.

'It's him,' he said, gritting his teeth, 'Jadea Jafil is Lifereaper.'

Chapter 50

As Crystal looked from Hugo to Jadea and back to Hugo her amber eyes narrowed.

'What are you saying, Hugo?' she demanded. 'Jadea came to Lovdiv to protect us from the vampanther who was massacring our village. Whenever there was an attack he was first on the scene, looking for clues to track down the monster.'

'Exactly,' said Hugo scornfully, his eyes locked on Jadea. 'But are you sure he arrived on the scene after the vampanther, or could he have been there all along? After all, the *very* first person on any crime scene is the perpetrator of the crime.'

Savage was staring at the signature in Hugo's hand, his ears and eyes open wide with shock. 'He was attacking these people all along,' he said, realization dawning. 'All the time they thought Jadea Jafil was protecting them he was just waiting for his chance to attack.'

Crystal gasped. 'I've just remembered the premonition I had the night we met. I sensed a tall dark stranger bringing misery and despair.'

'That's right. I guessed it was Jadea,' said Hugo. 'But

I thought the misery and despair referred to the news of Marcello's capture.'

Crystal finished Hugo's thought. 'Lifereaper leaves misery and despair in his wake wherever he goes.'

'You think you're so clever,' sneered Jadea, his voice swelling with triumph. 'Yes, I am Lifereaper. I am the vampanther. Now give me my Diamond Sword before I suck your blood until your body is no more than a desiccated husk.' With a sweep of his arm he pulled his headscarf off, threw back his head and let out a scream that resounded with pure evil.

As Jadea shrieked his whole body began to convulse, jerking violently as his shoulders grew broader and his ribcage expanded. He watched his own hands in apparent agony as they burst out of their gauntlets and hooked talons forced their way through his swollen fingertips. His chest burst through his shirt and dark hairs sprouted through every pore in his skin until his body was covered with velvety black fur that shimmered in the torchlight.

He threw his head back and yowled with fury as another violent spasm racked his body, but when he lowered his chin and met Hugo's gaze, his metamorphosis was complete.

The short smooth fur that covered Jadea's strapping shoulders had spread up his thick neck and over his head like a silk balaclava. Black eyebrows arched over

slanted green eyes that were almond-shaped and split by a vertical black pupil. His jawbones were elongated so that his mouth merged with his nose to form a short blunt snout. His thick moustache had flourished into magnificently long whiskers that twitched keenly and his petal-shaped nostrils flared with each furious breath.

The vampanther exuded power and evil as it studied Hugo. Its ears were thin membranes of skin fanned out by bony ridges and scalloped along their edges like two bat's wings, flickering eagerly in response to distant, imperceptible sounds. Slowly it stalked forward, every twitch of muscle rippling its silken hide like a shimmering black ocean.

Suddenly the monster's snout wrinkled into a snarl and its jaws opened wide to emit a vicious hiss, revealing jagged teeth that crowded around four magnificent fangs.

The icy blast from the monster's mouth ruffled Hugo's hair and tickled Savage's fur, filling their nostrils with the salty odour of stale blood.

'Oh dear,' murmured Savage. '*Someone's* breath could be a little fresher.'

The vampanther's hiss ceased as suddenly as it had begun and it fixed Hugo with its slime-green eyes as its voice boomed from its swollen chest.

'Give me back my sword – NOW!'

As an idea formed in his mind Hugo's confidence grew. 'I am holding the Diamond Sword,' he announced. 'So I am lord of all vampires now and I command you to lay down your own weapon.'

Immediately the vampanther lowered its sword until the tip of its curved blade was resting on the stone floor. Its shoulders slumped and its chin dropped to its chest. Hugo hesitantly took a step forward.

Suddenly the vampanther snapped back to life, at once lifting its sword and swinging it in a flat arc at Hugo's throat. The boy swayed on to his heel just in time for the blade to pass just inches from his neck.

Lifereaper's lips drew back into an evil fanged smile as an amused purr rattled in its gullet. 'I see that I had given you too much credit,' roared the vampanther. 'Were you really stupid enough to believe that I, Lifereaper, the original vampire, would fall under the spell of this sword like all of my underlings?'

Trembling, Hugo managed to shake his head at the monster before him. 'I'm going to kill you with this sword and when you are dead, or should I say deader, all the vampires in the word will perish.'

'You foolish boy!' boomed Lifereaper. 'You will never kill me. I am too strong and will vanquish you with ease. Give me the sword and I will let you live.'

'As a fellow – though I'd like to stress, distant – member of the cat family I feel I have a certain insight into his mind,' whispered Crystal. 'And my feline intuition tells me he's not to be trusted.'

'Your feline intuition, eh?' said Savage. 'Nothing to do with his lethal fangs and his reputation as a merciless bloodsucking monster?'

Hugo squinted into the vampanther's eyes. 'What about the mezzaghouls?' he asked.

Lifereaper shrugged. 'Their fate is sealed but you will be free to go if you do as I say.'

Hugo smiled at the vampanther. 'You make a very interesting offer,' he said. 'I can't make up my mind.'

'Give me the sword and you'll be safe.'

'I'm sorry, you misunderstand me,' said Hugo. 'I can't make up my mind whether to stab you in the heart right now or cut off your head first.'

As Hugo spoke he swivelled on the spot, swinging the Diamond Sword in a wide arc. As the blade flashed at Lifereaper's neck, the monster ducked out of its path and retaliated by stabbing his curved sword at Hugo's belly.

Just in time Hugo leaped to one side. But as he attacked his enemy again, the two blades clashed together with such force that Hugo lost his grip on his weapon.

The Diamond Sword flew into the air, somersaulting over Hugo's head and clattering on to the stone floor behind him. In a flash of teeth and sleek muscle the vampanther pounced. Before Hugo could even turn to retrieve the weapon he felt the cold hard metal of Lifereaper's blade pressing against his throat.

Keeping its crescent-shaped blade at Hugo's neck Lifereaper reached forward and slid Hugo's own sword from his belt, tossing it aside with contempt. Then the vampanther gripped the collar of Hugo's coat and, with one arm, lifted him effortlessly off the floor. Hugo kicked and punched but his enemy kept him at arm's length.

'Now you've really given me something to get my teeth into.' Lifereaper's voice burbled as it slid its curved blade back into its scabbard. A long pink tongue appeared from its mouth and rolled around its hairy chops, then it ran the back of a furry hand along the length of its whiskers.

'Look at him,' sneered Savage. 'He's like the cat that got the canary.'

With a flick of its finger the vampanther knocked Savage off Hugo's shoulder, sending him tumbling to the hard floor with a dull thud. Lashing out with one foot it sent Crystal skittering across the hallway with a screech.

'I should have killed you in the mountains when I had the chance,' spat Lifereaper.

'Why didn't you?' gasped Hugo, another idea forming.

'I planned to take that rodent's place and follow you here, but your cat tossed me over the cliff. Now you will all pay for that.'

'There was no harm done though,' argued Hugo. 'It takes more than a little fall to kill a mighty vampanther, doesn't it?'

Lifereaper snarled and lifted its tufted chin proudly. 'I've been searching for my sword for decades – do you honestly think I'd allow a mere child to stand in my way?'

Hugo patted his body. Blindly he ran his thumb down one of the straps across his body and felt the soft leather of his satchel.

'Listen, I was wondering,' said Hugo, running his thumb down the other strap. 'Would you care for an aperitif before you eat?'

The vampanther frowned angrily. 'What are you talking about?'

'I mean, would you like something to drink – you know, to wet your whistle?' Hugo asked, his hands finally resting on the swollen leather pouch they were feeling for.

There was a hollow pop.

'Uncle Walter likes a nice tankard of beer before his dinner.'

Holding the leather pouch in both hands, Hugo lifted it up to his chest.

'The only liquid I crave is the thick, warm fluid in your veins,' sneered Lifereaper.

'That's a pity,' said Hugo, sensing the icy breath on his neck as the vampanther lowered his gaping jaws towards his jugular. 'Are you sure I can't interest you in a nice cool swig of *holy water*?'

Hugo squeezed the leather water bottle in his hands, squirting a glistening stream into the vampanther's face.

Aghast, the monster immediately dropped him to the floor and staggered backwards, clutching its face and screaming, 'My eyes! My eyes!'

Hugo watched in horror as Lifereaper flailed blindly about, thrashing his head from side to side – his cloak billowing around him like a black cloud until finally he slumped into a heap on the stone floor.

'Some people just can't handle their drink,' noted Crystal.

'That holy water went straight to his head,' agreed Savage, scampering up to Hugo's shoulder. 'It's a shame though – I really liked Jadea.'

'Me too.' Hugo nodded. 'But something tells me he was about to become a real pain in the neck.'

'What are you waiting for?' urged Savage. 'Take his sword and kill him.'

Chapter 51

Hugo retrieved the Diamond Sword and hefted it in his hand. The weapon was about three feet long, with a straight double-edged blade that was stiff but incredibly slim. Its diamond hilt felt hard and heavy but the elegant blade was surprisingly nimble.

'I can't believe we've done it at last,' he whispered. His heart was scampering with joy. 'It's over.'

'Almost,' said Savage eagerly. 'You know what you've got to do.'

Hugo straddled Lifereaper's waist. Holding the sword vertically, pointing downwards, he rested its tip against the vampanther's barrel chest as if he were about to plant a flagpole.

'That's the spot,' said Savage. 'Let's kill this monster and go home.'

'This feels so weird.' Hugo hesitated. 'I know he's a monster but he looks so defenceless just lying there. It seems so . . . brutal.'

'Think of all the people Lifereaper has killed,' coaxed Crystal. 'They were all defenceless. Do it for Marcello and Lupus. Do it for Walter.'

With a deep breath Hugo gripped the Diamond

Sword with fresh resolve. Taking one last look at the vampanther lying beneath him he screwed his eyes closed. With all his strength he lifted his arms straight above his head, keeping the sword's blade vertical.

This is it, he thought. This is the end.

He froze as a sudden chill rippled through him.

'What's the matter now?' asked Savage impatiently.

Barely daring to breathe Hugo opened his eyes and lowered his chin. As his gaze ran down the vampanther's arm, he saw what he had already realized but had refused to believe. Wrapped round his ankle and gripping him with almost crushing strength was Lifereaper's hand.

Hugo kicked out his leg but the vampanther held tight, bringing its other arm up and grabbing at the sword. Hugo lifted the prized weapon out of reach and his enemy caught hold of his coat instead.

Savage scampered on to the vampanther's prone body and leaped on to its furry knuckle. With a groggy roar Lifereaper tugged on Hugo's coat, pulling himself into a half-sitting position. His icy breath rippled through Savage's fur, blowing his huge ears forward so they wrapped themselves around his face.

Flicking them away from his eyes with a toss of his head, Savage drew his cactus spine and stabbed it into the soft skin between Lifereaper's claws. The vampanther released Hugo's coat and fell back, hitting its head against the stone floor with a dull clunk. But as it collapsed it yanked at Hugo's ankle, toppling him backwards and sending him, together with Savage and the Diamond Sword, clattering across the chamber.

By the time Hugo had scrambled to his feet and recovered the sword, Lifereaper was on his feet and prowling towards him. Desperately grabbing the string of garlic around his neck, Hugo thrust the bulbs in the monster's direction.

'Oh no, my eyes, my poor eyes,' whined the vampanther sarcastically. 'Now the garlic has completely blinded me.' The beast began to rock as it emitted a deep, malevolent chuckle. 'You'll have to do better than that to fend off the famous Lifereaper.'

He stepped closer, head hung low, powerful shoulders hunched.

'We have to get out of here,' urged Savage. 'He's backing us into a corner.'

'Don't even think about escaping,' said Lifereaper with a chilling purr. 'The effects of that holy water have completely worn off. None of you will make it out of here alive.'

Hugo glanced at the stairwell over the beast's shoulder and swallowed.

'He's bluffing,' said Savage. 'I don't think he's feline too good.'

'I agree,' whispered Crystal. 'Let's split up.'

Hugo's hips swayed as he stepped deftly to his left. As Lifereaper pounced across his path, Hugo pushed back off his outstretched foot and darted to his right. Meanwhile Crystal darted to the left, distracting the vampanther just enough for Hugo to escape. By the time the monster focused on Hugo again he was halfway to the stairs and Crystal was close on his heels.

Chapter 52

'He must keep the mezzaghouls down here,' called Crystal as they spiralled deeper and deeper into the bowels of the castle.

'Maybe they can help us slay Lifereaper,' suggested Savage. 'What do you think, Hugo? . . . Hugo?'

But Hugo hadn't heard a single word. His mind was occupied pondering a notion that caused a tide of dread to well up inside him. As the pieces of his mental puzzle finally slotted neatly into place he was paralysed by a horrific realization. He slumped against the cold stone wall and slid to the floor, his lungs heaving.

'What are you doing, Hugo?' demanded Savage. 'Lifereaper is following us!'

Hugo's eyes stared blankly ahead. 'What's the point?'

Crystal turned and climbed back up the steps. Her friend's sad eyes reflected the flame of the wall-mounted torch like two small moons. 'Hugo,' she said calmly, 'what's the matter?'

'You were right,' said Hugo flatly. 'Your premonition was right.'

'I know,' Crystal purred softly. 'Jadea Jafil was the stranger bringing misery.'

Hugo shook his head angrily. 'No. Not that premonition,' he snapped. 'When you read my cards, you were right. Everything you said came true, didn't it?'

'No, Hugo. None of it was true,' cried Savage. 'Lupus stopped you eating the mushrooms in the forest, and he turned out to be a good friend even when he was hanging upside down, and you survived the battle in the bear's jaws. It was all wrong, remember?'

'No, it was all right.' Hugo sat upright, his eyes wild, his voice desperate. 'Crystal said that I would see a close friend upside down and realize he was my enemy . . . When I turned Jadea Jafil's signature upside down it spelled out the word Lifereaper. That's how I knew he was my enemy.'

Crystal was silent.

'But what about the poison?' asked Savage. 'You didn't poison anyone so she was wrong about that.'

'Actually, that's not quite true,' Crystal interjected. 'If you remember, when we went upstairs, Hugo did feed those mushrooms to Lupus so that the vampire guard would drink his poisoned blood.'

'See? I poisoned my friend. It's all true.'

'Well, she may have got lucky on that one but she was definitely wrong about the battle in the bear's jaws, wasn't she?' Savage tugged urgently at Hugo's collar. 'She predicted you would die in there and unless I'm sorely mistaken you're still very much alive.'

Hugo continued shaking his head.

'I didn't *actually* say he would die in there,' said Crystal apologetically. 'That's how you interpreted what I described. What I said was that when our group retreated from the fray, Hugo's footprints would be missing.'

'Meaning he hadn't survived the battle in the bear's jaws,' said Savage impatiently.

'Possibly,' said Hugo. 'Or maybe I'd leave no footprints because I would be carried from the battle.'

Savage and Crystal exchanged wide-eyed stares. 'Lupus carried you out because you'd injured your ankle,' the mouse said in an awed whisper.

Hugo nodded solemnly.

'So Crystal can see into the future after all,' said Savage dismissively. 'What's the matter? Oh, I get it, you're waiting for me to say I was wrong. OK, I admit it. I was wrong and she was right. Crystal, I'm sorry I didn't believe in your superfeline psychic powers but now I can see that when it comes to seeing into the future you are the cat's pyjamas.'

'I don't think Hugo was waiting for you to apologize to me,' said Crystal.

'Really? Then I take it all back,' gabbled Savage. 'So, what is the problem?'

'The problem,' said Hugo, 'is Crystal's fourth prediction, which I now see is destined to come true, no matter what I do to stop it.'

'The fourth one?' repeated Savage, his whiskers twitching curiously. 'Which one was that?'

Hugo gave Crystal a single nod, his blue eyes polished by tears.

'My fourth prediction,' she explained falteringly, 'was the one where Hugo's uncle dies.'

Chapter 53

Savage glanced anxiously up the stairwell leading to the hallway. 'Listen,' he said sternly. 'If Walter is a mezzaghoul already, the only way things can get worse for him tonight is if Lifereaper stabs him with his Diamond Sword.'

Hugo looked down at the weapon in his hands, his eyes focusing for the first time since he'd collapsed on the stairs. 'But I've got the sword,' he muttered, almost inaudibly.

'Exactly,' said Savage. 'Walter's future is in your hands.'

'Savage is right,' added Crystal. 'Forget about what I saw. Forget about fate. You can change the course of events if you put your mind to it. Make your own destiny.'

'So what's it to be?' asked Savage. 'Are you going to stay here feeling sorry for yourself and wait for Lifereaper to catch up with you or are we going to free the mezzaghouls and put the Vampire Lord to the sword?'

Hugo hauled himself to his feet and smiled resolutely. 'Let's put the Lord to the sword.'

*

The spiral staircase finally levelled out into a wide passageway, scarcely lit by the occasional torch on its granite walls. Hugo leaped the last four steps and followed Crystal into the gloom of the corridor. About thirty yards from the steps a heavy metal grille blocked their path.

Standing before the gate, their pallid skin riddled with veins and their blood-red eyes oozing pus, were two vampire guards. Sensing the group's approach their bodies stiffened and their mouths opened hungrily to reveal their pointed fangs.

'Oh great!' sighed Savage. 'Two more Stilton-faced freaks. What now?'

'Leave this to me,' said Hugo, striding purposefully towards the vampires.

'Wait!' urged Savage, clinging to Hugo's collar.

'Don't worry about me,' whispered Hugo. 'I know what I'm doing.'

'Who's worried about you?' retorted Savage. 'If you want to be a hero that's fine. But can't you at least leave me here with Crystal?'

Ignoring Savage's protest Hugo strode to within a couple of yards of the vampires. The monsters snarled and hissed as evil grins contorted their bloodless lips. Their fangs dripped saliva hungrily as they stalked towards him.

'Stop right there!' he commanded, holding the Diamond Sword before him. 'As holder of the Diamond Sword I am your lord and master and I command you to stand aside.'

The two vampires were entranced by the weapon for a few seconds then they shuffled past Hugo without a word and continued their retreat until the gloom of the corridor had swallowed them up.

'Well, they were quite a couple of chatterboxes, weren't they?' quipped Savage.

'I know what you mean,' laughed Hugo. 'They just seemed so *lifeless*.'

Holding a flame up to the iron portcullis Hugo peered into the darkness beyond. He could just about make out the outlines of figures huddled together in groups or aimlessly shuffling around in their shadowy tomb.

'The mezzaghouls,' said Crystal. 'Maybe they will help us defeat Lifereaper – if we could only open the gate.'

Gripping the metal bars Hugo heaved with all his might, but it was immediately clear that no amount of effort would shift the immense weight of the grille.

'There might be a hidden mechanism somewhere,' suggested Savage. 'Maybe in the walls?'

Hugo slotted his torch into a bracket on the wall to one side of the gate and examined the stonework, running his fingers over the cold flat slabs as he searched for any irregularity. Finding nothing he turned to the opposite wall, conducting his tactile search by weak torchlight.

'I've found something,' he gasped. 'Some sort of hole – it feels like a slot.'

'What's inside?' asked Crystal.

'I can't get my fingers in to it,' Hugo grunted. 'It's too narrow.'

'Maybe I can fit through,' said Savage, leaping from Hugo's shoulder and clinging to the opening in the stonework. For a minute or so his head and shoulders remained jammed in the slot while his hind legs scrabbled furiously at the wall as he tried to force himself through the narrow gap, his long tail wagging vigorously from side to side.

'It's no good,' he sighed at last, sliding out of the wall and dropping back on to Hugo's shoulders. 'I just can't get my hips through.'

'Maybe you should cut back on the Stilton,' said Hugo.

'Look who's talking. You couldn't even get your chubby little fingers in.'

Crystal, who had been studying the slot carefully throughout Savage's attempted incursion, cleared her throat. 'Could it be some sort of keyhole, I wonder?'

'Maybe,' said Savage. 'But we don't have a key.'

'Oh yes we do,' said Hugo, beaming.

Cocking his elbow so that the Diamond Sword was horizontal at shoulder height, Hugo pointed its blade at the wall. Squinting down the length of the weapon he slid it into the slot between the stone slabs. When the sword's hilt was just a few inches from the wall, Hugo felt some resistance against its tip – like the mechanism in a lock. Gently but firmly he pushed the blade further into the wall until its hilt pressed up against the stone. From deep within the stone came a single crisp click.

For a moment nothing happened. Then they heard the grinding of stone rolling over stone, accompanied by the metallic clanking of a heavy chain . . . and slowly but surely the metal grille began to lift.

The gate juddered to a halt, suspended above Hugo's head height by its hidden chains and pulleys. Tentatively he withdrew the sword from the wall, half expecting the portcullis to come crashing down again, but it remained put.

'Shall we?' said Hugo, gesturing for Crystal to lead the way into the dungeon.

'Oh no, after you,' she replied. 'I insist.'

Chapter 54

Hugo tucked the Diamond Sword safely into his belt and kept one hand firmly on its hilt as he ventured into the dungeon. The throng of mezzaghouls seemed un-moved by his presence as he pushed through the crowd searching for Walter. Some stepped out of his way without paying him any attention; others looked at him with empty eyes, blank expressions on their faces.

Hugo had never seen such a variety of nationalities in one place. There were plenty of characters with pale complexions wearing the simple loose shirts and doublets he was familiar with but they were interspersed with figures clad in an incredible range of weird and wonderful garments.

There was a woman wearing vivid-coloured robes and a young boy wrapped in grubby rags. A man with a neat beard wore an ornate doublet and a plump feather in his cap and an old man with narrow eyes and a shaved head had a bright orange robe wrapped around his body in swags.

Some had dark chocolate-coloured skin, others were yellowy or pinkish brown. There were wide flat noses and noses hooked like an eagle's beak. Faces were round and full, or slender and pointy; some features were rough, others refined.

'Lifereaper's vampires are spread across the world,' said Crystal, trotting at Hugo's side. 'But all their victims spend their first year drawn to the Diamond Sword, waiting for their soul to die.'

'Where would they go if Lifereaper were executed?' asked Savage.

'Legend has it that in the event that the Vampire Lord is killed, mezzaghouls will be transported to the place where they were attacked.'

As Hugo waded through the sea of faces something odd struck him. In spite of the wide variety of features, everyone wore the same dazed expression, halfway between bewilderment and insanity.

He strutted along on his tiptoes in an attempt to raise his head above the human tide, searching for a distinctive silver mop.

'Uncle Walter!' he called, turning his head from side to side. 'UNCLE WALTER!'

A flash of white caught his eye off to his left and he craned his neck to look over his shoulder, only to see it was the rather extravagant wig of a lady in a lavish ball gown. As he was turning to face the front again he walked square into someone with a hefty thud.

'I'm sorry,' he said instinctively then looking up at the face he yelped, 'Uncle Walter!'

His uncle looked at him blankly.

'Uncle Walter, it's me – Hugo.'

'Hugo?' Walter repeated, as if saying the name for the first time.

'Your nephew.'

'Ah yes, Hugo.' Walter's moustache twitched and his eyes crinkled. 'I'm sorry, my boy – I was in a daze.'

Hugo felt relief flush through his limbs. He reached out to grip his uncle's forearm but the feel of his icy flesh reminded him that Walter was not safe yet.

'We need to find Lifereaper,' Hugo said urgently.

Walter's eyes darted down to the weapon glistening on Hugo's hip. 'You have the Diamond Sword,' he said eagerly. 'How did you get it?'

'It's a long story,' said Savage. 'Now's probably not the best time.'

'I tried to kill Lifereaper with it, but I couldn't get near him,' said Hugo earnestly. 'We've stalled him with some holy water but he's still on the loose.'

'Give the sword to me,' said Walter. 'I've got a longer reach than you so I've got a better chance of finishing him off.'

Hugo slid the sword from his belt and held it across his body, resting it in both hands. As he looked down at the silver blade he saw his own eyes reflected up at him. Pausing for a moment he tilted the blade back and forth, twisting it along its length.

'Hugo,' said Walter warmly, 'Lifereaper will be here any minute – you'd better give me the sword.'

Hugo smiled briefly as if coming out of a trance. Slowly he held the sword towards his uncle. 'By the way, Jadea Jafil was here,' said Hugo casually. 'But it turned out he was a vampire.'

'Really?' exclaimed Walter, reaching for the sword.

'Not just any vampire,' added Savage. 'He is Lifereaper himself.'

'Jadea?' gasped Walter in horror. 'I can't believe it.'

'I knew when I first saw him that there was something strange about him,' Hugo remarked, absently pulling the sword back towards his chest. 'I think it was the way he used to arch one eyebrow all the time – remember?' Hugo raised an eyebrow at his uncle.

Walter laughed. 'Of course I remember,' he said, arching his left eyebrow.

Hugo giggled at his uncle's silly expression.

'Anyway, there'll be plenty of time to reminisce later,' smiled Walter. 'But now you'd better give me the sword.'

'Oh yes, of course,' said Hugo, running one hand along the weapon and gripping it by its diamond hilt. 'It's all yours.'

Then with one fluid motion he plunged the blade deep into his uncle's chest.

CHapter 55

Walter staggered back a few paces, staring down in disbelief at the blade impaled in his ribcage. Crimson blood oozed from the wound, coating his hands as they clutched the weapon helplessly.

Looking at Hugo with a mixture of anguish and confusion, a single word rasped in his throat. 'Why?'

Savage clung to Hugo's shoulder, his ears fanned out wide and his body rigid with shock. Then an awful question crept into his mind.

Am I actually perched on Lifereaper's shoulder? Did the vampanther somehow switch with the real Hugo during their duel upstairs?

Frantically he scampered across to Hugo's right shoulder and peered down at his sleeve. Tied round his right arm was the strip of red silk he'd torn from Crystal's scarf before they'd left Lovdiv. Savage was relieved but still so confused his little furry head was throbbing.

'Hugo?' he whispered. 'What have you done?'

Crystal's fur was so spiky she looked more like a silver-grey porcupine than a cat as she stared speechlessly at Hugo's stricken uncle.

Hugo held his breath and looked his uncle in the eye. His heart thumped in his chest, marking time as he waited for a sign.

Walter had just arched his left eyebrow at him but Hugo had remembered that his uncle could only move his right eyebrow on its own . . . unless he had learned the skill during their time apart.

As he watched his uncle drop to his knees Hugo realized that he was witnessing Crystal's fourth premonition.

Convinced he had made a terrible mistake, he rushed forwards, salty tears streaming into his mouth. But as he reached forward to pull the sword from his chest, his uncle rose to his feet and let out a hideous howling scream.

Frozen in his tracks Hugo watched the figure before him grow an extra two feet in height and at least as much across. His skin grew steadily darker until his torso was clad in silky black fur and a huge black cape unfurled around him, rippling in the arctic wind that now whistled through the dungeon.

The figure's face began to change as its devilish scream increased in volume and fury. Within seconds its bushy white hair had smoothed into a velvety hide and batwing ears had sprouted from its head. Its jade-green eyes bulged in agony above its puckered snout and strings of blood-streaked saliva swung from its fangs as it angrily thrashed its head, struggling in vain to remove the Diamond Sword from its heart.

'Lifereaper,' whispered Crystal in awe.

Hugo nodded, keeping his eyes on the vampanther.

'I knew it was him all along,' said Savage wisely.

Just as the vampanther's agonizing screech became so piercing that Hugo had to cover his ears, there was blinding flash that filled the whole chamber with brilliant magnesium white light.

Chapter 56

It was a few seconds before the light had faded enough for Hugo, Savage and Crystal to open their eyes again.

Taking his hands from his ears Hugo peered around, blinking like a mole in daylight. Where Lifereaper had fallen there was now a stone statue of a large cat, lying on its side with a scorched, blackened sword piercing its belly. As they watched the sword disintegrated, crumbling to the floor and leaving no more trace than a faint line of ash.

'He's gone,' he whispered.

'*Everyone*'s gone,' said Savage softly, unfolding his ears.

'Yes,' said Crystal. 'All the mezzaghouls have been transported back to wherever they were attacked.'

'And all the vampires in the world are gone?' said Hugo, hardly able to believe it was all over.

'You said it,' confirmed Crystal.

'Atta boy, Hugo!' Savage leaped in the air and kicked his heels together. 'You did it! You put the Lord to the sword.'

'*We* did. We worked as a team.' As Hugo reached

up to his shoulder and tickled Savage's chin he felt Crystal rubbing against his shins. 'I couldn't have done it without you two and Lupus . . . LUPUS!'

Hugo turned on his heel and set off at a sprint. He pelted out of the dungeon and along the dank corridor, skidding at the bottom of the staircase then climbing the steps two at a time.

He was blowing hard when he reached the hallway, closely followed by Crystal who seemed unmoved by the exertion. He paused for a couple of deep breaths and was just about to set off up the next spiral staircase when a beastly shadow on the curved wall froze him to the spot. Poised to defend himself, he waited for the creature to appear.

A wolf emerged from the gloom of the stairwell and skulked into the hallway. Its head hung low and its tongue lolled close to the stone floor. Locking its ice-blue eyes on to Hugo it charged suddenly towards him, reaching a terrific pace in just a few strides before lunging.

'Watch out!' called Savage.

But Hugo had seen the wolf in full flight and he reacted instantly.

He braced himself and held his arms out wide.

The wolf knocked Hugo over and pinned him to the floor, licking his face as he giggled and wriggled on his back. When he was able to, Hugo struggled to his knees and grabbed handfuls of the wolf's thick fur, rubbing it vigorously.

'Hello, boy,' he said huskily. 'We did it!'

Savage coughed. 'Excuse the intrusion, but do you two know each other?'

'Yes, and you know him too.' Hugo laughed. 'Savage, this is Lupus.'

'Lupus?'

'Turns out we got it wrong,' said Hugo. 'We always knew he was half man, half beast. It just turns out that he was all beast to begin with, then his tussle with a vampire left him part man.'

'Well, I didn't see *that* coming,' purred Crystal.

'But when we met him he was attacking those wolves in the forest.' Savage's nose twitched curiously.

'I don't think he was attacking them,' said Hugo, 'I think he was trying to play with them. They were aggressive towards him because he looked so different – isn't that right, Lupus?'

The wolf nodded and yelped excitedly.

'And we knew he was embarrassed about his ears – but he was embarrassed by their baldness rather than their pointiness,' Hugo added.

'Well, there's nothing wrong with having bald ears, I can assure you,' huffed Savage.

Lupus yowled and panted frantically.

'This certainly explains your mother letting you run

around the forest naked,' laughed Hugo.

'And feeding you raw meat,' added Savage.

Lupus rubbed his head against Hugo's tummy, then darted a few steps towards the exit and back again.

'I think he's eager to go and rejoin his pack,' said Crystal.

'Off you go then, Lupus,' said Hugo, ruffling the wolf's fur one more time. 'And thank you for helping us defeat the vampanther.'

Lupus licked Hugo's cheek. Then he licked Crystal and Savage, leaving the mouse drenched in saliva, before heading down the narrow passageway and into the outside world.

'I suppose I should have realized the truth when I saw him *wolf* down those mushrooms,' remarked Savage, a shining bead of dribble still hanging from his nose.

'His *husky* voice should have been a clue too,' purred Crystal.

'OK, that's enough wolf jokes,' smiled Hugo. 'Just *pack* it in.'

Hugo led the way down the corridor, under the row of mighty icicles and out into the night. Pausing just outside the entrance to the secret castle he breathed in the fresh, clean air. Peering anxiously across the frozen lake he saw something that made his stomach flip. It was a lean figure with a mop of wild grey hair and a thick moustache.

Hugo took a deep breath and yelled, 'Uncle Walter!'

CHapter 57

Hugo ran skidding across the frozen lake and threw himself into his uncle's open arms. Laughing with utter joy and relief, he buried his face in Walter's coat and hugged him as hard as he could.

'Steady on, Hugo,' laughed Walter. 'I can barely breathe!'

Hugo released his uncle from his bear hug and looked up at him from under his wavy fringe. 'Are you OK? Did those bandits hurt you? Do you remember anything about being a mezzaghoul?'

Walter's moustache twitched and he squeezed Hugo's shoulder. 'Don't worry about me, I'm fine,' he said warmly. 'Thanks to you and Savage and . . . Now then, who do we have here?'

'Uncle Walter, this is Crystal.'

'Hello, Crystal.' Walter bent down and ran a hand down the cat's back.

Crystal closed her eyes and purred, 'Hello, Walter – I'm delighted to meet you at last.'

Walter's eyebrows shot up his forehead. 'Goodness me – a talking cat!' he exclaimed. 'How extraordinary!'

'Have you seen Marcello?' asked Hugo.

Walter shook his head. 'I don't know how far he'd managed to get from the castle before the vampires caught up with him. Although I suspect he can't be far away.'

'Hugo killed Jadea Jafil,' gabbled Savage. 'It turned out he was the vampanther, so first he doused him with holy water. Then Jadea shapeshifted to look like you but Hugo stabbed him with the Diamond Sword. I knew he was an imposter all along.'

'Jadea Jafil the vampanther, eh? Well I never!' Walter stood up to address his nephew. 'I knew he was a vampire, but Lifereaper himself . . . Well I never!'

'When *did* you find out he was a vampire?' asked Hugo.

'The day I went to his room at the Sailors' Inn,' Walter explained. 'When Jadea answered the door to me I could see myself in an old mirror on the opposite wall, but I couldn't see him.'

'Was that why you didn't decode Marcello's map for him?' asked Hugo.

'Exactly. I told him the map was a mystery to me. Then the bandits kidnapped me from our house before I'd had a chance to warn you about Jadea. I'm sorry I dragged you into this, Hugo, but I didn't know what else I could do.'

Hugo gave his uncle a gappy grin. 'That's OK – I wouldn't have missed this adventure for the world!'

'You obviously managed to solve the clues I left for you.'

'Of course we did,' Savage piped up. 'It was easy cheesy.'

'I'm sure it was.' Walter's eyes crinkled into a smile. 'Well, you were all very clever to decode Marcello's map.'

'It wasn't until we were right outside the castle that I realized what the symbol made up of two diamonds meant. It just came to me out of the blue.'

'Ah yes. Marcello's symbol for our secret club – the capital M for Marcello on top of the W for Walter.'

Hugo nodded. 'I remembered you saying the symbol showed how you and Marcello were complete opposites, just as your initials are. Then I recalled that he always used the symbol on his coded invitations to your rendezvous and that he always waited for you at the highest point that venue offered.'

'*That's* how you knew we had to go to the top of the castle,' said Crystal with admiration.

'And that's why you sent Jadea Jafil downstairs,' deduced Savage. 'Did you already know he was Lifereaper?'

Hugo shook his head. 'No, I never suspected he was *that* evil. But something about his story didn't quite add up so I wasn't sure I could trust him. Then in the castle it all fell into place.'

'You were exceptionally brave,' said Walter, his moustache twitching as he spoke. 'Your parents would have been very proud of you, Hugo. I'm proud of you.'

Hugo smiled and a feeling of satisfaction swelled his chest.

'Shall we all go home?' suggested Crystal.

'Now, that is an excellent idea,' Savage enthused.

They were just about to begin the long climb out of the basin and on to the ridgeline when they heard a voice some distance ahead.

'Mamma mia! Walter Bailey – you saved my life!'

Hugo looked up to see a slight figure with tanned skin careering down the hill towards them, laughing hysterically as he bounded and stumbled his way through the deep snow.

Walter opened his arms wide and embraced the man, their hands slapping heartily on each other's backs. 'Marcello,' he said. 'It's good to see you.'

'Look who's speaking,' Marcello laughed. 'You are a sight for my painful eyes. I am sorry to have dragged you into this mess, my friend. When the vampanther killed all those people in Lovdiv I knew I had to do something. Then I heard about Margery, a witch in the village, who had seen a vision of the secret castle. I went to see her and she told me what she had seen and also gave me some good advice about dealing with vampires.

'I found the castle and saw the Diamond Sword but I was overheard so I fled. Fearing that my days had numbers I drew my map with coded directions in case it fell into the wrong hands. I knew that you would solve my riddle and know who to trust.'

Walter gripped his old friend's shoulders at arm's length. 'I can't take any of the credit,' he said. 'This is my nephew Hugo. He and his friends solved your riddles and discovered the castle and Hugo executed Lifereaper.'

'It's incredible. Hugo, you are a very brave boy.' Marcello winked kindly at Hugo. 'I bet you are the, how you say, the apples of your uncle's eyes.'

'I couldn't have done it without my friends' help,' said Hugo, blushing.

'Hello, Marcello – I'm Crystal.'

Marcello looked down in disbelief at the cat rubbing against his leg. 'No! My ears must be telling me lies. You are Margery's cat, no? Since when can you talk?'

'Margery put a spell on me soon after your visit. Some weeks later she too was killed by a vampire.'

'I don't believe it!'

'I know what you mean,' agreed Savage, cupping one paw to his mouth. 'I always thought cats were too stupid to talk too, but actually Crystal is considerably smarter than the average moggy – though between the two of us she's nowhere near as bright as yours truly.'

Marcello's eyes widened as he gasped. 'A talking mouse as well? Now I'm sure my mind must be playing the magic tricks on me.'

'Hugo can explain everything as we head back to Lovdiv,' suggested Walter. 'But first I'm dying to hear all about his adventures over the past four months. Start at the beginning for me, Hugo – and don't leave out a single detail.'

Savage scurried into Hugo's satchel. 'I'm just going to have a snooze,' he said, pushing the leather flap up with his snout. 'Wake me when you get to the bit where we steal the Diamond Sword.'

Hugo and Walter began the long trudge up the snow-covered slope, followed by Marcello and Crystal.

Hugo took a deep breath. 'Well, it all began when Savage and I came home and noticed that one of the chess pieces had been moved.'

Chapter 58

Instinctively Hugo scoured the rock face overhead, but his muscles relaxed when he saw what had dislodged the snow. The Abominable Orangofang was hanging from any icy outcrop, watching them pass with a broad grin across his rubbery face. Hugo raised a hand and smiled and the ape waved back, chattering excitedly.

'It seems even the Abominable Snow Monkey is almost cuddly, now that it's free of Lifereaper's evil,' said Crystal. 'It's more like the Adorable Snow Monkey.'

'Is it only humans that fall completely under the spell of the Diamond Sword then?' asked Hugo.

Walter shrugged. 'Possibly. That would explain why your friend Lupus didn't end up in the dungeon with me.'

'And why the vampoodle was able to revolt the way he did,' added Hugo.

Their shadows were just pools of deep blue around their feet when the travellers stopped for a bite to eat. As he chewed on berries that Marcello had picked, Hugo added the final details to his map of Demonica. With angular curves and choppy pen strokes he drew the circular basin – inaccessible but for the narrow ridge feeding into it. He sketched in the entrance to Lifereaper's castle entombed within decades of creeping ice and falling snow.

While Hugo drew, Savage pushed the flap of his satchel open just enough for him to poke his nose into the daylight.

'Pssst, Crystal,' he hissed. 'I've been thinking.'

'Well, there's a first time for everything.'

'Very funny.' Savage's words were slow and drowsy. 'I just wanted to make it clear that when we go back to the town, I think it's best if we keep our friendship a closely guarded secret. I have my reputation to think of after all.'

'Oh, dear Savage,' said Crystal. 'Dear sweet Savage. I can assure you that an acquaintanceship with a scraggy little rodent is not something I shall be doing *any* bragging about.'

'So you won't tell then?'

'I promise that you will forever be my grubby little secret.'

'You're too kind,' mumbled Savage, slipping sleepily back into the satchel.

The air was still and relatively mild and they made swift progress along the ridge and past the ledge where Savage and wrestled with himself, then they turned and headed north. They negotiated the steepest part of the mountainside with childish abandon, whooping with delight as they slipped and slid on their bottoms between the lumps of packed snow. As the slope became shallower they resumed walking, lifting their knees high as they trudged through the deep powder.

The setting sun dappled the ground through the forest of trees and highlighted the shimmering fur of the fangaroos bounding playfully through their habitat.

Night had fallen when they arrived in Lovdiv. Hugo diverted the group to the west of town where he hurried eagerly into the farmhouse stables. Grabbing Stilton's mane Hugo pressed his face against his neck while the pony whinnied excitedly and pawed the hay with one hoof.

'Hello, boy,' Hugo whispered. 'We're back –and not a moment too soon,' he added, peeking into Stilton's almost empty nosebag.

The village streets were deserted but flickering light spilled out of some windows and smoke puffed from the occasional chimney.

'At least some of the vampanther's victims must have been saved,' purred Crystal, pausing outside the windowless house. 'I wonder if . . .' As she pushed the door, a slice of orange light cut across the cobbled street. With a slink of her hips, Crystal disappeared into the house.

Hugo, Walter and Marcello waited outside for a few moments then Hugo eased the door open.

Kneeling by an open fire was a young woman with big hazel eyes and blonde hair that shone like gold. She was holding Crystal under one arm and tickling her between the ears with the other. On her head she wore a tall, pointed black hat.

'Come in,' purred Crystal. 'Margery, I'd like you to meet Hugo and Walter. Marcello, of course, you've met before.'

'Ahem!' said Savage, poking his nose out of the satchel.

'Oh – and this is Savage.'

'Pleased to make your acquaintance, Margery,' said Savage.

'Please,' said the girl, giving Savage a dazzling white smile. 'All my friends call me Madge.'

'Madge Ickspel?' mumbled Hugo. 'I – I thought you were a witch.'

'I am.'

'B-b-but you're so . . . young.'

Madge smiled. 'There are plenty of young witches around, Hugo. We're not born old and gnarled, you know – that comes with experience. We have to start learning our trade when we're young – just like mapmakers.'

'How did you know I'm a mapmaker?' asked Hugo.

'I know all about you,' said Madge kindly. 'Witches have incredible psychic powers.'

'So do their cats!' Savage interjected.

'What else do you know about Hugo?' asked Walter, who was rather intrigued by Madge's claim.

'I know that he has rid the world of vampires, saved my life and many others and, all in all, he's had quite a remarkable adventure.'

'What else?' asked Hugo eagerly, beaming at the young witch.

'I happen to know it isn't your first exciting adventure in far-off lands.' Madge Ickspel held Hugo's gaze with her pretty eyes and smiled. 'And I can tell you it won't be your last.'

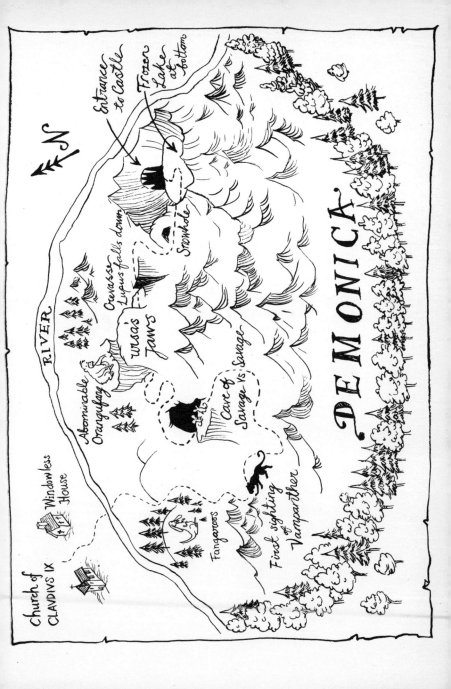

THE MAPMAKER'S MONSTERS

BEWARE THE BUFFALOGRE!

Rob Stevens

Here be maps, monsters and mayhem!

As newly appointed mapmaker for Admiral Rupert Lilywhite, Hugo Bailey is about to set sail for the very edges of the known world.

But even in his wildest dreams (or should that be worst nightmares?) Hugo hadn't imagined being stranded on an island where pigs fly, mice crack jokes and blood-thirsty BUFFALOGRES try to eat you!

Another book in this rollicking series about making maps, making friends and making some very quick escapes . . .

A selected list of titles available from Macmillan Children's Books

The prices shown below are correct at the time of going to press. However, Macmillan Publishers reserves the right to show new retail prices on covers, which may differ from those previously advertised.

All Pan Macmillan titles can be ordered from our website, www.panmacmillan.com, or from your local bookshop and are also available by post from:

Bookpost, PO Box 29, Douglas, Isle of Man IM99 1BQ
Credit cards accepted. For details:
Telephone: 01624 677237
Fax: 01624 670923
Email: bookshop@enterprise.net
www.bookpost.co.uk

Free postage and packing in the United Kingdom